INSPECTOR FRENCH:
THE END OF ANDREW HARRISON

Freeman Wills Crofts (1879–1957), the son of an army doctor who died before he was born, was raised in Northern Ireland and became a civil engineer on the railways. His first book, *The Cask*, written in 1919 during a long illness, was published in the summer of 1920, immediately establishing him as a new master of detective fiction. Regularly outselling Agatha Christie, it was with his fifth book that Crofts introduced his iconic Scotland Yard detective, Inspector Joseph French, who would feature in no less than thirty books over the next three decades. He was a founder member of the Detection Club and was elected a Fellow of the Royal Society of Arts in 1939. Continually praised for his ingenious plotting and meticulous attention to detail—including the intricacies of railway timetables—Crofts was once dubbed 'The King of Detective Story Writers' and described by Raymond Chandler as 'the soundest builder of them all'.

Also in this series

By the same author

*with other Detection Club authors

FREEMAN WILLS CROFTS

Inspector French:
The End of
Andrew Harrison

COLLINS
CRIME
CLUB

COLLINS CRIME CLUB
An imprint of HarperCollins*Publishers*
1 London Bridge Street
London SE1 9GF
www.harpercollins.co.uk

HarperCollins*Publishers*
1st Floor, Watermarque Building, Ringsend Road
Dublin 4, Ireland

This paperback edition 2022

1

First published in Great Britain by Hodder & Stoughton Ltd 1938

This novel is entirely a work of fiction. It is presented in its original
form and may depict ethnic, racial and sexual prejudices that were
commonplace at the time it was written.

A catalogue record for this book is
available from the British Library

ISBN 978-0-00-855406-4

Set in Sabon Lt Std by Palimpsest Book Production Ltd, Falkirk, Stirlingshire

Printed and bound in the UK using
100% Renewable Energy at CPI Group (UK) Ltd

MIX
Paper | Supporting
responsible forestry
FSC
www.fsc.org FSC™ C007454

CONTENTS

Contents

1

The New Job

Through gaps between the houses the sun blinked on Markham Crewe's taxi as it passed eastward through the maze of streets north of Piccadilly. The rays entering the windows shone intermittently on his old leather suitcase and bag of golf clubs, and indirectly lit up his dark handsome face, with its aquiline nose, sensitive mouth and innate stamp of breeding.

It was early May, and London looked cheerful, or at least less sombre than at other times of the year. The pavements had just dried after a shower, and were really clean, and the leaves on the trees in Berkeley Square showed a fresh tenderness in their green which it seemed incredible could have emerged from their black and gnarled limbs.

But Markham Crewe was obviously not considering these marvels. His face showed a certain anxiety, as if he were about to meet some crisis in his life. And indeed he was. As the taxi swung into Mount Street his heart gave a leap and began to beat faster. For that house which he was so quickly approaching represented the biggest milestone he had yet reached in his one-and-twenty years of life. He knew that on what happened in that house would depend his whole future career.

There had, of course, been previous milestones. The first which loomed out was that unforgettable morning when, as a child of Six, he learnt that his mother had gone away with 'Uncle Dick', a mysterious, black-moustached individual, who bore about with him an inexhaustible cache of sweets, and who had for some time been haunting the house. To young Crewe it seemed the end of everything, but at that age tragedy is of short duration. Life went on much as before until the great day arrived on which he first went to school. This, indeed, was a milestone. From school to college was another, though much less outstanding. He had spent two pleasantly slack years at Magdalen, and then still another milestone had come, this time a terrible one, which for a time left him completely overwhelmed.

Every moment of that dreadful day stood out sharp and vivid in his mind, when he had been called from a lecture to learn that his father, his jolly, easy-going, indulgent father, had been thrown from his horse when riding to hounds and instantly killed.

For a time grief overcame all other feelings, but soon he discovered that the loss of his father was not the only blow he had sustained. With the dead man had gone the vastly greater part of his money. Brigadier-General Sir Reginald Crewe had lived in such a comfortable, carefree way that no question as to the source from which this ease and security were derived had ever arisen in his son's mind. But after the general's death his affairs were found to be terribly involved. Part of the loss was the result of his own carelessness, but most was due to an unscrupulous solicitor who had taken advantage of his easy-going client to transfer the greater part of his capital to his own pocket. This man had been killed shortly before in a motor accident, but nothing could be recovered from his heirs, as he had managed to get rid of his illicit takings in speculations on the Stock Exchange.

When everything was settled up, Markham Crewe found himself alone in the world with an income of just under two hundred pounds a year; a fortune, indeed, to many, but to a young man brought up as he had been, a pittance barely sufficient for pocket money. To this he could add a healthy body and mind, some small knowledge of the classics, admirable manners and an easy ability to hold his own in society, together with a large number of very expensive tastes and habits. But of training for earning a living, he had none whatever.

When he discovered all this, he felt badly up against it. More money he must have if he were to live with what he called the merest necessaries, and as no one was likely to give it to him, he must make it for himself. But how? He could only sell his labour. But a few tentative efforts were enough to convince him that his labour was of a kind which no one wanted to buy.

Then, just as he was beginning to feel the first approaches of despair, old Colonel Hepplewhite wrote asking him to lunch at his club. Hepplewhite had been in his father's regiment in that other age before the War, and the two had remained friends. Crewe was about to decline on the ground that expensive Pall Mall clubs were no longer his *métier*, but a longing to enjoy once again his old surroundings overcame him, and he went.

The 'old boy' appeared glad to see him, and introduced him to some of his cronies. Lunch followed like a rite dating from the Conquest. But it was not till they were seated over coffee and cigars and the cronies had drifted aimlessly away that Crewe learnt that his host had more in view than a mere courtesy to an old friend's son.

'And what are you thinkin' of doin' with yourself now?' Hepplewhite demanded after a pause in the conversation.

Crewe smiled rather ruefully. 'Well, that's just it,' he answered. 'No one seems to want my perfectly good services.'

'Been lookin' for a job?'

'Rather. Everywhere. But as I say—'

Hepplewhite drew slowly at his cigar. 'I know,' he nodded; 'you young fellahs are all the same. Taught everything except how to earn an honest penny, eh? That's your trouble?'

'I suppose it is,' Crewe admitted. 'You see, till now I didn't expect to have to—'

'I know. No fault of yours, of course, nor of your father's, either.' Again the old man drew at his cigar. 'You're good at the social side, but a fool at business? That would sum it up?'

It was not the way Crewe would have put it, but he remembered he was the old man's guest and replied civilly.

The next moment he was glad he had done so. 'Well,' went on Hepplewhite, 'I asked you to come here because I had heard of a job that might suit you. Not a job I recommend, but it might start you off. What about it?'

'That's no end good of you, Colonel Hepplewhite,' Crewe answered gratefully. 'I can't just tell you how much I want it. What is it?'

'Not very pleasant, I'm afraid. Know that bounder Harrison?'

'Andrew Harrison, the millionaire?'

'Yes. He's a member here, though what the devil they

4

were thinkin' about to let him in, I don't know. Well, he wants a secretary.'

Crewe's hopes, which in spite of his better judgment had leaped up, sank like a stone in water. He shook his head with an unhappy smile. 'No go, I'm afraid. I know as much about secretarial work as of relativity.'

'I suppose you can't work a typewriter, by any chance?'

'Oh, yes, I can do that. You want it for everything nowadays, and I taught myself.'

'Better than I had hoped. You might suit Harrison all right.'

To Crewe it seemed hopeless. Hepplewhite meant well, but it was no good.

'You see,' the old man went on, after another of his slow pulls at his cigar, 'Harrison doesn't want a business man; he can get dozens of 'em for the pickin' up. He wants something much harder to come by. He wants a gentleman to run his social affairs.'

Crewe looked up with a requickening of interest.

'He pretends he wants someone to deal with his invitations and fix seatin' at his dinner parties, and so on; really, it's someone to tell him where to go and what clothes to wear and what to say when he gets there. Matter of fact, the blighter's lookin' for a peerage and he wants to know how to pull the ropes.'

Crewe chuckled. 'I could scarcely tell him that, I'm afraid.'

'Of course you could. Why not? After all, you couldn't well go wrong. Tell him to pay to the party funds. And if that doesn't do the trick, tell him to pay more. You wouldn't be fixed up forever, you know,' the old gentleman went on. 'You've got legs, and if you didn't like it, you could walk out.'

'Do you think I'd have a chance of it?' Crewe asked, less contemptuous of social climbers in the millionaire class than his host.

'I'll tell Comber to recommend you. Harrison would eat out of any lord's hand.'

So it came to pass that two days later Crewe presented himself at the head offices of Andrew Harrison, Ltd, armed with an appointment card to see the head of the firm. When he had become attuned to the magnificence of his surroundings he presented it, and was entertained to see the change of manner which resulted. The porter, to whom inspection was first granted, came down with a bang from lofty aloofness to respectful concern for Crewe's every convenience. Other personages to whom he was passed, like some registered and highly insured letter, and who obviously became more and more eminent the further he progressed, vied with each other to do him honour. He felt like a celebrated entertainer about to give a command performance before royalty—until he reached the great man's private secretary, and knew himself for what he was. This young woman's haughty glance made him feel that he was a rather nauseous, but otherwise negligible, bit of jetsam that some hitherto unsuspected current had washed up on the office carpet, and her tone when at last she realised his presence did little to dispel the illusion. Nothing brought home so vividly to Crewe the dizzy height to which Harrison had attained, as the fact that with even this radiant young creature his writ ran. She took Crewe's card, glanced at it as if it was in an advanced stage of leprosy and, opening a door—at which she actually knocked—announced him.

Andrew Harrison was a short, stocky man, with a square face, a mouth like a trap, and eyes shrewd enough to set thinking those whose point of view he had accepted in any negotiation. His face was clean shaven, his hair white, his expression unpleasant, and his age about sixty.

'Good morning,' he began, stretching out his hand, but not rising. 'I suppose Lord Comber told you what I had to say to you?'

Crewe shook hands and took the chair indicated. 'My father's friend, Colonel Hepplewhite, told me you wanted a social secretary, and that Lord Comber had been good enough to recommend me.'

Harrison nodded. 'And what can you do?' he asked laconically.

This seemed at first a question which would allow Crewe plenty of scope, but he soon saw that if it had been put in its negative form it would have been easier to answer. After all, what could he do? Mix a good cocktail, dance, play bridge and cricket, poker and tennis, row a little, flirt with a safe discretion, put together on emergency a few well-chosen but meaningless words on any given subject, and, of course, type, though this latter not, perhaps, very well. As he thought of this typing, he took courage. Yes, he had at least one of the qualifications of a secretary.

As he replied, going over his points as he might those of a horse he had entered for the Derby, he was conscious that Harrison was watching him keenly. When he had finished, the magnate made no reference to his statement. He sat without speaking for a few moments, then leant back and made a stabbing gesture with his right forefinger, which Crewe later learnt was characteristic.

'Now see,' he began, and this also proved a characteristic opening, 'it's about all this social stuff. I have my business to attend to, and I find it's enough for any one man. I've neither time nor inclination to be bothered with the other. I want someone to run the social side of things. I want him to sort out the invitations, accepting those that are socially worthwhile and refusing those that aren't. I want to be advised, without having to think of it for myself, about what I should go to, and the minimum time I need stay. All that sort of thing. Also issuing our own invitations and fixing up dinner seating, and so on, so as everyone is pleased. See? And Mrs Harrison would want some help with her correspondence and that. Got the idea?'

It seemed to Crewe that he could do the job. He admitted that he had grasped what was required and, judging his man, asked about terms. These were cut and dried and were stated without ambiguity. He would live with the Harrisons as one of the family and would have the ordinary facilities of the household, such as the use of a car when he wanted it. He would be his own master and could take what reasonable leave he wanted, provided the work did not get behind and he was available when required. His salary would begin at four hundred pounds. If he gave satisfaction this would be increased. If he did not, he would leave at a day's notice. Of his satisfactoriness, Harrison was to be the sole judge. Was that all right? Then he might sign this form of agreement.

Crewe felt as if he were walking on air when once again he reached the street. This jolly old world was not so bad a place as he had been inclined to think. The streets seemed to him brighter, the people on the pavement cheerier and more kindly. He collided with a man who turned a corner too quickly. The man took it as a joke; smiled and nodded amiably. Marvellous, Crewe thought, the amount of good there is in everybody, if you only look for it.

Presently he began to think with less exuberance. Thanks to Colonel Hepplewhite, he had landed a fine job. From the point of view of externals it left little to be desired. He would carry on the kind of existence he had been accustomed to, and to some extent mix with his former friends. His material needs were provided for, and he felt he had little fear of failing to satisfy his employer. His natural shrewdness, together with Harrison's reaction to his early inquiry about terms, told him the attitude to adopt. A certain superiority of manner, a not too completely veiled contempt for all he saw, and an absolute refusal to kowtow to anybody would go down best. He realised, in fact, his amazing luck.

And yet there was another side to the picture. He had been making inquiries about Harrison, and the result was by no means reassuring. The man had an unpleasant reputation. His brilliancy in business was admitted on all sides. Even his obvious enemies admired, if ruefully, his financial dexterity. Never could his deals be touched by the law. But of his humanity and honesty, Crewe heard not one word. 'Crooked as they make them' was perhaps the most flattering description he received. 'Dirty lying swine' was an easy average, while those remarks with real feeling behind them scarcely lent themselves to the printed page.

However, it was silly to meet trouble halfway. He had taken the job, and it was as a result that on the afternoon of the fourth of May he was driving with his suitcases and golf clubs to begin work in the Harrisons' house in Mount Street.

The door was opened to him by a butler who, while perfectly professional, yet contrived to instil into his manner something human and kindly. Crewe had a large experience of butlers, and he took to this man instantly. Competent and reliable looking, respectful but not obsequious, his mere presence suggested to Crewe that Harrison in the home must be a pleasanter proposition than Harrison in the counting-house.

'Mrs Harrison's expecting you, sir,' he said when Crewe gave his name. 'Perhaps you would like to see your room first? Or will you go direct to the drawing-room?'

Crewe was agreeably surprised by his first view of the interior. A spacious and dignified building he was expecting—the house was of the best of a good period—but the furnishing was not so guaranteed. However, it delighted Crewe. Simplicity and restfulness was the keynote of the decoration, and the furniture was sparse, of admirable design, and arranged with real taste. 'Who,' Crewe asked himself, 'have they had to do it for them?' and immediately felt ashamed of himself.

His room, which looked out from the back over a wilderness of roofs and chimneys, was on the sixth floor, but in the light of the two automatic lifts height did not matter. He was delighted to find it supplied with modern fittings: an electric fire, built-in wardrobe, and connecting bathroom. From the material point of view he saw that he was going to be in clover.

Hearn, the butler, was waiting for him when he went down, and led him to the drawing-room, a large first-floor room overlooking the street.

Three women stood in a little knot in front of the fire, which the day was just cold enough to make pleasant. Two evidently belonged to the house, but the third was dressed in outdoor clothes and seemed to be just leaving. This last was by far the most striking-looking of the three. Flamboyant was the word that shot into Crewe's mind as he glanced at her. He had also a sense of familiarity, as if he had seen her before, though he could not remember where. She had large, generously curved features whose natural colour remained a mystery to the observer. Her clothes, Crewe thought—and he considered himself a connoisseur—were impressive, though not exactly loud. She spoke in a high-pitched and penetrating voice, strengthening her points with gesticulation which made her rather exuberant jewellery flash and scintillate.

Of the other women, one was middle-aged and one young. The former was obviously the mistress of the house, for she turned and greeted Crewe in a dry, formal manner. She was tall and trim, with well-cut tight-fitting clothes which showed off to the best advantage her magnificent figure and carriage. In face she was good-looking rather than beautiful. But her expression was contemptuous and unpleasant. Beneath her conventional smile her face was hard and cruel. She seemed very young to be the girl's mother, and Crewe assumed she must be Harrison's second wife, an assumption which proved correct.

The girl was a complete contrast as far as features went, though these bore a very similar expression. She was pretty in a mild way, and in build took after her short and sturdy father. She was a girl at whom one would scarcely look a second time, were it not for her eyes. They held Crewe. He had often come across the expression 'smouldering' as applied to eyes, but up to the present had never seen what it was supposed to describe. But now that he saw it, he realised that smouldering was the only adequate word. Gloria Harrison's eyes smouldered, as if behind them were enclosed a seething mass of resentment and hate. They were evil eyes which remained unpleasantly in the imagination.

He was introduced also to the flamboyant woman, Miss Morland, and when he heard them call her Blanche he could not understand how he had failed to recognise her. She was a well-known actress, and he had seen her in more than one production.

'Well, I must run,' she said, when the introductions were complete. 'I don't suppose I shall see you much before Henley. When do you go down?'

'About ten days before the time, I should say,' Mrs Harrison returned. 'Andrew's always in a fever to get on the water.'

'So should I be if I owned the *Cygnet*,' the actress declared, and with the help of Crewe and Hearn took herself off.

'The *Cygnet*'s Mr Harrison's new vessel,' went on Mrs Harrison. 'We call her a vessel because no one knows what kind of a ship she really is. He had her built to his own ideas, and she's a sort of cross between a motor cruiser and a houseboat.'

'Sounds rather fascinating,' Crewe considered. 'You use her on the Thames?'

'At Henley time, yes. But she's been across the Channel, and we've done the Rhine and some of the other waterways in her. Rather tiresome, I thought. A river's all right for a time, but one soon gets enough of it.'

'I canoed across France once,' said Crewe, glad to have stumbled on a congenial subject. 'Three of us from Winchester. We had no end of a good time.'

Mrs Harrison pursued the subject in a half-hearted way, carelessly polite, though obviously uninterested. But her step-daughter did not speak, remaining buried in thought and looking rather sullen. Crewe decided to see what could be done about it, and at the first pause turned towards

12

her. 'Ever done any canoeing, Miss Harrison?' he asked directly.

She glanced at him negligently. 'A little,' she admitted. 'I'm not particularly interested in it.'

This was not helpful, but Crewe persevered.

'It's rather sport if you go through the right country. Where have you done it?'

'Canada.'

'Oh, I haven't done that,' he went on. 'That would be proper canoeing. I've just knocked about the Continent a bit,' and he struggled on valiantly.

Presently tea came, and the conversation grew general. It was a rather unsatisfactory conversation, of which Crewe bore the greater weight. Both women were polite enough in a careless way, and, of course, he could expect no more. But there was a strain in the atmosphere, a lack of spontaneity the talk, which jarred. Something was wrong. He could not tell what it was, but he felt it. Some unhappiness somewhere. Was there some secret weighing on the minds of these two? Or was it hate? Hate for each other, or hate for some third person? Those smouldering eyes and that air of resentment looked like hate, but it was impossible to be sure.

When after tea Crewe excused himself he felt vaguely disquieted. It seemed to him that his new job had not opened too propitiously. There was evil lurking beneath the surface in this house of wealth. However, he told himself, he must expect snags. He would go ahead and make good.

Almost desperately he repeated that he must make good. He had now the chance of a lifetime. He mustn't throw it away. If he lost this job, the very losing of it would make it infinitely harder to get another. No, at all costs he must make good.

2

The Harrison Household

It was not until the evening that Crewe met the other members of the household. Dinner was at eight-thirty, and shortly before that hour he went down to the lounge. It was empty save for a young man with dark hair, horn spectacles, and a thin, anxious face. He looked questioningly at Crewe.

'Are you Crewe by any chance?' he asked doubtfully.

Crewe reassured him.

The young man nodded. 'I'm Entrican,' he went on. 'I'm your opposite number on the business side: Harrison's private business secretary. I heard you were coming.'

'Yes,' Crewe returned. 'It was fixed up two days ago. I'm not sure that I know exactly what I'm to do.'

'I don't expect the old man knows himself. You're a new idea, you know.'

'You mean that I'm the first of my species?'

'Yes. There were girls, a whole series of 'em, private secretaries to Mrs Harrison, but none of them survived. They usually arrived on a Monday and departed in tears on the following Tuesday.'

Crewe smiled. 'You're encouraging,' he pointed out.

'Oh, you'll be all right. The girls gave way to the old lady and she trampled on them. You'll stand up to her and she'll treat you decently.'

'A pretty useful hint.'

'Besides,' Entrican went on, 'as the old man engaged you, he'll be on your side. They fight like blazes over everything.'

Crewe's reply was cut short by the entry of a young man of about five-and-twenty. He lounged in, slouching along with his hands in his pockets and the suspicion of unsteadiness in his gait. He was like old Harrison, so like that there could be no doubt as to his identity, but he was taller and had better features. But those features were already becoming coarsened. His face was not indeed pleasant, with its sullen expression, shifty eyes, and unmistakable stamp of dissipation. Entrican looked over at him.

'Come along, Rupert, and meet Crewe,' he invited.

'How do?' the newcomer nodded ungraciously, and his voice was more than a trifle thick. 'Though what the hell you've been fool enough to come to this—hole for, I don't know.'

Entrican looked at him anxiously. 'Oh, Crewe'll be able to look after himself, never fear. But I say, old man, you go and have a rest and come down later. There's no one interesting tonight, and you won't miss anything.'

Rupert Harrison steadied himself and faced the other. 'Will you,' he said slowly, 'mind your own—business?'

Entrican went over and took him by the arm.

'Come on, old bean,' he urged. 'Come along up with me and have a spot and you'll feel better.'

The young man drew away his arm and answered with a careful choice of words: 'Do you—think—I'm drunk?'

'Drunk? Of course not.' Entrican spoke pleasantly and again took his arm. 'But you know your father'll think so. And none of us want another row. Come along and have that spot.'

Young Harrison hesitated, but Entrican's suggestion seemed too strong for him, and he allowed himself to be led from the room.

The two had scarcely disappeared when another door opened and a buzz of conversation swept in. Mrs Harrison and Gloria ushered in three nondescript women, and Harrison senior followed with a tall, well-groomed young man with a vacant, good-humoured face. They bunched together in the middle of the room and then Harrison saw Crewe and beckoned him over.

'Well,' he greeted him not unpleasantly, 'so you've arrived? You've seen Mrs Harrison? Then come and meet Lord Algy Mannering.'

There was a little delay before dinner, and things hung fire slightly. They chatted in a desultory way. The elder woman visitor had met Crewe's aunt and was full of reminiscences of the occasion. Lord Algy, it appeared, also knew some of his friends, and Crewe was amused to observe how his prestige with the Harrisons increased accordingly. Then Entrican entered hurriedly, and with him a young man, evidently a stranger to the party, whom he introduced as Johnnie Fortescue. On their heels came Hearn with his impressive 'Dinner is served.' There was no sign of Rupert Harrison, and Crewe wondered with some amusement whether the delay had been due to the providing of a substitute. If so, he thought, it threw a curious light on relations in the household. However, he was had no time to indulge in speculations, as he found himself beside the elder lady and realised that the subject of his aunt had obtained a new lease of life.

Lord Algy was evidently the guest of honour. He sat between Mrs Harrison at the foot and Gloria. Crewe was interested to watch their reactions. It was clear that Mannering was attracted by Gloria, and equally clear that she was bored by him. Indeed, she was enough of a cold douche to have put off anyone who was not head over ears in love with her. The girl seemed unhappy and was at no great pains to be pleasant.

With Harrison, Crewe was agreeably surprised. Not only did he look better in evening dress than Crewe would have believed possible, but except on one point his manners were unexpectedly easy and good. He made an admirable host and had the gift of really listening to what was said to him. If anything, he was rather silent, but when he did speak it was to the point and worth hearing. In fact, had Crewe not heard so much against him, he would have been rather attracted.

The one point was his bearing towards his wife. He spoke to her as little as possible, and when he did it was in a short and dictatorial way. But she gave him as good as she got. She similarly addressed him only when she could not help it, and then with not too carefully veiled sarcasm. Though their words and actions were outwardly correct, it was impossible to avoid the conclusion that they loathed each other. Neither, moreover, was particularly polite to Entrican, who belied his own advice and was altogether too obsequious.

After an uneventful dinner and some extremely dull bridge, Crewe was about to go to bed when he heard Entrican's voice: 'Come and have a drink before you go up.' He followed the young man to a snug little room at the back of the house, furnished partly as a sitting-room and partly as an office. Entrican threw some logs on the dying fire and drew up two armchairs.

'This is where I work,' he explained, as he brought out from a cupboard a decanter, syphon and glasses.

'Jolly comfortable,' Crewe commented, helping himself. 'Are you kept busy?'

Entrican pondered this, as if anxious to give a strictly accurate reply. 'On the whole, no,' he pronounced at last. 'Work comes in spates. You know, the old man has a private secretary at his' office, or, more probably, a dozen of them. I perform only when he gets an extra special fit of energy and works at home. But that occurs more often than you might think.'

'I should have thought that would clash with the office work.'

'No; apparently I do a different kind of stuff. He has political aspirations and gives expert evidence before Parliamentary Committees and so on. I'm always getting out figures.'

'Interesting, I should think.'

'Might be worse,' Entrican admitted without enthusiasm.

Crewe sipped his whisky. 'I wondered if that was a brilliant conjuring trick you performed before dinner?' He smiled. 'Kidnapping the son and heir and producing a perfectly good substitute all quite correct and at a moment's notice.'

Entrican did not smile. 'That young fool, Rupert!' he exclaimed. 'There'll be an unholy bust up one of these days and the ass knows it, and still he goes on drinking.'

'If it gets a hold on you—' Crewe suggested.

'I know all about that. But the old man has threatened to throw him out on the street and cut off his money if he doesn't keep sober. And when the old man threatens, it's not empty words. He'll do it.'

'And what would Mrs Harrison say to that?'

'Oppose it on principle. Not for love of Rupert, but because Harrison wanted it. They hate each other like hell. I can tell you, Crewe, it's not what you'd call a happy household. There'll be murder done before we're very much older, unless they look out for themselves.' He made a gesture of weary disgust. 'Oh, damn! Sorry, but one gets fed up at times.'

Crewe was surprised at all these intimate revelations on what was virtually a first meeting, but he now realised that Entrican had himself taken a little more than was good for him. He was not drunk; just somewhat less circumspect than normally. Crewe felt he should not be discussing his employer's family in this way, but he could not resist going on.

'It struck me that Miss Harrison wasn't too pleased with life either.'

But on the mention of Gloria's name Entrican shut up like a clam. He scowled at Crewe and abruptly changed the subject.

'That ass Mannering would put anyone off,' he declared. 'By the way, you didn't do so badly at bridge. What did you make?'

They discussed the game, and then Crewe turned the conversation on to Entrican himself. When some half-hour later they went to bed he had gleaned quite a lot about the household into which his turn of luck had brought him.

Harrison, he gathered, was out for money, and so long

as he got it, he cared little as to the means. Apart from money he was not too bad, or so Entrican said. Mrs Harrison did not care about money as such, provided presumably she had everything that money could buy. Her ambitions were social, and she was climbing as rapidly as she could. It was she who had spurred her husband on to take an interest in politics. She was sharp enough to see that his special knowledge could be useful to the Government, and that this would give him the *entrée* into otherwise closed circles. Entrican had not mentioned the idea of the peerage, but Crewe felt sure from what he had heard that old Colonel Hepplewhite's hint was the truth.

Rupert, so Entrican said, was a likeable enough fellow when sober. His father's ambitions had ruined his life. He had wanted to go to sea. Had his predilection been for the Navy, a grudging consent might have been obtained. But Rupert had no use for the Navy. He favoured the Merchant Service—not exactly work in tramps, but as a deck officer in one of the good passenger lines. The idea was anathema to old Harrison, and he vetoed it absolutely. Rupert's choice was submission or a complete break with his family and the loss of all his expectations. He hadn't the stamina for this latter, and gave way.

But as he wasn't allowed to work in his own way, he decided he wouldn't work at all. When he came down from Cambridge he drifted into a fast set about town. They taught him to gamble and drink, both to excess. Unless some very drastic change took place, Rupert was a ruined man.

Crewe wondered about Gloria. Entrican's sudden silence at the mention of her name was interesting. What did it portend? That he was in love with her? From her elders' point of view Entrican would be no match. Could she be fond of him, and so find herself in a position parallel to that of her brother? Well, it was no business of his.

His thoughts went on to Entrican himself. He, at least, seemed a decent sort. And yet, Crewe was not so sure. He hoped he was not censorious, but he had to admit to himself that he did not greatly take to Entrican. He wondered if he was wholly trustworthy? There was a look in his eye that seemed rather too sharp to be wholesome. And, somehow, his cheery, welcoming manner did not quite ring true. Crewe hoped he was wrong, as it looked as if Entrican was going to be his chief companion in the household.

He pulled himself up. He had done enough criticising for one evening. Presently he turned over on his side and went to sleep. And immediately it was daylight and a maid was at his door with his morning tea.

At breakfast only himself, Harrison and Entrican put in an appearance. Harrison emerged from his paper, wished Crewe a curt good morning and once again became buried. He had little to say during the meal, and that grumpily, then with a short nod to the others he took himself off.

'Worried about his stocks,' Entrican volunteered when the door had closed. 'They're falling and nobody seems to know why. There have been all sorts of rumours lately that things were not too rosy in the house of Harrison, and the markets have reacted.'

'Any truth in the tales?' Crewe asked.

'He says not, and I believe him. But nobody really knows except himself. And credit's a very dicky thing. If a rumour gets believed, it may play old Harry with the soundest business.'

'Faith the most important thing in finance?'

Entrican shrugged. 'Sometimes it looks like it,' he admitted.

'Though faith wouldn't get me this breakfast if I couldn't pay for it.'

'Well, you don't pay for it.'

'Don't I? The old boy sees to that all right.'

Crewe smiled. 'I suppose he does. Is this drop in the stocks serious?'

As on the previous evening, Entrican paused for thought, as if to ensure that his answer would be strictly accurate. Crewe gradually found it was a habit.

'No, I shouldn't say so. An average of about six points. The nasty thing is that it has been going on more or less steadily for about a fortnight. This morning they're down another half point. That's what upset the old man. He can't understand it—or says he can't.'

Before Crewe could answer, the door opened and Rupert appeared. He was sober and looked better than on the previous evening. He stared with a slightly puzzled expression at Crewe, then went over and held out his hand.

'You're Crewe, aren't you?' he said. 'Did I see you last night? Yes? Bit under the weather, you know. Better today.'

Crewe took this as a rather handsome apology for his manner of the previous evening, as indeed it was.

'We're all that way at times, I'm afraid,' he declared, smiling.

Conversation became general and less interesting. Rupert was clearly not quite over his binge, as he began with a brandy and soda and then went on to coffee, which ended his meal. However, he was pleasant enough, and Crewe met him more than halfway. Indeed, Crewe took more to the young man than to any of the other occupants of the house, except perhaps Hearn, the butler.

When an hour later at Mrs Harrison's request he joined

her in her sitting-room, Crewe found there was a good deal more work to be done than he had expected. It took him the whole morning to clear off current matters, without touching the baskets of arrears which were stacked everywhere. However, he saw that once things were brought up to date he would not have too difficult a time.

Lunch proved a quiet meal with Entrican alone, but Mrs Harrison and Gloria were at home for tea. There were three callers, two women and a man. To the man Crewe took an immediate and instinctive liking.

He was a tall, thin young fellow, of some three- or four-and-twenty, with a friendly and honest but extremely plain face. He seemed rather overwhelmed by the four women and greeted Crewe's arrival with a look of ill-disguised relief.

'I'm Coleman and I live at Henley,' he announced, moving beside Crewe. 'I don't think I've met you here before?'

'No,' said Crewe. 'I only turned up last night. I'm going to do social secretary work for the family.'

'Oh, yes, rather. Gloria said someone was coming. I hope you'll like it.'

For a moment Crewe was uncertain of the spirit in which this benediction had been given, but a glance at the rather dog-like face told him that it was in good faith.

'Thanks, I expect I'll like it all right,' he answered. 'I've heard them speaking of Henley already. They're going there shortly, I understand.'

'Yes; that's to the *Cygnet*—Harrison's motor houseboat, you know. You've not seen her?'

'No. What sort of craft is she?'

The young man glanced round and sank his voice 'Like nothing earthly,' he declared. 'But you'll like her, all the same. He had her built to his own design, and whatever he may be with stocks, he's no naval architect.'

'What size is she?'

'Maximum for the Thames. Hundred and thirty feet by seventeen. She's a sort of barge, really, a flat-bottomed houseboat, with a small Diesel engine. They've had her across the Channel—selecting their weather, of course. But I'd be afraid of her in a sea.'

'Turn turtle?'

Coleman nodded significantly. 'I think so. But for sheltered water she's safe enough. And pretty good inside. Fitted up like the Ritz, you know. Everything posh to the nth degree.'

'You've been a lot on board?'

'Well, yes, in a way. They moor opposite our ground, you see. We live along the river, on the actual racing reach in fact, so it's rather a good pitch.'

'Then we'll probably meet down there. I expect I shall be going with them.'

'Sure to.'

As they sat chatting, Crewe could not help following the direction of his new acquaintance's eyes. Coleman could scarcely keep them off Gloria. He looked at her with a sort of adoring longing, and when at last a general move made it possible, he shot like an arrow to her side. He left Crewe in the middle of a sentence, evidently entirely unconscious of anything but the prospect of getting near her.

During intervals in a rather pointless conversation with one of the women callers Crewe could not help speculating on the situation thus revealed. Coleman loved Gloria. Entrican, he imagined, loved Gloria. From their actions on the previous evening it looked as if Harrison and his wife wished her to marry Mannering. What was Gloria's reaction to this tangle? Though he did not wish to see anyone hurt, Crewe promised himself some quiet amusement in watching developments.

That evening when he came down for dinner he found Harrison talking to two strangers in the lounge. The elder, a stocky man of about fifty, was, of this unattractive crowd into which Crewe had penetrated, the most unattractive he had yet seen. His close-set, shifty eyes provoked an instinctive distrust, and his lowering expression and heavy jaw suggested that no nice points of aesthetics would turn him from his purpose, whatever that might be.

His companion was younger: fortyish, Crewe thought. He looked more affable and less capable, though not a whit more trustworthy. Both were well groomed and had easy, not unpleasant, manners.

Crewe was introduced at once. The elder was a Mr James Stowe and the other Sir Richard Moffatt. There was no indication of who they were or what they did, except such as might be deduced from the fact that they spoke only of higher finance. Entrican followed into the room on Crewe's heels and greeted the visitors as old friends.

Once again there was a delay in the serving of dinner. Then Hearn came in to say that Mrs Harrison had just rung up to say she was sorry she could not be home for dinner. Inquiries revealed the fact that Gloria and Rupert were also out.

Crewe could see that Harrison was annoyed as he apologised to his guests and declared cynically that an occasional stag party was every man's right.

As on the previous evening, the dinner was admirable as far as food and service went, and the conversation dull to the verge of tears. At least to Crewe it was dull because he understood very little of it. On high finance Harrison laid down the law, Stowe for the most part agreed, Moffatt said very little, and Entrican threw in an occasional word, usually to supply some exact figure which the others knew, or pretended to know, only approximately. No ordinary topics were touched on: books, music, the drama, politics, the international situation (save for its financial ramifications) might never have existed. Indeed, only once Harrison descended to a conventional remark. He said, 'We'll soon be going up the river; Henley, you know. You must both come and spend a day or two with us.' After dinner he took his guests to his library, apparently to go more fully into financial details. Entrican and Crewe were left to fill in the evening as best they could.

'Who on earth are those two?' Crewe asked when they had ensconced themselves in Entrican's lair.

The young man laughed. 'Oh, they're big enough pots really. At least Stowe is. Moffatt is his partner. They're financiers, same as the old man, but they're minor planets to his sun. They're all right, both of them. I meet them sometimes at a club I occasionally go to for a spot of play. You must come some night. Not tonight: the old man might want me for something.'

Crewe said he would be delighted, and they spent the remainder of the evening in desultory chatting and reading.

3

The Westminster Guardian

The next day passed without incident, save that in the evening a more peaceful spirit reigned in the house, owing to Mrs Harrison dining out, Harrison having gone to France, and Entrican to a theatre. Crewe had dinner with Gloria and Rupert. Both were pleasanter than previously. Rupert in particular seemed good-hearted, and Gloria for the time being had lost her grievance.

Entrican looked next morning into the room in which Crewe was at work. 'Doing anything tonight?' he inquired. 'The old man won't be back and I'm going to that club I mentioned. Care to come?'

'Love it,' answered Crewe.

'Then after dinner I'll look out for you.'

'Where is the club?' Crewe asked as they set off.

'Not exactly West End,' Entrican smiled. 'It's over a house agency in Brigadier Street off Wardour Street. An old house, but quite comfortable. It's a small private club, of course, but perfectly regular: registered and licensed and all that.'

'What do you play?' Crewe asked curiously.

'Oh, well, anything you like. Personally I'm fond of a spot of roulette.'

Crewe smiled. His suspicion was confirmed. 'I can't join in that,' he protested. 'I couldn't afford it.'

'You needn't play if you don't want to,' Entrican rejoined easily. 'It's quite interesting to look on.'

'All hopelessly illegal, I suppose? Ever been raided?'

'Oh, Lord, no! It's very mild. Technically, I suppose it is against the law, but actually it's all right. We don't play for high stakes and no one's any the worse.'

They presently arrived at the address. The door bore two names, that of the house agents and a small, dirty brass plate with the legend 'Abruzzi Club'. The door was shut, but Entrican produced a key and they let themselves in.

A faint light from a street lamp shone in through the old-fashioned fanlight and revealed a dirty passage with doors at either side. Entrican tapped an S.O.S.—three short, three long, three short—on one of the doors. It was promptly opened and they entered a small waiting-room. A huge man with the thickened neck and ears of the prize-fighter was in charge. He said 'Good evening' to Entrican and looked inquiringly at Crewe. 'My friend, Mr Crewe,' said Entrican. The man bowed, took their coats, and unlocking a second door, stood aside for them to pass.

This door opened on a staircase. They mounted it and entered a room which appeared to stretch over the entire first floor. In one corner was a bar with white-coated attendant, and round the walls were spaced armchairs and settees. In the centre were two small roulette tables. Round each of them a knot of people were gathered, while others sat about with drinks.

It was at once obvious to Crewe that the 'club' was a

highly illegal undertaking, and that if the police were to call, all present would find themselves under arrest. He wondered why Entrican had introduced him, a stranger, without at least a promise that he would keep the secret. Somehow he could scarcely imagine it was mere disinterested kindness, but he could not see what object the young man might have in view.

'Oh, here's Jepton,' came Entrican's voice behind him. 'Let me introduce you.'

'Mr Peter Jepton' was a young man resembling closely enough Entrican himself. He greeted Crewe with some effusion and immediately suggested a drink.

'This your first visit to the Abruzzi?' he asked as they sank into the luxurious corners of a settee.

'Yes, I never even heard of it until Entrican asked me today. But I'm here under false pretences really. I can't afford to play.'

Jepton made what might be called a semi-French gesture. 'Oh, that's all right,' he said reassuringly. 'A lot of us don't play. I myself only do it very occasionally. I come here to watch. It's a change, at all events.'

'I should gamble if I had money enough,' Crewe declared. 'I tried it once at Monte and enjoyed it. But I lost everything I staked, and that rather put me off.'

'You're bound to if you go on long enough. The thing to do is to stop if you get a stroke of luck.'

'But nobody does.'

'That's it,' Jepton agreed.

At intervals as they chatted fresh people entered. The room was now well filled. Every seat round the tables was taken, while a ring of observers stood behind the players. Presently Crewe saw the two people with whom he had dined a couple of nights before—Stowe and Moffatt. Stowe caught his eye, hesitated for a moment, and then came forward.

'Good evening,' he greeted Crewe. 'I didn't expect to see you here. Have you been playing? Evening, Jepton.' He turned to Moffatt. 'Here's our friend that we met at Harrison's.'

Sir Richard nodded and they pulled up chairs and called for drinks.

'How did you hear of this place?' Stowe asked. 'I don't think I've seen you here before.'

'Entrican kindly brought me. But as I've been saying to Jepton, I'm a fraud. I can't afford to play.'

'Don't let that worry you. It's a free country, and you're not bound to play unless you want to.'

Crewe enjoyed his evening in a mild way, except that it lasted too long. He was tired and wanted to go to bed, but it was nearly three before he could get Entrican away. 'I'm broke and I'm winning, so I must go on,' Entrican invariably declared when he approached him. But at last they left.

'That's a pony to the good, at all events,' Entrican said as they hailed a belated taxi. 'The first time I've won for weeks.'

The young man had taken more than was good for him. He was garrulous in the taxi. And he would talk of nothing but his employers and their household. He was very outspoken in his strictures. No member of the family escaped criticism.

Harrison, he now said, was a complete crook and liar, overbearing and aggressive, and utterly relentless if he got his knife into anyone. Nor was he above looking elsewhere for the sympathy his wife refused him. Entrican spoke darkly of lady secretaries.

But if Harrison was the Compleat Cad, Mrs Harrison was the Compleat Snob. For herself and her social advance she would sacrifice her nearest and dearest. According to Entrican she kept her husband shadowed by detectives, in the hope of collecting evidence for a divorce. Harrison knew this and was torn by the desires, on the one hand to supply the evidence and be rid of her, and on the other to withhold it so that she might be disappointed. It appeared, however, that she was not above reproach herself. For years past her 'name had been coupled' with someone called Locke, though Entrican thought the attachment was more on his side than hers.

About Gloria Entrican was more guarded, though even here his potations had loosened his tongue. Gloria was unhappy with her family, and particularly with her stepmother. She and young Jasper Coleman were in love and wanted to be engaged, but the Harrisons wished her to marry Lord Algy Mannering. Harrison had informed her that if she married Coleman he would cut her off-with a shilling. As Coleman had no money to speak of and only a poor job, matters had thus drifted into a condition of stalemate.

Next day Harrison returned from Paris. He had, Entrican explained, frequent business there, being interested in the financing of French Government loans. But his journey on this occasion was not connected with that. He had gone to try to trace the source of the rumours which were depressing, his stock, with what result Entrican didn't know.

A week later Harrison went to Paris again. He left on Sunday afternoon and was due back by the day service on Tuesday. But on Tuesday a wire came saying he was delayed and would cross by the eight-twenty service on Wednesday.

Crewe had a quiet day on that Wednesday. He had got through his work in the forenoon, and, everyone else being out, had lunched alone. In the afternoon he had called on no less than three lots of people, all of whom were out. Slightly disgruntled, he returned to Mount Street about six o'clock. Hearn opened the door.

'The *Westminster Guardian* people have been on the phone two or three times, sir,' he said. 'They have asked if Mr Harrison has yet returned, and when I answered that he had not, they asked to speak to one of the family. But no one was in. There,' the telephone bell came stridently, 'I expect that's another call. If so, would you speak to them?'

'Right,' Crewe agreed.

'Yes, sir, it's the *Guardian*,' Hearn went on presently. 'I'll put you through.'

Crewe went into the telephone cabinet and said: 'Hullo!'

'Sorry to trouble you,' was the reply. 'This is the *Westminster Guardian*. Can you give me any information as to the whereabouts of Mr Harrison?'

'None,' Crewe returned helpfully.

'We understood he had gone to Paris?'

'Yes. He was in Paris yesterday, and there was a wire that he was leaving by the eight-twenty service this morning.'

'We understood that also. What I am inquiring about is whether he made any change of plans?'

'Not to my knowledge. I suggest you ask his office.'

'I have done so. They know nothing further.'

'Well, I know nothing further, either.'

'It's rather urgent,' the voice insisted, 'otherwise I shouldn't trouble you. Might I ask who is speaking?'

Crewe told him.

'I wonder if you would be good enough to make quite

sure that no message has come from Mr Harrison; a message might have been taken by somebody else. As I say, it's really urgent.'

'I haven't had anything,' Crewe returned. 'But hold on a moment and I'll inquire.'

Hearn was still hovering in the distance. Crewe called him over.

'That's what they asked me, sir,' the man declared. 'There has been nothing.'

'No letter from Mrs Harrison or Mr Entrican?'

'No, sir; I saw all the letters and there was none from Mr Harrison.'

Crewe repeated this. 'But he should be here at any time,' he went on. 'What's all the excitement?'

There was a slight hesitation. 'As a matter of fact, we are informed that he came today from Paris as far as Dover, but left the train there. We were anxious to confirm or otherwise.'

Crewe was growing slightly annoyed. 'Well, I can't help you,' he said shortly. 'I don't see that it matters to either of us. Suppose he did leave the train; isn't it his own business?'

'Oh, yes, quite,' the speaker agreed. 'But if you do hear, I wonder if you'd be so kind as to ring us up. As I said, it really is rather urgent.'

Crewe rang off, but when Mrs Harrison came in a few minutes later, he told her of the inquiry.

'Damned impertinence,' was her comment. 'I hope you told them to mind their own business?'

'Yes, or words to that effect.'

Mrs Harrison nodded, and the subject dropped. But it was revived later in the evening.

At dinner-time, Harrison had not turned up and had sent no message. In view of the newspaper inquiry, Crewe began to wonder if anything could really be wrong. No one else, however, appeared to give the matter a thought.

The meal was just over when Hearn appeared and called Entrican mysteriously from the room. He was absent for a few minutes and then returned, looking worried.

'There's a representative from the *Westminster Guardian* in the morning-room,' he told Mrs Harrison. 'He appears upset about Mr Harrison—thinks that something may have happened to prevent his returning. He's extremely anxious to see you, if you could spare him a minute.'

'Happened?' returned the lady. 'What does he mean?'

'He wouldn't say, except that his business was urgent.'

'I should have thought it was your business to deal with such matters,' she said unpleasantly. 'However, I suppose I'll have to see him.'

Entrican did not reply, but held the door open for her and followed her out.

'What's it all about?' asked Rupert. Crewe told of the previous inquiry.

'It sounds serious,' Gloria commented. 'They've got hold of something. Wonder what it is.'

'Looks like it,' Rupert agreed. 'He hasn't turned up and a lot of trains from Dover must be in by now.'

Though Crewe felt vaguely uneasy, he resumed a story which had been interrupted by Hearn. They chatted for some minutes, and then Mrs Harrison and Entrican came back. She was looking furious and he more worried than ever.

'What do you think?' she began indignantly. 'These wretched *Guardian* people have started a cock-and-bull story that your father has disappeared.'

There were exclamations of surprise and protest.

'They say,' Mrs Harrison continued, 'that they have

34

information that he travelled from Paris to Dover by the eight-twenty service, and that he went into the station at Dover as if he was going to the train, and then turned suddenly and walked out into the street.'

'But why shouldn't he, if he wanted to?' asked Rupert.

'That's what I asked the man, but it didn't seem to satisfy him. He said that if we had been expecting your father, and he hadn't turned up or let us know, that it looked as if their information was correct.'

'It does,' Gloria agreed. 'But what is that to the *Guardian*?'

Mrs Harrison made a gesture of anger. 'This,' she declared fiercely: 'They say your father's such an important man that anything about him is news. If we can't satisfy them about him, they're going to make a scoop of his disappearance tomorrow.'

Rupert leant back in his chair. 'But they can't do that,' he drawled. 'They forget the law of libel.'

'That's what I told the man, but he said there would be no libel in the matter. Their report would be the actual truth on a matter of public interest.'

'Funny we haven't heard, all the same,' Gloria put in more thoughtfully. 'You know it's not like father not to phone us if he changes his plans.'

Rupert shrugged. 'He's seen somebody he wanted to have a chat with, and stopped off, intending to come by a later train. Probably he forgot to wire, or wired so late that we've not got it yet.'

'I feel sure that's it,' Entrican ventured. Mrs Harrison turned on him. 'No doubt, but that's not the point. What we want help in is to get this cursed newspaper from making a scare about it. He'll be perfectly furious if they do. Besides, that's not the sort of publicity any of us want.'

Gloria tossed her head. 'He needn't be furious. If there is publicity, it'll be his own fault. Why didn't he let us know?'

Mrs Harrison frowned at her. 'I expect to see him walk in any moment.' She glanced round questioningly and lowered her voice. 'I think if we can't silence the *Guardian* in any other way, I'll telephone that he has come home.'

Crewe left them discussing this novel method of dealing with the problem. It certainly was strange about Harrison. And when later on Entrican came in for a chat, he could see that he took a serious view of the situation.

'I've been with Harrison now for nearly four years,' he declared, 'and I never knew him to do such a thing before. He's a methodical man and keeps to the day's programme he has arranged. If he does change his plans, he invariably informs all concerned.'

'It doesn't look too well to me, either,' Crewe admitted.

'It's this newspaper affair that's so disquieting. They know something they haven't told us.'

'You think so?'

'I'm sure of it. I wanted to go round and see the editor and find out what it was, but Mrs Harrison wouldn't hear of it. She declares she will tell them she has had a message from him that he is staying the night in Dover. I urged her not, but she wouldn't listen.'

'It would keep the paper quiet.'

Entrican considered this with his air of weighing all the possibilities before pronouncing judgment.

'It might,' he said slowly, 'or again it mightn't. If they know something, it probably wouldn't. Besides, if there really is anything wrong, giving this false information might look very badly later.'

Crewe crossed to a cupboard, took out his decanter and

siphon and put them beside his companion. 'You, then, do fear something serious?' he asked.

Entrican helped himself to whisky. 'Well,' he said after another pause, 'I feel that if he has taken some drastic step, his family should give all the help to the authorities from the start.'

'What do you mean by drastic step?'

Entrican seemed suddenly to think that he had gone too far. He, as it were, withdrew into himself. 'Nothing special,' he parried. 'I mean simply that if anything has happened, it would be wiser not to give the impression of trying to keep it dark. But perhaps I'm wrong and it's all a false alarm.'

'Let's hope so. Is anyone going to sit up?'

Entrican thought not. Crewe, at least, did not see why he should, so after arranging with Entrican to come and tell him if there were developments, he turned in.

4

The Missing Financier

When Crewe went down next morning he found that the household was taking the affair much more seriously than on the previous night.

He met Hearn in the hall. 'Any news this morning?' he asked.

The man shook his head gravely. 'No, sir. No information of any kind has been received. But there's a notice in the *Guardian*.'

Crewe passed on to the breakfast-room. Mrs Harrison seldom came down for breakfast, but she was there this morning, looking worried and, he thought, the least little bit alarmed. Entrican was also there, evidently very much upset. They nodded absently as Crewe took his place.

'Seen that?' Entrican passed over the *Westminster Guardian*, his thumb marking a paragraph.

A single column in the middle of the centre page—the *Guardian*'s chief news page—was headed in large letters:

WELL-KNOWN FINANCIER MISSING.
MR ANDREW HARRISON DISAPPEARS
DURING JOURNEY FROM PARIS.
HIS WHEREABOUTS UNKNOWN.

Crewe whistled soundlessly. The *Guardian* had taken the plunge all right. The paragraph beneath, however, was more restrained.

Mr Andrew Harrison, the financier, *it read*, disappeared yesterday while travelling by the 8.20 service from Paris to London.

It is believed that he reached Dover, for a man closely resembling him was seen to leave the station just after the start of the boat train. Since then all trace of him has been lost.

Mr Harrison had intended to return on Tuesday, but on that day a wire was received from him saying he had been detained in Paris and would come by the service mentioned on Wednesday.

The missing gentleman is known to have been working at high pressure recently, and it is feared that he may be suffering from loss of memory.

This was followed by some notes of Harrison's career, the whole being expanded with journalistic skill to form a full column of highly readable matter.

'I wonder if that's all they know?' Crewe commented.

'I think so,' Entrican replied. 'It's all they would tell us at all events. Mrs Harrison and I went round to see the editor after I left you last night.'

'He was most offensive,' the lady broke in with venom.

'I asked him quite directly not to insert the paragraph and he refused. Actually refused my request to my face!'

Crewe imagined this wasn't a frequent experience, and smiled inwardly. 'Well,' he pointed out, 'it would be big news for his paper, and he'd naturally want to make the most of it. Any of the other papers got it?'

'None.' Entrican indicated a pile on a side table. 'I've been through them all.'

'But that won't matter,' Mrs Harrison put in. 'Everyone will know from this.'

'Very distressing,' Crewe said sympathetically. 'And I question if there's any remedy. The *Guardian* people have had their eye on libel when they wrote.'

'Yes,' Entrican agreed. 'It's skilfully done.' As they talked, Crewe could watch Mrs Harrison's annoyance ebb and a certain fear taking its place. At length, after a period of silence, she turned to them and burst out: 'I'm worried about all this! It's not like him not to have let us know. I wonder if we should do anything?'

'Well,' Entrican returned, 'I'm afraid there's only one thing that you can do. I don't know what you think, Crewe,' he looked across the table, 'but it seems to me rather early to take such a step.'

'You mean to inform the police?' asked Crewe, who disliked hints.

'Yes; I don't see what else is possible.'

Crewe hesitated. 'I don't see either. Unless,' he went on after a pause, 'you happen to know his business in Paris? Any good ringing up whoever he saw? What do you say, Mrs Harrison?'

Entrican made a gesture of impotence. 'If I knew whom he met I would have suggested that long ago. But I don't. He didn't tell me where he was going.'

Mrs Harrison was listening with attention. 'Perhaps Mr Kemp knows,' she suggested. Kemp, Crewe had heard, was the head of the office staff, Harrison's second-in-command.

Entrican rose. 'I've rung him up. He knows nothing. Perhaps you'd like him to come round?'

'Yes; ask him to. And he had better bring Mr Harrison's secretary, Miss What's-her-name?'

'I'll arrange it at once.'

Mrs Harrison was always more gracious to Crewe when they were alone. She turned to him now in an almost friendly way.

'Unfortunately, I don't know where he went either. He discusses social matters with me, though not business; which is quite correct, for I shouldn't understand business and should be bored.'

'Of course,' Crewe agreed. 'Did he know anyone in Dover?'

'Not to my knowledge. But Mr Harrison knows everyone. He might have met a dozen friends at the station.'

'Quite,' Crewe agreed.

'What do you think, Mr Crewe? Should we tell the police? I mean, if Mr Kemp can suggest nothing?'

Crewe hesitated. 'I hardly like to advise. I think, on the whole, I should wait till lunch time. Mr Harrison may have sent a message which has miscarried. But he won't know it has miscarried until he sees the *Guardian*. As soon as he sees the *Guardian* he'll send another message. If he doesn't do so, I think a report to the police would be justified.'

'You're probably right.'

'But,' Crewe went on, 'I shouldn't report to the nearest station. I should get in touch with someone high up in Scotland Yard, who'll understand that the inquiry must be handled discreetly.'

Mrs Harrison looked impressed and slightly surprised at Crewe's common sense. However, she did not reply, as Entrican entered at that moment.

'Kemp and Miss Lavender are coming round at once,' he reported, 'though they know nothing.'

Crewe was not present at the interview, but Entrican later repeated what had been said. Harrison had told Kemp that he was going to Paris and would be out of the office on Monday and Tuesday, though he had not mentioned his business. Both Kemp and the secretary had believed it was in connection with the rumours which were depreciating the stocks, which were thought to have originated in Paris. Neither, however, could state this positively.

The morning dragged through leadenly, and at lunch the question of going to Scotland Yard was reopened. But Mrs Harrison decided against it. 'I'm sure he's all right,' she declared. 'I feel satisfied he sent a message which has gone astray. And he may not have seen the *Guardian*. He may have read *The Times*. No, I think we'll wait a little longer.'

Crewe disagreed with her, as did Entrican, though less emphatically. But she could not be moved, and both Gloria and Rupert backed her up.

The evening papers quickly made her change her mind. All had heavily-headed headlines, and all made the disappearance their most important news item. They were circumspect in language, stating directly no more than the *Guardian*—that Harrison had left Paris on the previous morning and had not reached London, and that his whereabouts was unknown. But with a life history, interviews with various people, and more or less veiled suggestions, all padded up with infinite journalistic skill, they made the affair one of major importance. The *Standard* had three columns, the *Star* two, and the *News* a half page.

All devoted space to the effect of the affair on the stock markets. Though Entrican had kept all day in touch with the office, the family had scarcely realised how serious was the position. Harrison stocks were simply tumbling. If Harrison did not soon turn up, it looked as if there might be a complete collapse.

It was this news which forced Mrs Harrison to a decision. 'Apart from ourselves, half the people in the country will be ruined,' she said to Crewe and Entrican. 'I think that justifies me in acting. Will you two gentlemen go to Scotland Yard and see someone? Get them properly stirred up, and tell them not to make more publicity that they can help, though, of course,' she added with a bitter look at the pile of papers, 'that scarcely matters now. I suppose neither of you know anyone at the Yard?'

Entrican shook his head, but Crewe had a suggestion. 'I don't know anyone myself,' he said, 'but my father's old friend, Colonel Hepplewhite, knows Sir Mortimer Ellison, one of the Assistant Commissioners. I could get an introduction to him if you liked.'

Mrs Harrison thought this an excellent idea, and Gloria and Rupert agreed with her.

Presently the two men set off, and having obtained the introduction, reached the Yard. After a short delay a young constable led them up to Sir Mortimer's room. It was furnished like an office, save for the couple of rather worn armchairs at either side of the fireplace. At a table desk sat the A.C. He rose as they entered.

'Mr Crewe?' He held out his hand. 'I knew your father. We met I don't like to think how many years ago when I was in India. He was major then, I remember.'

'Yes, he was on the Viceroy's staff.'

'So was I—in a different branch. And this is Mr—?'

'Mr Entrican. And when I tell you that we're both secretaries to Mr Andrew Harrison, you can guess our business.'

Sir Mortimer waved them to the armchairs and passed over his cigarette case. 'Ah, yes. I thought when I saw the papers that unless Mr Harrison turned up soon we should hear more about it. A very well-known man, Mr Harrison. Did you decide to come here on your own responsibility?'

'No. We suggested it, but Mrs Harrison, of course, had the final word. I should say that she's very anxious that there should be as little more publicity as possible. That's why we're troubling you instead of going to the local police.'

'A neatly turned compliment,' Sir Mortimer said dryly. 'She wishes the affair to be handled with circumspection. Well, we'll try to do so. And now, as time may prove of value, we'd better waste no more on preliminaries. Just one question before we begin: Why did you not come to us earlier?'

Crewe explained.

'And you think that as he hasn't sent a second message it's because he is unable to do so?'

'That was our idea.'

'Probably quite sound, too. Now will you begin at the beginning and tell me all you can about the affair?'

Crewe glanced at Entrican. 'You know more than I do, I think? Hadn't you better—?'

'Right,' said Entrican. 'Well, I should begin by explaining just what we both do,' and he mentioned their position in the household, going on to tell of Harrison's journey to France and its possible object.

Sir Mortimer gave him a keen glance from his heavy

lidded eyes. 'This may require some looking into,' he said, 'so we might have an officer in.' He picked up his desk telephone. 'What are you doing French? . . . Well, can't Willis finish that off? . . . Right, then; come along here, will you, and bring a stenographer.' He replaced the receiver. 'That'll save you repeating your story twice, Mr Entrican.' He smiled. 'If you can satisfy Chief Inspector French about details, you'll satisfy me.'

He chatted on till the door opened and a blue-eyed, kindly-looking man of slightly below middle height entered, followed by a tall young fellow, obviously a constable in plain clothes. The A.C. introduced French. 'I've been telling these gentlemen you may have to make some inquiries, so should hear their statement from the beginning. It's about the disappearance of Mr Andrew Harrison, which you may have seen in the papers,' and he summarised what Entrican had said. 'Now, Mr Entrican, just go ahead and tell us all you can about those rumours. The chief inspector will then ask his questions.'

'How long is it since they began, sir?' French said as Entrican seemed to be at a loss how to start.

'I don't know exactly. About a month since I heard them. But of course they probably were circulating some time before they reached my ears.'

'Can you remember who mentioned them first?'

'I heard them from a number of people. I'm not sure, but I think Mr Kemp was the first. That's Mr Harrison's general manager.'

'And just what form did they take?'

Entrican favoured his questioner with one of his ruminative pauses. 'Very hard to put into words,' he said at length. 'There was more a general suggestion that something might be wrong than a definite statement. Someone would come up to me and say: "Look here, old man, I don't want you to give away cabinet secrets, but I've got most of my little all in Harrison's, and you know what's being whispered. For the love of Mike give me the straight tip if I ought to get out, strictly on the q.t., of course." That sort of thing, you understand. Nothing to take hold of, but a suggestion of trouble.'

'No one put into definite words what was suspected?'

'No. There were hints and sly references to Kruger and the Swedish Match Company and all that. Suggestive, but not actionable, if you know what I mean.'

'Clearly, sir. Now these rumours had an effect on the stocks?'

'A very considerable effect,' Entrican rejoined with decision. 'They had dropped something like eight points before this present affair.'

'Do you think it was the rumours which caused the drop, or the drop which caused the rumours?'

'Obviously the first. It wasn't until after the rumours were in circulation that the drop began.'

French nodded. 'Now here,' he said, 'is a more difficult question, and I may just mention that all that passes here is confidential except what proves to be material evidence in a case of crime. How much truth was there in the rumours?'

Again Entrican spoke with decision. 'So far as I know, absolutely none. Only Mr Harrison himself could definitely answer the question, but I myself do not believe a word of them.'

'From his confidential financial secretary that's pretty strong evidence, sir. I suppose if anything did go wrong it would be a pretty serious matter for a lot of people?'

'I should just think so! Ruin to thousands.'

'Hence the nervousness of the holders?'

'It's not hard to understand. If all your savings were in a concern that you heard was shaky, you'd sell, no matter at what loss.'

'Quite so, sir. Now where does Mr Harrison usually stay in Paris?'

'At the Miranda Palace.'

'And can you give me a list of his friends there?'

'I can make a list from my letter-books, but of course I can't say that it will be exhaustive.'

'It may be a help, sir. I would like also the wire he sent saying he would return on the Wednesday instead of the Tuesday.'

'I'll enclose that too.'

'Can you also give me a list of Mr Harrison's special English business friends?'

For the first time Entrican laughed, though it was mirthlessly. 'The members of the Stock Exchange and financiers in the City of London and elsewhere,' he returned. 'No, chief inspector, I'm afraid I can't answer that. His operations were very large and he knew a very large number of people.'

French paused, and Crewe saw him exchange a rapid glance with his chief. The latter very slightly shook his head. French relaxed his attitude.

'Well, we're much obliged to you, Mr Entrican, for your patience. I think that's all at present. I will put some inquiries in hand, and if I want more from either of you gentlemen, I have your address.'

'Yes,' Sir Mortimer added, 'we'll do what we can. And you may tell Mrs Harrison that if we hear anything we'll let her know at once.'

Mrs Harrison seemed a little disappointed that Scotland Yard had not then and there produced her husband, and was disparaging about their promises. However, nothing more could be done, and she was obviously relieved that the matter was out of her hands.

The later editions of the evening papers came out with fresh headlines and rearranged columns, but with no additional information. But the mere fact that so much more time had elapsed since the disappearance had a very distinct bearing on the situation. Every hour that passed made things look worse. The more Crewe thought of it, the more likely accident or something even more sinister became. Evidently also Scotland Yard took a serious view if they had put a chief inspector on the case. Then Crewe wondered if he were right in this. Their action might have been due simply to Harrison's position.

Entrican also appeared increasingly anxious. 'It looks badly,' he said; 'very badly indeed.' He shook his head solemnly.

'What do you fear?' asked Crewe.

Entrican flung himself into an armchair. 'What about a spot of that whisky of yours, old man?' he suggested. 'I'm just about tired out.' He sat for a moment staring before him into vacancy, then returned: 'What do you fear yourself?'

Crewe poured out a couple of stiff tots. 'I don't know what to think,' he admitted, 'except that no trivial explanation will cover the thing.'

'You've said it.' Entrican tossed off his whisky. 'And that opens up some nasty possibilities.' He put down his glass. 'Do you know what they're saying tonight?' Entrican sank his voice. 'That he's seen a crash coming and cleared out while the going was good.'

'Well,' retorted Crewe, 'and is it impossible?'

'They're saying,' went on Entrican, 'that it'll be found the coffers have been cleared, and though there may be thousands ruined, he'll be all right.'

'Is it impossible?' Crewe repeated.

Entrican made a sudden gesture. 'Of course it's not impossible. But,' he paused, 'it's darned unlikely.'

'You think he's not capable of it?'

Entrican laughed scornfully. 'I think it's exactly what he'd do. No, it's not that; it's because I think the stock is sound.'

'What's been in my mind is that a great many people have reason to dislike Harrison.'

'Foul play?' Entrican shook his head. 'I don't think you need consider that. If what those *Guardian* people told us is true, he was seen walking out of Dover Pier Station. That looks to me like a voluntary job.'

'He might have been got away by some trick.' Entrican gave another scornful laugh. 'Harrison? Not a blinking chance! He's not the bird to be caught with chaff. No, if the Guardian story's true he's gone off voluntarily.'

'But you've just said you didn't think so, because the stock was sound.'

Entrican glanced at him questioningly. 'No,' he declared; 'I said I didn't think he had gone off with other people's cash. I didn't say he hadn't gone off.'

"Well, you've got me beaten now. Just what do you mean?'

'I think it's clear enough. Harrison's a man like the rest of us. He wants the same things. He has no home life here—not to call home life. You've seen how he and Mrs H. and Gloria hate each other. My belief is,' again he lowered his voice, 'that he has gone off with a woman.'

Crewe looked surprised. 'Are you serious? You know, I shouldn't have said he was that sort of man.'

'We're all that sort of man,' Entrican pronounced. 'Besides, it's just a man like him who would make a break—when he's worried with business and dog tired.'

Crewe pondered. 'You may be right,' he admitted at length. 'But even so, it would play old Harry with his stocks. They'd drop just the same and a lot of people would be ruined.'

'Probably thousands. The stock would come right again, but these people would sell when it had slumped.'

'Make a difference to the family.'

Entrican made a savage gesture. 'Hang the family! The family'd be all right. But somebody else would suffer. Who do you think?'

Crewe nodded. 'I know. I've been thinking of that. Whatever happens, we're likely to be out of a job.'

Entrican slapped his thigh. 'That's it! That's what has been worrying me since it happened. I know what it is to be out of a job, and I don't want to experience it again.'

'I know it, too.'

'That's the trouble,' Entrican repeated. 'It doesn't really matter to us very much what's happened to Harrison: he never made himself so popular with us that we should care. But if there's any scandal it won't help us to another job.'

Crewe agreed and put forward once again his theory of murder. This Entrican scouted, and arguing their respective viewpoints, the two men drained their glasses and went up to bed.

5

The Undelivered Message

The disappearance had got on Crewe's mind, and he could not sleep. Though he had met tragedy before—the fatality to his father was still comparatively recent—this was the first time in which an atmosphere of mystery and suspicion had touched him. And very trying he found it. Ignorance of what was happening and the fear of some unknown blow produced a gnawing sense of suspense and unrest. In spite of Entrican's scorn, he could not help pitying the family. Apart from possible feelings of affection for Harrison, they must be dreading loss of money and position and perhaps a shameful notoriety. To Mrs Harrison such would be almost worse than death, and it would also fall hard upon the young people.

Crewe's thoughts turned to the disappearance itself. The more he considered Entrican's theory of Harrison and a woman, the less likely it seemed. Harrison was one of those fighters who loved the money game for its own sake. Though no doubt he felt the need of feminine sympathy, he was unlikely to give up the financial battle to obtain it. Besides, feminine sympathy—or what passes for it—could be had without any such sacrifice. Harrison could do as so many in his position did—keep a second establishment. No, Crewe felt a growing certainty that whatever had happened, it was not this.

Then what was it?

Escape from an impending crash? This certainly seemed more likely. Such an event had been paralleled in countless instances in the past. How many a man, seeing his circumstances growing desperate, had realised all the cash he could, and cleared out before the deluge. While Crewe felt that Harrison was not the man to sacrifice his career for a woman, he was exactly the type who in a crisis would seize all he could for himself and get out, careless of what those he left behind might suffer.

If, however, Entrican were correct that the stocks were sound, it knocked the bottom out of this theory. Admittedly Entrican couldn't know this with certainty. But, Crewe asked himself, who had a better opportunity of forming an opinion on such a point than a man's own private financial secretary?

Assuming for argument's sake that Entrican were correct, it made it very unlikely that Harrison had disappeared voluntarily. And precise similar arguments tended against the idea of suicide. Accident seemed even more improbable. Where in the neighbourhood of Dover Station could Harrison meet with an accident unknown to other persons?

But if voluntary disappearance, accident and suicide were ruled out, it left only the theory that Crewe had himself put up—that Harrison had been the victim of foul play. As Crewe weighed this idea he saw that at least there was no lack of motive for murder.

How extraordinarily well Harrison's death would suit almost everyone with whom Crewe had yet come in contact!

First there was Mrs Harrison. She apparently wanted a divorce and could not obtain the necessary evidence. If so, her husband's death would solve her problem. It might well be the thing of all others she desired. If she were really in love with someone else, the motive might grow overwhelmingly strong.

Gloria, too, had a very similar reason for wishing her father's control at an end. She was in love with young Coleman. But he had no money, and if she married him her father would cut hers off too. Therefore her happiness, like her stepmother's, could best be obtained by his death.

Much the same applied to Rupert. His father's opposition overcome, he could go to sea. He could adopt the profession he so much desired, without having first to give up his home and inheritance. Not perhaps so strong a motive for murder as in the other two cases, but still sufficient.

Crewe, of course, did not suspect any one of the three. That was not the point which had occurred to him. It was rather that Harrison had given each of the three persons who were nearest to him a motive for murdering him. When this was true of the members of his own family, how much more would it be true of his business rivals, of those he had crippled and ruined in his own success? An unscrupulous and relentless financier is universally hated. How many people must have become Harrison's bitter enemies? How many were prevented from killing him only by fear of consequences; another way of saying that, given the opportunity, they would take it.

It grew increasingly obvious to Crewe that this was the only theory of the disappearance which would cover the facts. And he did not think that Entrican's objection to it was really material. Suppose the *Guardian*'s statement were true and that Harrison had walked out of the Dover Station of his own free will. In spite of Entrican's belief in his shrewdness, he could have been tricked. It only meant thinking out a good enough story: surely not an impossible achievement. And if he had been so tricked all the facts would be accounted for.

Next morning all restraint had vanished from the newspapers. They plunged into the affair with avidity. They wallowed in it. The rumours of insolvency were no longer confined to whispers and asides. They were printed openly, and though the actual statement was avoided, it was conveyed plainly enough that in it lay the explanation of the whole affair.

Though probably so vague as to avoid grounds for legal action, every reader was given to understand that the Harrison stock was cracking, and that he had foreseen it and cleared out while there was still time.

'That'll about put the lid on things,' Entrican said gloomily. 'No stocks could stand against such panic mongering. You'll find that perfectly good investments are worthless before the day's out.'

His prognostications seemed about to be justified. All that morning news kept coming in of tumbling prices and ruined fortunes. Every time the telephone rang it was to announce that a new low level had been reached. In vain Kemp and his assistants issued reassuring statements. Panic had gripped the public, and all that they wanted was to turn their holdings into cash, no matter at how great a loss.

Crewe did not see the Harrisons. But Entrican told him that at last their calm had vanished. The panic had now spread to them and they could now visualise nothing less than complete ruin. Crewe kept at work, answering the more immediate letters, but he felt that he might just as well save his trouble for all the attention they would receive.

Then, just before midday he became conscious that something was happening. The telephone rang incessantly and hurried steps ran to and fro. He went out into the lounge. Entrican was telephoning excitedly. As Crewe went forward he replaced the receiver.

'Can you beat that?' he asked, his features moulded into an expression of amazement.

'What?' Crewe returned.

'Gosh! Have you not heard? He's all right.'

'All right?' Crewe repeated stupidly.

'All right! Can't you understand English?'

Crewe gaped. How could the words have their literal meaning?

'I don't know what you're talking about,' he said. 'Do you mean Harrison's well?'

'Of course I do! Absolutely all right in every way.'

'Then why—oh, come on, Entrican, I'm not a thought reader. What's happened?'

Entrican came down to earth. 'He has just rung up,' he explained, 'from Folkestone. Said he had only now seen the papers. The whole thing's a mistake. He'd been out with a friend in a yacht.'

Crewe made a gesture of exasperation. 'But that doesn't explain it, you owl! Why didn't he let us know?'

'He did let us know—or says he did. He wrote a telegram and gave it to a porter at Dover.'

'And the man destroyed it and pocketed the fee.' Crewe whistled. 'It's not like a porter, I will say.'

'Well, there you are. The old man says he gave it to him. Then he went out sailing with the friend and never heard a thing about the excitement till he landed today.'

The story seemed to Crewe extraordinarily improbable. Even in the short time he had been with Harrison he had observed how tenaciously he adhered to his plans. If the man had intended to return to London by the afternoon train on the Wednesday, he would have done so, unless prevented by something over which he had no control. And he had intended to return. Suddenly to change his mind for so trivial a reason as to go sailing would be quite unlike him. And if to that were added the equally improbable statement that a porter had failed to send a telegram with which he had been entrusted, the result was surely beyond credence.

'Doesn't sound frightfully likely to me,' Crewe observed mildly.

Entrican shrugged. 'Well, that's what he says,' he repeated. 'It would seem to cover the facts.'

'We don't know the facts,' Crewe countered. 'Did he ring up here?'

'No; to the office. Kemp rang us up. But that was all right. He wanted to talk to Kemp, and it's quicker to get one trunk call and a local than two trunks.'

'His stocks?'

Entrican nodded. 'He wanted his return known at once to try and stop the run.'

'Too late, surely?'

'I don't think so. I wish I had about a hundred thousand. I'd buy, and in two or three days I'd be a rich man.'

'How are they taking it?' Crewe asked with a gesture towards the upper rooms.

'Relieved, I think. Mrs H. is grousing that we went to Scotland Yard. I've just been ringing them up.'

Crewe shook his head. 'It's what I call fishy,' he concluded. 'I'll bet there's more in it than meets the eye.'

But when a little later he read Harrison's full statement in the evening papers, he had to admit it was not so improbable as he had imagined. The financier began with a declaration that while he had acted with the best intentions and, he believed, with scrupulous correctness all through, he still desired to tender a very full apology and an expression of deep regret for the misunderstanding, to all those who had suffered or been in any way inconvenienced thereby. Owing to the unusual circumstances he felt he must explain exactly what had taken place, though this meant revealing a fact which he had intended to keep secret.

Some time previously, the statement went on, he had been approached by two men with a very old story. They had, they said, a military invention of the greatest value, and they wanted money to develop it. They believed that not only would it put this country in a very advantageous position if war unhappily broke out, but also that they would be able to sell it to the Government for a very large sum. As a rule he, Harrison, paid no attention to such requests, but these men explained enough of their idea to make it appear both feasible and valuable. Some negotiations took place, and Harrison at last agreed that he would witness a demonstration with a model, and if favourably impressed would finance the construction of a full-sized machine. For obvious reasons this demonstration could only be made in the greatest secrecy. The men suggested hiring a yacht and making the tests in the open sea, out of sight of land or shipping. To this Harrison agreed.

He had kept them advised of his movements, so that they could summon him to join them at short notice, the tests being possible only in exceptionally calm weather. When in Paris he had received a note from them saying that everything was at last in order, and that the test could be made if he would break his journey back to London. Should the weather remain suitable one of them would be on the platform at Dover Station when his train was leaving. This man would not attempt any communication, as their association should remain unknown, but his presence would be an intimation to Harrison to proceed to a rendezvous upon which they had already agreed. For the same reason the sailing and return of the yacht would be from a deserted spot on the coast.

When Harrison reached Dover he saw his acquaintance waiting for him. He had written out two messages, one to his family, the other to the office, and before leaving the station he gave them to a porter to send off. It was evident the porter had failed to do this. The man was reliable looking, and Harrison did not believe he had destroyed them to obtain the money. Rather he imagined he might have lost them and have been afraid to report it.

The tests had duly been carried out on the Thursday and Friday morning, and then he, Harrison, had been put ashore. But it was not till he saw a paper that he realised what had happened. Immediately he had rung up his office, explaining the circumstances, and instructing his staff to communicate with the Stock Exchange and the Press. He gave his personal assurance that his stocks were in a perfectly satisfactory condition, and ended by once again expressing his great regret at the incident.

Most of the papers printed leaders on the subject. They

moralised on the supreme importance of credit and character in business life, then pointed out that while sympathy must be felt for those who had suffered through the falling stock, those who had refrained from selling would doubtless find their potential losses made good. Finally they took the general line that the episode was closed, all being well that ended well.

Crewe was interested to notice the reactions of the various members of the household to the news. Entrican, whom he saw first, was obviously delighted. 'We've not lost our jobs, at all events,' he chuckled. 'I feel as if a ton had been lifted off my mind. And the help we gave during this time should improve our position with the family.'

The others he saw at lunch. Mrs Harrison was in a very unpleasant humour. Instead of expressing relief that the prospect of disaster had vanished, she appeared to resent the fact that her anxiety had been unnecessary. Crewe felt that Harrison would presently hear her considered opinion on the policy of trusting porters with telegrams, instead of going oneself to the office to ensure their proper despatch. She was short with Crewe, apparently blaming him for having suggested an unnecessary appeal to Scotland Yard, and specially for having obtained the introduction to Sir Mortimer Ellison. To Entrican, who inadvisedly stated his satisfaction at the closing of the incident, she was extremely rude.

In Gloria's and Rupert's cases also irritation seemed the predominant emotion. Crewe, indeed, was a trifle shocked to discover that both were sorry their father was not dead. Perhaps, he thought, he was wrong to judge them. Both had seen the liberty they longed for, and which they believed was in their grasp, suddenly snatched away.

Altogether lunch was not a happy meal, and Crewe was glad when it was over. He longed to have a chat over things with some of his own old friends, but extra work kept him busy all the afternoon. Indeed, he was hard at it until it was time to dress for dinner.

It was when he was upstairs that an unpleasant incident occurred. When he reached the fifth storey on his way up to his room he saw Gloria waiting for the lift to go down. He therefore stopped to give her preference, intending to go up the remaining flights on foot. She looked annoyed and disgusted.

'They're scrapping away worse than ever,' she said with a grimace, as Crewe held the door open for her.

He was surprised that she had mentioned such a matter— the first time she had been so intimate. But her reason immediately became obvious; there was no possibility of keeping it private. On this floor were the Harrisons' bedrooms, and through a closed door he could hear Harrison's voice raised in wrath. The sounds were muffled and he could not distinguish the words, but the tone was horrible.

Crewe told himself that the Harrison quarrels were no concern of his, and he was passing on to the stairs when the door of Mrs Harrison's room opened and Harrison swung out. His face was dark with rage and he slammed the door furiously behind him. He gave no sign of Crewe's presence, but passed like some whirling storm cloud across the lobby and into his own room, the door of which he also slammed.

Crewe was startled. Really, the man seemed scarcely sane. With an expression of that kind he looked capable of murder.

Fortunately by dinner-time passions had burnt themselves

out. An undercurrent of bitterness and hatred remained, but no one made any reference to what had happened, and outwardly the meal passed off conventionally.

Next morning the papers took the same tone as those of the previous afternoon. They had a good deal to say about the affair, but the only fresh information they gave was that the Harrison stocks had made an extraordinary rally, and that it was believed they would shortly recover to their previous level.

There had been, however, some terrible cases of loss. Already three suicides had taken place as a result of the slump, and countless people who had sold during the panic had lost almost all they possessed.

During the forenoon Crewe had occasion to go to the bank, and it was while he was there that he first heard a fresh and very unpleasant rumour. While waiting for the teller's attention he bumped into Tony Bagshott, with whom he had shared rooms at Magdalen and who was now secretary to a Ministry of Transport official. The two men had not met for some time, and withdrew from their respective queues for a chat.

'And what are you doing with yourself now?' Bagshott went on after reminiscences had been adequately discussed.

Crewe told him.

Bagshott whistled. 'Lord!' he exclaimed. '*That* bounder! Then you're news at present.'

Crewe said he hadn't realised it.

'Yes, everyone connected with Harrison is news, or soon will be. I'll bet you anything there's going to be trouble.'

'How do you mean, going to be? I thought the trouble was over.'

'Over, my eye!' Bagshott looked at him more closely. 'Do

you mean to tell me you haven't heard what they're saying now?'

'This is the first time I've been out of the house since Harrison came back. I've heard nothing.'

'You might have guessed it for yourself.' Bagshott glanced quickly round and dropped his voice. 'They're saying he did it on purpose.'

Crewe was puzzled. 'But of course he did it on purpose,' he rejoined. 'What do you mean?'

'You ass, Crewe; you've got slow in the uptake, as they say in Ireland. They're saying the whole story of the launch and invention is a yarn—that he hid deliberately and stayed hidden.'

Crewe starred. 'You mean—'

Yes. Done deliberately to juggle the stock about and make a pot. In other words, rob all those unfortunates who have have gone under.'

Crewe did not reply. He had not thought of this, but the moment it was suggested to him he realised its probability. The difficulties he had already seen in accepting Harrison's story occurred to him with redoubled force. But if this theory were true, Harrison had not changed his plans and the porter had not failed in his duty.

'A jolly ingenious idea,' went on Bagshott, adding as a sop to his conscience, 'if it's true. Just see how it would work out. Harrison is perhaps short—what he would consider short, I mean. He sees how he can make a pile. He starts rumours that his stock is unsound. He has countless agents in his power, and nothing would be easier. Then he sells, regularly and steadily. The stock begins to fall. That in itself strengthens the rumours, which depresses it still further. He stops selling, but other people have now got the wind up and are beginning to get out, so it continues to drop. Then when he thinks the psychological moment has come, he does this disappearing stunt. Attention must be called to it at once, so he rings up the *Westminster Guardian*, knowing that if he has given them the hint they'll do the rest.'

Crewe swore. 'That's why they were so mysterious about it,' he ejaculated.

'Oh,' Bagshott said eagerly. 'I didn't know about that. What do you mean?'

'Why, that we couldn't get any satisfactory statement from them. They were mysterious because they said they didn't know who had rung them up, or why.'

Bagshott nodded. 'There you are. Unexpected confirmation. Well, Harrison no doubt keeps closely in touch with the market, and when he considers things have have gone far enough he reappears. At once he buys—as much as he can. The stocks rise. By the time the thing is finished he'll have cleared out hundreds of small investors and transferred their little all to his own pockets.'

'Dirty swine, if he has,' Crewe declared indignantly. 'But look here, Bagshott, we don't know that he has. You can't condemn him unless there's proof.'

'You can't get proof in a thing like that. Even if he would tell the alleged inventor's name and the nature of the invention—and he has already supplied himself with a reason for not doing so—I bet he has arranged for people to come forward and swear he was out with them in the yacht. Perhaps he was. And it would be easy enough to give the nature of the invention. He would only have to say what it did; not how it did it.'

Crewe lit another cigarette. 'I see you've made up your

mind. But I'm not so sure. I think I should want some more facts before being convinced. But you said there was going to be trouble. Just what did you mean about that?'

Bagshott made an impatient gesture. 'What's happened to you, Crewe? Can't you see that for yourself? If this rumour is believed, and I think it's sure to be, someone of all these ruined people will see red. Look, for instance, at those suicides. If Harrison's guilty, he has murdered them. He hasn't a charmed life himself. What I mean is, if you want it in brutal words, someone will murder him before either of us is very much older.'

As Crewe walked slowly back to Mount Street, and after that as he sat in his room staring vacantly over his typewriter, he kept turning the story over in his mind. And the more he did so, the more likely it grew. As a statement it was certainly cohesive and logical, and it covered all the known facts. Was there, he wondered, any test by which its truth or falsehood could be demonstrated?

He thought there was. Could they find out whether Harrison had sold his own stock while it was high and re-bought it when it was low? If he had not done so, he was innocent of this crime. But if he had, so surely he was guilty.

Crewe was amazed to find that Entrican had not heard the rumour. It had an extraordinary effect on him. He stared at Crewe with goggling eyes and slapped his thigh. 'They're saying that, are they?' he exclaimed in a low voice. 'I believe they're right! It's exactly what the swine would do.'

But Entrican knew nothing of sales or purchases of stock. 'That's nothing, of course,' he pointed out. 'If the old man were on to a game of that kind, he'd never let Kemp or me know. He'd act through other agents. I don't know whether we could find out either—probably not.' He shrugged. 'But hang it all, Crewe, I don't want to know. I'm not responsible for his morality: that's his look out. I want my job and my salary and I'm not going to meddle in anything outside my own business. And if you're not a darned fool, you'll do the same.'

Crewe had to admit that there was a certain worldly wisdom in the advice.

6

The Vessel Cygnet

Next day the household settled down into its normal slightly unhappy life. Little reference was made to the crisis, and whatever the various members felt about it, they kept their own counsel. To Crewe the affair meant a lot of extra work, but as this was part of the price he was paying for the retention of his job, he did it thankfully.

It wasn't till a couple of days later that he had any intimate talk with Entrican, but then the financial secretary had some news.

'I was thinking over that theory we discussed,' he began; 'I mean whether Harrison vanished deliberately to depress his stocks. Well, it seemed to me that one piece of evidence, if we could get it, would settle the point.'

'I thought of that piece of evidence, too,' Crewe put in. 'Whether he sold out and then bought again?'

Entrican nodded. 'That's it. You asked the question, you remember, but I couldn't answer it. I've heard since.'

'You have?' Crewe's interest suddenly increased. 'And had he?'

'Kemp told me this morning. The old man's phone came about nine. He told Kemp to keep it dark that he had heard from him, and to buy, buy, buy. Then as soon as Kemp had cleared the market he was to ring up Mrs H. and release the good news.

Crewe whistled. 'I don't see how you can get over that!' he declared.

'Kemp says they've cleared well over £100,000 as it is, and they're not done with it yet. If the stock continues to recover they'll make ever so much more.

Crewe was usually extremely moderate in his language, but now he swore luridly. 'The unmentionable swine!' he exclaimed. 'Can you believe it? That a man with more money than he knows what to do with should ruin hundreds of poor struggling devils just to get a bit of amusement—for he can't have needed the cash. What he wants is hanging. Hanging's too good for him.'

'That's all right,' Entrican returned, 'but it takes people different ways. You're upset, but Kemp was delighted. Full of admiration! Said it was just like the old man; that he was a complete top-notcher; more than a match for any combination of people he could meet. And Kemp's not usually enthusiastic. I expect he's getting a share of the swag.'

'I'd rather he was getting it than me.'

'I shouldn't. You're an ass, Crewe, with your lofty ideals and all that. We've got to live in the world. If I can get money, I take it. And what's more, I ask no questions about where it comes from.'

'I don't believe you, Entrican. If you knew your money meant someone else's ruin and death, you wouldn't take it.'

'Like a shot I would. Someone else should have looked

after himself better. If he didn't take the trouble, he can't squeal if he gets nipped.'

Crewe knew this was the view of many and did not press the subject. 'I wonder if Scotland Yard will smell a rat?'

'Probably. But what if they do? The old man has broken no law.'

'Obtaining money under false pretences?'

Entrican shook his head. 'I doubt it. In any case they'd have to begin by disproving his statement, and I don't see how they could do that. All he'd have to do would be to keep his mouth shut. He's put up a good story, and trust the old man to leave it at that and not give himself away.'

Crewe felt that this was true. If suspected, it was exactly what Harrison would do.

His thoughts turned to a more personal matter. If Harrison had really done this thing, should it make any difference to himself? Should he remain in the service of such a man? Crewe's outlook was ordinary and decent, but it was not wholly on a point of morality that he was considering the question. He was afraid of sharing Harrison's reputation. He didn't want to stay all his life where he was, and if his name became associated too closely with his employer's he might find another job not too easy to get.

But after all, was the affair completely proven? 'What about sales?' he asked sharply. 'Had Harrison been selling before he disappeared?'

Entrican paused to sip his whisky. 'That's what was worrying Kemp,' he replied. 'Kemp knew nothing of any sales. Of course that's not conclusive. The old man has so many channels he could sell the entire caboodle and no one would be any the wiser.'

'But surely that sort of thing can be found out? It's always known who holds stock.'

'That's true, and I don't say it couldn't be found out—I say it hasn't been.'

With this Crewe had to be content. He was firmly convinced that the affair had been a deliberate coup on Harrison's part, but the evidence just stopped short of proof. Perhaps, he thought, the man should be given the benefit of the doubt.

At all events Crewe took no action about it. As the days passed relations in the household grew more normal. Outside also the affair was being forgotten. The rumours had died down. The stock had reached its old level. Harrison had been neither murdered nor assaulted. The idea of throwing up his job grew more and more quixotic to Crewe.

Then, some fortnight after the affair, there came a break in the family routine. The day arrived for the move to Henley. Crewe was pleased with the prospect, for it was a fine summer and Town was dusty and hot. Also he was tired of Mount Street and looked forward to the river.

It was arranged that he and Entrican should go down early in the forenoon; the family following later. Accordingly, with the back of the large Daimler stacked full of secretarial equipment, the two young men set off.

It was mid-June and a brilliant day. The country, when at last they reached it, was looking its best. The foliage was fully matured, though still young and fresh and vivid. In the shadiest parts of the fields the cattle stood motionless, save for an occasional switch of their tails, and the very atmosphere was heavy with a somnolent peace. Even in what we now call built up areas, glimpses through gates and over fences revealed the blazing colours of massed flowers.

'This is the Colemans',' said Entrican at last, steering the car into a drive between gates which bore the legend Amalfi.' A few yards brought them to the house, where Entrican pulled up.

'We can't take the car any farther,' he explained. 'We shall have to walk down. Take your most precious possessions and we'll send Higgins up for the rest. That's the steward, you know.'

'Curious arrangement having no proper approach to the boat,' Crewe considered.

'It's not so bad really. It's pretty private here, and if a wharf is wanted, we've only to run up the river. The old man has made some arrangement with Coleman to use his ground.

From the house the lawn sloped down to the Thames, which accommodatingly made a re-entrant bend at the place; thus furnishing a delightful view of the reach. First there were flower beds, then a tennis court, and beyond that the river. The tow path was at the other side, and the Coleman ground ran down to the actual water. At the sides of the little estate herbaceous borders melted into first shrubs and then trees, which practically hid the houses up and down stream.

To their left as they walked was the Colemans' small boathouse, and to the right, connected with the shore by a long gangway, lay the *Cygnet*.

Crewe gazed at her with interest. She certainly was a strange-looking craft, a sort of combination of barge and houseboat. She was long and wide and square, like an elongated biscuit box. Towards the blunt bows was a small group of deckhouses, with a tiny navigating bridge. The remainder of the hull was divided into two roughly equal

70

parts. That next the bridge carried a deckhouse, stretching for the full width of the ship, then came an expanse of deck, flat and unbroken, save for a companion right aft. Two boats were carried forward on patent davits. The minimum freeboard was considerable, about six feet, Crewe judged, and along the side was a row of round portholes.

'You can dance quite a big party on this deck,' Entrican observed as they went aboard, 'and there are all sorts of portable screen arrangements to head off any wind that might be so untactful as to blow. 'Bout time they had the awning up.'

There seemed to be no one about, but on Entrican's shout of 'Higgins!' a young man dressed in a steward's uniform of white linen with blue facings ran out of one of the deck-houses.

'Morning, Higgins. Our stuff's in the car. You might bring it along.'

At the sound of voices a rather distinguished looking man with thin aristocratic features and an alert expression appeared from the same place. He was dressed in a blue gold-braided uniform, and moved with an unassuming but assured air of authority. 'Royal Navy, retired,' thought Crewe, who knew the type.

'Hullo, captain,' Entrican greeted him. 'Here's the first contingent. Let me introduce you to Captain Collison, Crewe. When did you come up, captain?'

Crewe was considerably surprised to find that the *Cygnet* carried a captain, and yet a moment's thought showed him its necessity. Someone would have to live aboard and take charge. Crewe wondered what Harrison had paid to induce a man of this type to take such a job.

'I expect you're ready for a drink,' Collison suggested

presently in just the cultivated voice which Crewe expected. 'Come to my cabin. They're still cleaning the lounge.'

Captain Collison's cabin was in the forward deckhouse. It was tiny—just held the three of them and no more, but it was furnished luxuriously. Even an ex-Navy captain might be comfortable enough in such a place. It had windows looking both forward and aft along the deck, and a second door and narrow flight of steps led to a tiny wheelhouse. Crewe looked up with interest.

'What a splendid place!' he exclaimed. 'I really must go up.

Collison smiled. 'Come up and be welcome,' he invited, leading the way. 'You see it's arranged as a one man's show, though we always have two on duty when we're moving. Are you anything of a sailor?'

Crewe knew just enough to appreciate what he saw. The wheelhouse, which opened on to a tiny bridge, was sufficiently raised above the deckhouse to give a view over its roof to either side and astern. In front was a quite hefty binnacle, the only object of any size in the room, with behind it a wheel of gleaming brass. To the left, within easy reach of the helmsman, stood a diminutive Chadburn, or ship's telegraph, double-faced for two engines. On its shaft was an array of small handles.

'With those,' Collison explained, 'you can really drive the motors. We've got twin screws with Diesel motors. But one wouldn't dream of insulting our engineer by using them.'

'Who's that talking about insulting the engineer?' asked a voice with a suspicion of the pleasant roughness of Scotland, and a stout, kindly-looking man in a blue uniform entered.

'No one. You must have been dreaming, Donald,' the

captain told him. 'This is Mr Crewe: Mr M'Gregor, our chief engineer.'

'Chief, second, third and fourth in one, Mr Crewe,' declared the newcomer, holding out a slightly horny hand. 'You meet, in fact, our entire engine-room staff, barring one greaser.'

'Glad to meet you all,' Crewe returned, thinking the phrase permissible under the circumstances.

'We're a happy family. Wonderfully few quarrels in the engine-room.'

Crewe took to M'Gregor at once. He looked straight and capable. A good friend, Crewe felt sure he would prove, as well as useful in a tight corner.

Presently Collison asked Crewe if he would like to see over the ship, and they started on a leisurely tour of inspection, beginning at the bows. Right forward were housed the crew of six: two deck hands, a greaser, a cook and a bedroom and a dining-room steward. Next came stores and then the engine-room.

'It's Mr Harrison's design, you understand,' the captain explained as they walked. 'He put the motors well forward, so as to get the noise as far away from the living quarters as possible.'

'It means two pretty long shafts.'

'Yes, and that's a nuisance, because there's no draught for tunnels. The greasing has to be done by lifting floor plates. However, we don't move about a great deal.'

'How long do you stay here now?' Crewe asked.

The captain looked at Entrican.

'Till the regatta's over, I believe,' the secretary answered. 'Then I heard them say they were going farther up the river. About a month on board altogether.'

'A month? Splendid!' Crewe exclaimed. 'Nothing would suit me better. But are we to be with them all the time?'

'Oh yes, I think so. The old man goes up to Town fairly regularly, but Mrs H. sticks to the ship. But they're never alone on board. The place is crawling with guests all the time. Too many of them for me. What do you say, captain?'

'Yes, it gets a bit hectic at times,' Collison agreed.

Above the engine-room were the deckhouses, where the captain and engineer slept, and behind it was the kitchen, pantry and bathrooms, then the dining saloon and two rows of staterooms, five on each side, and each with its bathroom. All were small, but exquisitely furnished. Labour and space-saving devices of all kinds were installed, and though the decoration was simple, it was highly effective. The deckhouse aft of the bridge was divided into two rooms, a music room and a large and luxurious lounge.

'It's absolutely perfect,' Crewe declared enthusiastically, when they had seen it all. 'When I'm as rich as Harrison I'll have just such another.'

'I'm afraid there's one snag so far as you are concerned,' Entrican put in. 'You can't get a cabin to yourself. You'll have to share with me.'

'I'll live through it,' Crewe answered, 'if you can.'

'Good! Then let's go and get unpacked and settle down before the others turn up.'

By the time they had stowed their gear lunch was ready. Collison and M'Gregor joined them. Both officers proved themselves pleasant companions. The captain had been with Beatty at Jutland, and had an amicable disagreement about the tactics of that engagement with M'Gregor, who had served in the engine-room of one of Jellicoe's ships. This, Crewe afterwards found, was a stock bone of contention, which the two men brought out whenever they could get a fresh audience. But in addition Collison had sailed over most of the world and could talk interestingly of what he had seen, while the engineer's dry humour added a spice to all he said.

After lunch the awning was up, and subsiding into easy chairs on deck the four men chatted desultorily in a slightly somnolent atmosphere. Then just before tea the arrivals began.

First came Mrs Harrison, Gloria and Miss Blanche Morland. Miss Morland was the actress, the flamboyant woman with the penetrating voice and impressive clothes who had just been leaving the house in Mount Street on Crewe's first arrival. These were followed shortly by Rupert and Lord Algy Mannering in the former's sports car, and they had scarcely come aboard when a Mr Graham Locke was announced.

This was the man, Crewe soon discovered, about whom Entrican had spoken in connection with Mrs Harrison. He was an insignificant little fellow, with a large head, a mop of untidy hair and a pathetic expression. 'Weak and might be mulish,' was Crewe's mental comment as they were introduced. No one appeared particularly pleased to see him, not even Mrs Harrison. Her greeting was insufferably condescending, indeed it was contemptuous. Crewe happened to catch the look he turned on her in reply and felt slightly shocked. It was a look of utter adoration mixed with misery and fear. The man was in love with her to an almost insane degree. The whole party had evidently been on the *Cygnet* before, as when Crewe joined them at tea he found all sharing reminiscences of previous visits.

It was not till close on dinner-time that Harrison arrived.

He brought with him two financiers, Stowe and Moffatt, whom Crewe had met at Mount Street and at Entrican's gambling club.

'Stowe and Moffatt are only staying one night,' Entrican volunteered as they were dressing. 'Only for them we should have separate cabins.'

'What do we do all the time?' Crewe inquired. 'I mean when the regatta's not on.'

Entrican shrugged. 'We do what people on yachts generally do,' he returned. 'Boat and bathe and eat and drink and flirt and talk scandal and dance and squabble and—'

Crewe laughed. 'A little of that goes a long way with me.'

'You'll be wanted to dance. Otherwise you can do what you like. But beware of the Morland. If you're not careful she'll have you running round all the time like a prize lapdog.'

Crewe said dryly that he would take the hint. But at dinner he was not at the lady's table, and somehow he did not come across her afterwards. The party drank a good deal and grew noisy, and when later there was dancing on deck some of the members were not very steady on their feet.

Next morning everyone began to carry out the programme outlined by Entrican: eating, drinking, flirting, squabbling, and so on. Harrison remained on board, and during the day they went for a cruise upstream, returning to their moorings just before dinner. Though Crewe had a good deal of correspondence to get through, he found the little trip delightful. He brought his typewriter up on deck and settled down forward of the wheelhouse, where he was undisturbed. Progress was delightfully peaceful: the motors were not being pressed, and were running silently and with practically no vibration. They floated gently along between the well-wooded banks, one charming reach opening out after another, with occasional pauses to negotiate locks. A delightful change from Town!

One of the pleasantest factors in this new phase of Crew's life was his acquaintanceship with the Coleman family. On the second day after his arrival he ran into Jasper while walking out to the road. This was the young man with whom Gloria was supposed to be in love.

'Hallo!' Jasper said with a friendly smile. 'You've come down after all? We met at Mount Street, you remember, and you weren't sure that you'd be here.'

'I've come all right,' Crewe assured him. 'And very glad of it. It's better here than in Town.'

'Rather. I always like the river about this time, though we pay for it in winter with the floods. But come along in and have tea. We're alone, though; only the mater and I, if you can stand that.'

Crewe said he would be delighted, not realising that it would be the truth. But the more he saw of Jasper Coleman, the more he liked him, and he fell instantly in love with his mother. Mrs Coleman seemed to him the personification of all an elderly woman should be: well preserved without aping youth, dignified and natural, sympathetic and kindly, tolerant and sincere and obviously capable. Crewe felt at home the moment he entered the room, and before long as if he were a second son.

He took also to Mr Coleman, when a couple of days later the two men met. Like his wife and son, he also was kindly, unassuming and sincere. The Coleman household, indeed, seemed to Crewe one of the happiest he had ever visited, and he admired Gloria's taste in wishing to marry into it. More and more Crewe took to spending his spare time with the family.

One evening shortly after the move to the river the Colemans came to dinner on the *Cygnet*. But their visit was not a great success. They obviously lived in another world to that of the Harrisons, a world of books and music, with fewer cocktails and less noise. The Harrisons were polite, but far from cordial, and the Colemans left as soon as they could.

A couple of evenings later Crewe obtained involuntarily a further sidelight on this not very pleasant household. He had a slight headache, and after the dancing and drinks which he had been unable to avoid he felt he wanted some air. He therefore slipped on deck when the others went below to their cabins. He leant over the rail, enjoying the coolness and the silence, and then he made the unfortunate discovery that if one were immediately over an open porthole, one could hear anything that might be said in the cabin concerned. What he did hear was disconcerting. The cabin was Mrs Harrison's, and Locke was there and was speaking. Crewe did not deliberately listen, but before he could move away he heard enough to learn the essential facts. It seemed as if Mrs Harrison were in love with Locke as well as he with her. Locke was pleading with her to leave Harrison and go abroad with him. 'Andrew would divorce you,' he said with urgency; 'you know he wants his freedom. Then we could be married. You'd love Rio, and we could either settle there or travel about.'

Crewe stepped noiselessly back. Here was another complication and more misery. These poor people, all grasping for what they thought they wanted, and so missing happiness! A tragic affair and full of potential danger.

But not, Crewe sternly reminded himself, any concern of his. His job was to do his work and mind his own business and let other people do the same.

Soon the days on the *Cygnet* began to pass as quickly as had those in Town. And then dawned the week of the great social event for which ostensibly they had come. On the Monday Stowe and Moffatt dined, scarcely, Crewe thought, a fitting prelude for festivities. However as they afterwards disappeared with Harrison, presumably to talk finance, he soon forgot this cold douche. In a blaze of glory the regatta opened on the Wednesday. His prospects of enjoying it seemed admirable. Splendid weather, a crowd of visitors almost up to pre-War standard, entries to ensure a brilliant series of contests, and the most perfect grandstand imaginable.

Crewe looked forward to a very pleasant time indeed.

7

The Drifting Death

Henley Regatta lasted till the Saturday and proved to be just as successful as had been anticipated. But pleasant as are these functions, one is very like another, and it is unnecessary for us to follow in detail all that took place. It is sufficient to say that the days passed in a whirl of social engagements, and that Crewe's hopes of a pleasant time were more than fulfilled.

Next day, the Sunday following the festivities—the last of their stay, for on the following morning they were to move upstream—an event took place which went far to mar the previous satisfaction. The party had grown a little smaller. Blanche Morland and Lord Algy Mannering had left. Entrican had gone up to Town for the night, to dine and do a show with a newly arrived Australian cousin. Locke had stayed on, but when the trouble occurred he and Rupert were out for a stroll.

Whether it was due to the family being alone—for the first time since coming to the river—or to some other cause, Crewe did not know, but later that night a terrible quarrel broke out between Harrison and Mrs Harrison on the one side, and Gloria and Jasper Coleman on the other.

How it began Crewe could not gather. After dinner he had spent half an hour going through some cruising arrangements with Captain Collison. A point arose on which Harrison's ruling was required, and it was when he entered the music room on his way to get this that he heard the raised voices in the lounge.

'I tell you I won't have it,' Harrison was saying angrily. 'You haven't been invited here and you can just get out!'

Then came Gloria with a sharp edge to her voice which Crewe had not heard before. 'You know that's not true! He was invited! I invited him and he'll stay as I want him!'

'He'll go now, and what's more, he'll not come back!' Harrison shouted threateningly.

'I'll go, Gloria,' came Jasper's voice. 'We can't have this. I'll go at once.'

'If he goes, I'll go too! I won't have him spoken to like that!' Gloria cried.

'Don't be a fool!' Mrs Harrison's voice, though scarcely raised, was the most malicious and biting of them all. 'Can't you see that all he wants is your money?'

'He won't get that,' snarled Harrison. 'And what's more, Gloria, if you go now you can stay away, and your money comes to an end: both your allowance and your inheritance.'

Gloria's voice rose suddenly. 'You devil! How I hate you! If I had a gun I would shoot you! Shoot you! It's what you deserve!'

'Hush, Gloria, don't say things like that,' Jasper appealed. 'I'm going. I must, after what they've said. You stay where you are and we'll settle this later.'

'No, I'll kill him!' Gloria shrieked, as if her self-control had suddenly snapped. 'Look out for yourself, you devil!'

There was a moment's silence and then a babel of voices broke out. 'Stop her! Stop her!' shouted Jasper, while Mrs Harrison screamed. 'Gloria! Pull yourself together!' and there was a sort of deep growl from Harrison. Then Mrs Harrison's voice came sharply. 'Get her out into the air!' There were steps next door and Crewe, fearful lest someone should enter the music room and find him listening, slipped back to the captain's cabin.

'There's a fine old shindy going on in there,' he explained, deciding he mustn't hide the fact, but anxious to minimise its gravity.

Captain Collison shook his head. 'At it again, are they? I've heard them before now. They're not very careful and one can't help it sometimes. Well, it's not our business,' and he went on to talk of other matters.

Crewe stayed for half an hour and when he returned to the lounge all was quiet. Apparently things had quieted down with no one very much the worse.

Crewe was not sleepy and decided that before going down he would have a stroll in the cool on deck. It was deserted and he paced up and down, his rubber soled shoes making no sound on the planking.

Suddenly, as he paused for a moment at the side, the same thing happened as had a few nights before: he heard voices from the porthole of the cabin just below him. This time the cabin was Harrison's and the voices were those of the owner and his wife.

Though Crewe knew that they occupied separate cabins, there was nothing remarkable in their meeting for discussion in one of them. But it was not the fact of the discussion

82

that instantly riveted his attention. It was the tone. Clearly the two were quarrelling bitterly. They kept their voices low. But there was a distressing suggestion of repressed evil in the sound. Crewe could not hear the words and indeed he did not wish to. Instead, he crept back noiselessly and went down to his cabin.

A miserably unhappy family, he thought as he slowly undressed. There seemed to be nothing between the members but mutual hate. In the dispute with Gloria her father and mother were in agreement and supported each other. But it was now clear they were no better friends for that. They loathed each other! Only so could such a tone be possible between them. What a tragedy if the only thing their wealth brought them was loss of the power to enjoy it!

And it was a dangerous condition too. Crewe did not exactly fear violence, believing that social training and environment would prevent it. But he knew that if hate is allowed to fester in the heart, there is no gauging the result. Apparently Gloria had lost her self-control that evening and made some attack on her father. Others were present and no serious consequences ensued. But given the same break under other circumstances, no one could be sure it would pass off as easily.

However, as Collison had said, it was not Crewe's business. With a mental shrug he dismissed the subject and took up his book to read for a little before going to sleep.

Next morning he had lost the feeling of oppression induced by the unpleasantness of the previous night. They were going cruising, which would be delightful. Moreover the party would be small and he thought he would have little or nothing to do. Basking on the deck with a book while the wooded banks of the Thames dropped slowly behind, appealed to him as an ideal antidote to the social surfeit of the last few days. Only one small matter must be attended to before they left—itself also a pleasure. He must call on the Colemans to say goodbye and return thanks for their hospitality, and dissociate himself from any slight which might have been offered to the family.

It was a brilliant morning. His porthole looked out over the Colemans' ground. The sun brought out vividly the greens of the grass and trees, the splashes of deep colour from massed flowers, and the mellow russet of bricks and tiles. Aromatic scents floated in, mingling with the clean smell of earth moistened by dew. Little sounds of swirling water combined with the singing of birds and the soft hum of insects. A charming setting for what would doubtless be a charming day.

It was still rather early, but Crewe felt wakeful. He dressed in a leisurely way, intending to go for a stroll before breakfast. But just as he was leaving his cabin he met Higgins, the steward.

'Beg pardon, sir, but I wondered if you knew if Mr Harrison had made any special plans for this morning? He didn't answer when I knocked and he's not got up.'

'Sleepy, I imagine. When did you knock?'

'At his usual time, sir; seven o'clock.'

'Does he always get up promptly?'

'Always, sir. I've never known him more than five minutes late for his bath, and see, now it's getting on to eight.'

'I expect he's just sleepy.'

'He's very sound asleep in that case, sir. I've knocked him loudly twice, because I was afraid he might be annoyed if he was let sleep too long, but I can't get any answer.'

'Why not go in and see?'

'I can't, sir. The door's bolted.'

Crewe felt a sudden qualm of misgiving. 'Does he always do that?' he asked more sharply.

'Oh yes, sir, always. And I understand he locks his bedroom at Mount Street.'

Crewe considered. Higgins was hanging about with an expectant air, as if he had transferred his responsibility and was awaiting a lead.

'Come and knock again,'Crewe said. 'I'll be responsible if he's annoyed.'

Relief showed in the man's eyes. 'Thank you, sir,' he said moving off.

They knocked loudly at Harrison's cabin and Crewe called out and shook the door vigorously. There was no reply.

A very real anxiety had now taken possession of Crewe's mind. This silence seemed terribly suggestive. It fitted in too horribly with his thoughts of the night. However he controlled his fears and spoke in a normal manner.

'Is Captain Collison about yet?'

'Yes, sir, I saw him forward just now.'

'Then wait here and if Mr Harrison opens the door come and tell me. I'm going to speak to the captain.'

A few seconds put Collison in possession of the facts, to which he listened with an uneasy frown.

'I was wondering if we should break open the door,' Crewe continued. 'If he's all right, he'd be furious, but if he's ill we shouldn't delay.'

'He's not all right or he'd have answered,' the captain returned. 'But if you don't want to make a fuss breaking open the door, I think we can find out otherwise. Our portholes are only about four feet above the water line. If you wait a couple of minutes I'll have a boat overboard and we can look into the cabin from the outside.'

'By all means,' Crewe agreed. 'Good idea.'

Collison called his two deck hands and the three of them swung out one of the light dinghies and lowered it to the water. Crewe dropped in beside the captain, and one of the deck hands manoeuvred the painter as the current drifted them slowly along the *Cygnet*'s side. Presently they came to Harrison's porthole and Collison signed to the man to make fast.

The porthole was closed, which seemed strange to both men. Though the previous evening had been chilly, it was not really cold, and Crewe felt sure that everyone on board would sleep with his porthole open. However Harrison's practice on the point could be ascertained later.

While Crewe considered the point, the captain was standing up, looking through the glass. He stood peering for some seconds, then motioned Crewe to look in his turn. His face was grave and Crewe's apprehensions redoubled.

The cabin seemed black after the blazing light without, but presently Crewe's eyes adjusted themselves and he was able to make out a good deal.

Harrison was in bed. He was lying on his back, apparently motionless. But what immediately struck Crewe was the colour of his face. It was a livid, almost leaden shade.

Crewe whistled soundlessly. 'He can't be dead?' he said involuntarily lowering his voice to a whisper. 'Not with his face that colour?'

'I'm not so sure,' Collison returned in the same low tone. 'What about some sort of fit? But it settles our difficulty. We must break in at once.'

'Yes, and have a doctor,' Crewe answered. 'I'll run to the Colemans and ring up, if you'll carry on here.'

'Right. I'll get the door open.'

They climbed aboard and Crewe raced to the house. He saw Jasper and hurriedly explained.

'Dr Jellett's your man,' Jasper exclaimed. 'I'll ring him up.'

Two minutes later Crewe was back on board, Jasper at his heels. As they reached Harrison's door M'Gregor had just forced it open, and they followed him and Captain Collison into the cabin.

A glance in the better light told Crewe that they were in the presence of tragedy. Harrison was dead. He was lying on his back in a natural position, his face undistorted and calm as if he were asleep, normal in every way except for its dreadful colour and complete immobility. Crewe raised the clothes and touched the breast.

'Cold,' he said in a low voice. 'He's been dead for a considerable time.'

For a moment all four men stood staring down at the motionless form. Harrison had gone to his account. No longer would he dominate his home and the money market. No longer would his deals leave a trail of ruined homes and make his rivals sweat with fear. Never again would he quarrel with his wife and make his daughter curse him. His day was over.

For a moment these thoughts passed through Crewe's mind, and then he roused himself. 'The doctor'll be here directly,' he said in the same low tone as Collison.

His words broke the spell. The captain made a slight gesture and took charge.

'You'd better tell Locke,' he said to Crewe, 'and get him to see Mrs Harrison. He knows her better than the rest of us. Perhaps you might tell Rupert and Gloria, too, or get

Rupert to tell Gloria. You stay here with me, Donald, till the doctor comes. And you, Higgins, go ashore and show the doctor the way.'

Crewe hated his job. However, with Locke he had no trouble. He was half-dressed when Crewe went to his cabin, and he stared incredulously when he heard the news.

'My God!' he faltered. 'Harrison! You don't say *dead*! How awful! How—how—did it happen?'

'We don't know,' Crewe returned. 'It looks like apoplexy or some kind of fit. The doctor's on his way.'

Locke seemed very much upset. Crewe rather cynically looked for some involuntary expression of satisfaction, but to the man's credit he did not find it.

'I couldn't—have believed it,' Locke went on. 'He was not—at all full-blooded.' Then after another pause: 'Mrs Harrison—will be—terribly upset.'

'Will you tell her?' Crewe put in.

Locke shrank back. 'Oh, no—I couldn't. Oh, please don't ask me. The captain will tell her.'

Crewe felt annoyed, and with a curt nod left the cabin. It was sorely against his will, but in the end he himself broke the news to all three members of the family. All reacted as he would have expected. All showed extreme surprise, but there the similarity ended. Mrs Harrison was by far the most affected. She seemed turned into stone, while the blood drained slowly from her face, leaving it white and drawn. He hated the expression in her eyes. It was one he had not often seen, particularly in the eyes of a woman. It was naked fear that showed. Whatever she thought had happened, Mrs Harrison was mortally afraid.

The other two received the news more normally. Rupert was cool about it, as if the matter scarcely concerned him.

'He never gave us the chance of getting fond of him,' he said with bitterness. 'How could we be expected to weep?' But Gloria took it more to heart. 'Oh,' she cried, 'and I had that row with him only last night. It was only that I was annoyed for the moment. I didn't really mean it. And now I can never tell him!'

While Crewe was talking to Locke he had heard the doctor arrive, and since then there had been other comings and goings. But now as he went with Rupert to the dead man's cabin he heard heavier steps on the deck. Two pairs of dark blue legs appeared descending the companion, and presently the bodies of an inspector and sergeant of police came into view. An elderly professional looking man, obviously the doctor, looked out into the alleyway, and after saying 'Morning, Pollock! Morning, Speers!' in a pained voice, vanished again into the cabin. The two policemen stalked heavily after him.

There was obviously no room for Crewe or Rupert, even if their presence had been permitted. They therefore went forward to look up Collison.

'I'm sorry,' the captain answered their question, looking particularly at Rupert, 'but we had to have the police. The doctor insisted on it.' He paused as if tacitly asking Rupert's approval, then, before receiving it, went on: 'And there's another unfortunate matter. The doctor isn't sure of the cause of death, and—again I'm sorry to tell you—there'll have to be a post mortem.'

Rupert's face fell. 'That'll be rough luck all round. Are you sure it's necessary? Is this doctor any good? What about getting another?'

'That can be done if you like. But it wouldn't help. Unfortunately, Jellett is the police doctor, and they're certain to support their own man. If he says he wants a P.M. they'll insist on it.'

'They can insist, I suppose?'

'I imagine so. But the coroner certainly can.'

'Jellett doesn't give any opinion?' Crewe put in.

The captain hesitated. 'You may as well hear the whole story at once,' he said slowly. 'You'll know it soon enough in any case. He thinks it was carbon dioxide gas.'

'Carbon dioxide gas?' Crewe exclaimed incredulously. 'But how—? I don't understand.'

Crewe was aware that deaths from carbon dioxide— otherwise carbonic acid gas or CO_2—were frequent. CO_2 poisoning was one of the commonest ways of committing suicide. But so far as he knew the CO_2 was invariably obtained from ordinary coal gas. Why, the very phrase 'head in the gas-oven' meant suicide by carbon dioxide. And of course lots of people died of it by accident. But there was no such gas on the *Cygnet*.

Rupert's thoughts were evidently traversing the same ground. 'The man's a darned fool,' he declared, only 'darned' was not the word he used. 'How could it be gas when there's none on board?'

Collison made a little gesture. 'Let me finish. Jellett thinks there was gas on board. On the table at the head of the bed was a bowl full of scraps of marble, which gave clear traces of having been acted on by acid. There was also a small decanter of hydrochloric acid. And hydrochloric acid on marble produces carbon dioxide gas; or so he says.'

The three men exchanged glances. 'Oh, Lord!' exclaimed Rupert, looking at last a good deal distressed. 'And you say the portholes were shut and the door fastened on the inside?'

'I'm afraid so,' Collison answered in a lowered voice.

There was silence for a few moments. Once again Crewe's thoughts raced ahead of the conversation. Poor Harrison! Behind his overbearing manner and apparent selfishness what intense unhappiness there must have been! With the natural urge for life we all have, only complete despair or madness will drive men to suicide. And Harrison wasn't mad. The dispute with Gloria must have hurt him infinitely more than anyone could have believed. No doubt it could not have been the cause of his suicide, but it might well have been the last straw which made a terribly unhappy position no longer bearable. And poor Gloria! If her conscience was smiting her already, how would she not feel when she learnt the truth? In the whole situation Crewe saw tragedy, not only for the life which had gone, but for those which remained also.

Presently Rupert broke the silence. 'I just can't believe it!' he declared, also in a lowered voice. 'Suicide! I should have said the old man would have been about the last in the world for that.' He looked at Collison. 'I suppose there's no possible chance it was an accident?'

The captain shook his head gravely. 'We can't be sure of anything till the police have made their inquiries,' he pointed out. 'But of course it looks badly.'

Badly! Crewe thought. To him what had happened was clear beyond doubt or question. There was the saucer of marble chippings and the bottle of acid in the cabin, proving premeditation in the providing of the gas. There was the closed cabin: no one could pass anything in or out with the door and portholes shut. No one could place the marble and the acid on the table and then leave the cabin. And most of the facts he had seen for himself. No, there could

91

be no doubt as to what had happened. Whatever the reason, Harrison had committed suicide.

'I'm afraid,' Crewe said to Rupert, 'this is going to upset Mrs Harrison and your sister pretty badly. Perhaps until we're quite sure we'd better not suggest anything to them?'

'I don't see that it matters,' Rupert returned. 'It's pretty clear what has happened, and they've got to know of it sooner or later. What do you say, captain?'

'I think I should do as Crewe suggests,' Collison replied. 'Whatever we may think ourselves, we don't actually know what took place. The police may find something that will put a different complexion on things. I suggest we wait for their report—it can't make a deal of difference.'

Rupert shrugged. 'Oh, all right, if you both think so.' He moved uneasily. 'I think I'll get properly dressed,' he muttered, and with a short nod he left the cabin.

'A bad business, Crewe,' the captain went on when they were alone.

'Terrible. A terrible end for a man of that kind.'

'Yes.' Collison paused. 'And it will be the end of a good deal more than himself.' He made a gesture including his surroundings. 'All this, for instance. One shouldn't think of oneself, of course, and all that, but you and I'll be out of a job because of it.'

Crewe, to do him justice, had up to now thought more of the survivors of the family than of himself. But the captain's words brought home to him his own position. Yes, before long he would be among the unemployed, and this business would not help him to another job. And Entrican, too. Crewe knew Entrican's fear of unemployment. Entrican would be terribly upset.

As if in answer to his thoughts, as he glanced out of the

aft window he saw Entrican crossing the gangway. He jumped up.

'There's Entrican coming aboard,' he exclaimed. 'I must go and tell him before he butts into anyone.'

Entrican was carrying a large envelope; Harrison's mail, Crewe supposed. He looked anxious.

'What's up?' he asked as Crewe approached. 'You look like a mute at a funeral, and I saw through the porthole that no one has had breakfast.'

'S-h-h!' Crewe warned him, then in a low voice told him. 'There's bad news. It's Harrison. He's dead.'

Entrican looked dumbfounded. For a moment he could scarcely speak. Then rather hoarsely he asked for details.

Crewe told him what was known.

'It's incredible,' Entrican kept on repeating. 'I could have believed it sooner of anyone else on board. But not Harrison. No, Crewe, he was not the man to take his life. Are they sure?'

Crewe shrugged. 'We've not heard the police view,' he explained. 'But I've told you what we found. You can draw your own conclusions.'

'It beats me,' Entrican insisted. 'I've known the old man now for four years, and, as I say, I can't see him committing suicide. However, I suppose I'm wrong. What was the trouble, do you think?'

'He had some fairly nasty quarrels last night with Gloria and Mrs H.'

'What sort of quarrels?'

Crewe gave him a short summary.

Entrican dismissed the idea with a gesture. 'Nonsense!' he asserted with scorn. 'Nothing of the kind! You don't know the man. No,' he glanced round and sank his voice, 'if he's really done what you say, it's because his money's gone. He would only take his life if he saw absolute and final ruin coming. Like that Swedish match man, Kruger.'

Crewe's thoughts had been so much taken up with the family that he had forgotten this side of Harrison's life. Now he saw that Entrican's view must be the right one. A financial crash certainly would explain more reasonably what had happened.

But if so, it meant even more serious trouble for the family. If Entrican were correct, they would have nothing. As paupers they would have to start life again. Whatever happened, the family was going to suffer.

Crewe's reflections were brought to an end by Higgins. 'Mrs Harrison's compliments, gentlemen, and would you both go down to breakfast? It's served now.'

She was there before them, white and tight-lipped and still scared-looking. 'What do they say?' she inquired as the two men entered.

'They haven't made any report as yet,' Crewe answered. 'I think the police are still talking to the doctor. I need scarcely say that anything we hear will instantly be put before you.'

'I wish you'd ask them before we begin. It won't take a minute.'

Crewe did so, but the police said very little. The sergeant made a clumsy but well-intentioned speech of regret for what had happened and of sympathy for the family, adding that he was sorry, but that the law required an inquest. All present might be required to give evidence, and must therefore please remain on board. Further, he regretted he must later on ask for a statement from everyone, so that the coroner might know what their evidence was going to be.

But of theories or ideas of what might have occurred he gave no hint.

Crewe finally took him aside and asked him the direct question.

'Well, sir,' the man answered politely, 'I think you know as much about it as we do. Weren't you there when the door was broken open?'

'Yes, I was.'

'Then you saw everything for yourself. In fact, sir, I'm hoping you may be able to give us some information about the deceased gentleman which may help us to find the motive at the back of the affair.'

Crewe gave it up. If the police had any counsel, they were evidently keeping it.

8

The Coroner's Inquest

Breakfast proved a silent meal. When Crewe reported on his interview with the police, Mrs Harrison nodded, but made no reply. The others tried nobly to keep up a spasmodic conversation, but the pauses grew longer and longer, until they practically joined. Only once general interest flickered up, when Entrican asked if he should not ring up Kemp and tell him the news.

'I know we ought to do that,' Mrs Harrison agreed, 'but I've been funking it. Is there not a danger of another slump in the securities?'

Entrican admitted that he also feared it, but added that he didn't see how it was to be avoided. He thought the fullest publicity would be best in the end.

'He's right,' Rupert said unexpectedly. 'Any suggestion of hushing things up would be more damaging than the truth.'

This seemed common sense to Crewe, and when Mrs Harrison looked at him as if to ask his opinion, he said so.

'Then you had better phone to Mr Kemp,' she decided,

transferring her gaze to Entrican. 'Then I think you should go up and see him.'

This also Rupert approved, and the matter was settled.

'We ought to settle what we're going to do ourselves,' Rupert went on. 'I don't suppose you want to stay on here. What about closing down and going back to Mount Street?'

This struck a sympathetic chord. All present were in favour of leaving the *Cygnet* at the earliest possible moment.

'What about after lunch?' Mrs Harrison suggested. 'The police will surely have done with us by then.'

Rupert apparently hadn't meant anything so drastic. 'Remember you've got to be back early tomorrow,' he pointed out. 'What about sleeping the night here and going up after the inquest tomorrow?'

'Yes, that would be best,' Mrs Harrison agreed. She was about to leave the table when Crewe stopped her.

'There's just one other point,' he remarked. 'It's not my business, of course, but I haven't heard it mentioned. Do you wish for your solicitor to represent you at the inquest?'

This also they thought a good idea, and Crewe was told to arrange it.

The first thing after breakfast was the removal of Harrison's body by the police. Then they sealed Harrison's cabin, and, to Crewe's great surprise, left a constable to watch the door. Next they established themselves in the music room and began to take statements. Entrican was interrogated first, so that he might go as soon as possible to town. Higgins was the next to be questioned, and then it was Crewe's turn.

A very mild affair Crewe found his examination. He had read something about American third degree methods, and though he did not expect anything of that kind, he did fear some offensive personal questions. But none were put to him. Inspector Pollock was politeness itself, and seemed to take it for granted that Crewe was doing his best to help. He asked what was the first Crewe had heard of the affair, and led him to describe Higgins' call, the knocking at the door, the taking out of the boat, the breaking open of the door and the calling of the doctor and police. So much Crewe expected, but the next series of questions took him slightly aback.

'Thank you, Mr Crewe; that's all very clear. Now let us turn to another point. I want you to tell me all you can about the quarrel which took place last night.'

'Except that there was a quarrel, I really don't know anything about it,' Crewe answered, wondering how Pollock had obtained his information. 'I wasn't present.'

The inspector looked at him as if weighing him in a pair of mental balances.

'How did you know that a quarrel had taken place?' he asked presently.

Crewe could not but admire the cleverness of the question. Smoothly it penetrated his defences, leading directly to: Whose voices had he overheard? and, What had each of them said? At this latter question he baulked slightly. He omitted to mention Gloria's threats. However, Pollock already knew of them, for he asked directly if Crewe had not heard anything of the kind. Crewe lied, but he had an uneasy feeling that the man was aware of it. However, he made no comment, but went on to ask the equally unpleasant question: Was that the only quarrel Crewe knew of?

This time Crewe told the truth. He described what he had heard of the apparent row between Harrison and his wife.

Pollock however seemed to think his testimony of but little importance. His manner was perfunctory as he read over Sergeant Speers' notes of the evidence and asked Crewe to sign them.

'Thank you, sir, I'm much obliged for your help,' he ended up. 'That's all I want until the inquest. Perhaps as you go out you'd be good enough to ask Captain Collison to come down?'

Crewe had scarcely done so when the next phase of the affair began. He was called to the telephone at the Colemans' to hear the first question from the first newspaper correspondent. The burden of the conversation was short. Was the tumour of Harrison's death true? It was? Found dead in bed? The police had been called in? Right, he'd be down straight away.

Before the morning ended Crewe discovered there were more representatives of British newspapers in Henley than he had believed existed in the whole of England. He quickly arranged with the Colemans to have their telephone disconnected and got Collison to draw in the gangway. But slight checks of this kind had no effect on the assailants. They came round the *Cygnet* in skiffs and punts as natives encircle a liner in an Eastern port. At last, on the advice of Rupert, approved by Mrs Harrison, he brought them all into the lounge and handed them over to Pollock.

He could not but admire the way the inspector dealt with them. In a pleasant, leisurely way he assured them that both the family and the police were out to help them, and said he was sure that they in return would observe a reasonable reticence in their reports. He told them quite accurately the details already known to Crewe, other than those of the quarrels. He explained that the inquest would be held on the following day, when everything known would be put before the coroner. In an atmosphere of peace and goodwill they thanked him and hurried off to the nearest telephone.

When at last the evening papers came, reticence did not seem to Crewe the word he would have chosen to describe their efforts. They had included everything the inspector had told them, together with a good deal that must have been pure surmise. There were descriptions of the boat and its lavish fittings, and its position on the river, with pictures of both. (Inset, Captain Collison, R.N.R., who acts as skipper.) There were portraits of Harrison and his family, a human interest story of his life, and a description of his vast financial interests. Two of the three London evening papers spoke guardedly of his death, but the third threw discretion to the winds and had a three-column heading: 'Suicide of Mr Andrew Harrison.' The only thing they did not put into words was the theory that he had killed himself because his stock was worthless.

Presently Entrican arrived, looking extremely gloomy. 'Its worse than I could have imagined,' he whispered to Crewe, before going in to report to Mrs Harrison. 'The stock's absolutely tumbling. As sure as we're alive there'll be a panic on the Exchange tomorrow, unless we can do something.'

'What can we do?'

Entrican shrugged. 'Kemp is issuing a statement to all the morning papers that everything is in order. He has arranged with Morton & Clotworthy, perhaps the biggest chartered accountants in the City, to go into the books immediately and publish what they find, and he's advertising this. Various steps of that kind can be taken, and he's taken them all. Tell you more when I've seen Mrs H.'

By this time telegrams of condolence and sympathy were beginning to pour in. Crewe had to deal with these, besides consulting Mrs Harrison about the funeral and other matters, and putting in train the arrangements she approved. It was not indeed till they were turning in that Crewe had an opportunity for discussion with Entrican. He turned at once to the financial situation. But Entrican had little fresh to tell, except that Kemp was very pessimistic, as he was himself.

Entrican seemed unduly worried, but Crewe soon discovered that it was not the fate of Harrison's stocks which was upsetting him, but his own prospects. 'I don't know how long you'll last,' he said. 'If Mrs H. sticks to her money and her social climb she might wish to keep you. But my time's up. Whatever else she'll want, it'll not be a financial secretary.'

'You don't know,' Crewe told him. 'Someone must take Harrison's place, and no one would be more useful to him or her than yourself.'

Entrican brightened up. 'I hadn't thought of that,' he observed. 'I hope you're right. She'll probably marry Locke now and he'll want someone. I don't like Locke, he's a helpless worm. But to work with he'd be better than the late lamented.'

'Is there something in the wind there?' Crewe asked, not wishing to mention what he had overheard.

'Lord, yes!' Entrican returned. 'Hadn't you twigged it? Locke's a sort of permanent appendage. He's been wanting her to leave Harrison and marry him for donkey's years. And Harrison was hoping she'd do it, to get rid of her. What she can see in the fellow I don't know, but she's certainly fond of him.'

Next morning, shortly before ten-thirty, the party set off for Henley, where the inquest was being held. They found the hall crammed to suffocation, but as potential witnesses, seats had been reserved for them.

Mr Campbell, of Campbell, Campbell and Heavyside, Harrison's solicitors, a cadaverous man with a face like a horse's, came up at once and greeted the members of the family impressively. 'A very dreadful affair,' he declared, shaking his head solemnly. 'Dreadful! But of course today's proceedings are purely formal. I tried, Mrs Harrison, to induce the coroner to excuse your attendance, but unhappily without avail. However, even if you are called, it will only be for a moment.'

Kemp's chief assistant, Walpole, was also there, sent by Kemp. He was looking worried and, Crewe thought, more than a little frightened.

'It's terrible!' he whispered to Crewe and Entrican, while Campbell was talking to Mrs Harrison. 'I've just been on the phone to the office. Our stocks average twelve points down already and they're falling. It looks like a complete collapse. If it can't be stopped, we'll all be ruined.'

'What's Kemp doing?' Entrican asked.

'Buying, buying, buying: all the time. But he can't stop the run.'

'The verdict here won't help things much.'

'Not if it's suicide,' Walpole agreed. 'I suppose that's a foregone conclusion?'

Entrican nodded. 'Not the ghost of a chance of anything else. If they could make it out accident, or even murder for that matter, it might save us. But suicide!' He shrugged expressively.

'I know. That's what Kemp says.' He moved off to speak

to Mrs Harrison, and Crewe settled himself beside Entrican and began to look about him. The room was evidently a public hall of some kind, a fine chamber with an elaborate hammerbeam roof and oak panelling black with age. A table ran down the centre with chairs at each side, and at this were accommodated the Harrison party, Mr Campbell, some official looking persons whom Crewe did not know, and a number of pressmen. Behind were Captain Collison, M'Gregor, Jasper Coleman, Higgins and others. Three chairs at the head of the table were reserved, as Crewe supposed, for the coroner, his clerk, and the witness under examination.

Sergeant Speers was seated near the witness chair, and at the door and elsewhere in the hall stood policemen. In a little group on the coroner's right were seven empty chairs: obviously for the jury, if one were called. All the other chairs in the hall were occupied, presumably by spectators, and behind and around them were standing crowds whose faces bore an expression of pleasurable anticipation. The coming entertainment was evidently popular.

By the time Crewe had taken in these particulars it was half-past ten. As the hour struck there was a movement at the door, the constable held it open and saluted, and a short stoutish man with a round florid face entered, followed by a second, tall and hatchetty, and carrying a despatch case.

'That's Mr Digby,' said a voice into Crewe's ear, and he found that Inspector Pollock had moved in beside him. 'The coroner's ill, and he's acting.'

'Oh,' said Crewe. 'What is he?'

'Solicitor in the town. Very well thought of, for all he doesn't look the part.'

The round-faced man bowed to the assembly and took his seat at the head of the table, his companion settling himself at his right hand. The latter now opened his case and took from it several papers, which he spread before his chief. Digby beckoned to Sergeant Speers and a whispered conversation took place.

'I've decided to sit with a jury,' Digby announced. 'Will you, sergeant, make the necessary arrangements.'

Speers called certain names and seven persons, six men and a woman, left their places in the audience and moved to the clump of vacant chairs. They were, Crewe thought, a representative lot. The man at the end, the foreman presumably, was a thick-set individual with a heavy red face, blue jowls and a sharp 'no nonsense' expression. He looked to Crewe—who could be fanciful enough at times—as if he ate too much meat, and he put him down as a working butcher. Beside him was an elderly man in Harris tweeds and a brown pullover, evidently retired, whom Crewe could picture in no more appropriate setting than sauntering along a river bank with a pipe in his mouth and a fishing rod in his hand. The other four men looked like small shopkeepers or tradesmen, and while differing extraordinarily in personal appearance, agreed only in their look of self-conscious importance. The woman was elderly and stout, with a placid kindly face.

Various preliminaries were now put through and the jury were sworn.

'You may view the remains if you think it desirable,' the coroner told them, 'but you are not bound to unless you wish it.'

Upon this the jury consulted importantly among themselves, and then the red-faced man said they had decided to do so. This led to a delay while they tramped out to a room at the back. When at last they settled down, the proceedings proper began.

The first witness was Rupert Harrison. He had seen the remains upon which the inquest was being held, and they were those of his father, Andrew Harrison. He had last seen his father alive about ten o'clock two evenings previously. He seemed then in his ordinary health and spirits. He, Rupert, had gone out about that hour for a stroll in the cool with one of their guests, a Mr Locke. When they returned to the *Cygnet* everyone seemed to have gone to bed. He knew nothing of his father's death till informed next morning by Mr Crewe.

William Higgins was the next witness. He gave his qualifications and said he had been steward on the *Cygnet* since she was built, two years earlier. Though the family spent comparatively little time aboard, he remained there constantly to keep the vessel clean and aired. He had also seen the remains and identified them as those of his employer.

Higgins then told of the discovery of the tragedy: the knocking at the cabin door, the consultation with Crewe, his waiting while the boat was taken out, and finally, the breaking open of the door.

'You'll hear from another witness what was found,' the coroner told the jury. 'But on that point I wish to ask this witness one question. You knew that a decanter containing hydrochloric acid had been found on the table at the head of the deceased's bed?'

'I saw the decanter, sir, and I heard what was in it.'

'Did you recognise that decanter?'

'Yes, sir; it had been taken from the sideboard in the dining saloon.'

'Is it one of a set?'

'Yes, sir, there are four. Two of them were in use, filled

with whisky and brandy. The other two stood empty on the sideboard. This was one of the empty ones.'

'How were you able to identify it?'

'The size and pattern, sir. That and the fact that one of the empty ones on the sideboard was missing.'

'Can you form any opinion as to when it was taken from the sideboard?'

'It must have been about ten days ago, sir.'

'How do you fix the date?'

'I clean the glasses on Saturday mornings. It was gone on last Saturday week. But I hadn't missed it before that, and I think I would have done if it hadn't been there.'

'I follow you. Then, as this is Tuesday, it would have been missing for just ten days, you said. Did you make any inquiries when you missed it?'

Higgins grew slightly more uneasy. 'No, sir. I was afraid I should be blamed for not looking after it, and I hoped whoever had taken it would put it back.'

'Very well. Now let me turn to another point. Was it the deceased's habit to bolt his door?'

'Yes, sir; always.'

'Do you know why?'

'No, sir, but I understand he locked his room in Mount Street in the same way.'

'Never mind what you understand. Tell us only what you know yourself. Now was it his habit to keep his portholes open or shut?'

'Usually open, sir. He was very keen on fresh air.'

'You say usually. Were there any exceptions to the rule?'

'Yes, sir. He was in the habit of taking a warm bath before stepping into bed, and he didn't like the bathroom porthole open at that time. He said it made a draught.'

'I see. Was that the only exception?'

'Yes, sir. I always shut it when I was doing the room in the evening, and opened it again when I called him in the morning.'

'Now take this particular evening—the evening before his decease. Did you do the room that night?'

'Yes, sir; just as usual.'

'About what hour was that?'

'A little after nine, when the dinner things were cleared away.'

'Very well. When you left the cabin in what position were the portholes?'

'The sleeping cabin porthole was hooked up, fully open. The porthole in the bathroom was closed.'

'Was it screwed fast?'

'Yes, sir.'

'That seems quite clear. Now tell me, when did you last see the deceased alive?'

'Just before ten, sir, when I took some drinks into the lounge. He was there. Unless I was told otherwise, that was the last thing I had to do at night, and I was then free to go to bed.'

'And did you go to bed?'

'Yes, sir; about half-past ten.'

'Where were you from ten to half-past?'

'I was about the pantry for a while, tidying up. Then I went on deck for some air before going to bed.'

'During that period did you hear anything unusual? Any discussion or raised voices or anything of that kind?'

Higgins hesitated, glancing in a half-frightened way at Mrs Harrison. His thought was obvious. That the coroner followed it was shown by his next remark.

'I have here a statement you made to the police that you heard raised voices in the lounge as if a quarrel were in progress. Is that statement true or false?'

Again Higgins glanced deprecatingly at Mrs Harrison. 'It's true, sir,' he said at last in a low tone.

'Well, that's all right,' the coroner rejoined a little testily, 'I'm not making a mountain out of a molehill; I only want to know what took place. Whose voices did you hear?'

Higgins was obviously very uncomfortable. Little globes of sweat showed on his forehead and he twisted uneasily on his chair. It was clear that he feared the loss of his job if he went on, and being branded as a liar on someone else's testimony if he stopped. At last he appeared to come to the conclusion that the truth would serve him best. 'There were Mr and Mrs Harrison and Miss Gloria and young Mr Coleman,' he answered unwillingly.

'Quite.' The coroner had a paper in his hand, at which he glanced. 'You heard what they said?'

Again Higgins twisted on his chair. 'I accidentally overheard a word or two. I didn't listen. It wasn't my business.'

The coroner nodded. 'Quite. I don't want you to repeat anything you heard. But, broadly speaking, did you hear enough to learn the cause of the quarrel?'

More unwillingly than ever Higgins admitted that he believed so.

'Then in that broad way, and without repeating actual phrases, you might tell the jury what was being discussed.'

Crewe felt a little sorry for Higgins, or he would have done so had he not feared that his own turn was coming. He could see the man was now bitterly reproaching himself for admitting any knowledge of the affair. However it was too late for that now, and the coroner soon had his information.

108

Jasper Coleman, it appeared, had told Harrison that he wanted to marry Gloria and that Gloria had accepted him. But as she was under age Harrison's consent was necessary. Jasper had asked for this all quite politely and respectfully. But Harrison had refused in an extremely offensive way. Then Gloria had intervened with a remark which had further incensed her father, and before long all three Harrisons were going at it, hammer and tongs. Then Jasper had left and the affair had apparently blown over.

Judging by the fragments he had himself heard, Crewe saw that Higgins must have been listening before the quarrel broke out, and had kept on eavesdropping to the very end. Crewe felt he had no further sympathy for the man. If Mrs Harrison sacked him afterwards, it was only what he richly deserved.

Asked if quarrels were frequent in the Harrison household, Higgins said they were not, but admitted under pressure that this was by no means the first. Whatever his intention, when his evidence was over he had succeeded in painting life on the *Cygnet* as discordant and unhappy.

It seemed to Crewe a pity that the subject had been discussed at all. He did not see what business of the coroner's it was. His duty, as Crewe understood it, was to find the identity of the deceased, the cause of death, and whether blame was anywhere accruing. Perhaps consideration of circumstances which might tend to bring about suicide were germane to the inquiry, but Crewe doubted it. There had been some time previously a lot in the papers about coroners exceeding their powers, and it looked as if this were a case. If so, it was hard lines on both families.

His ruminations were brought to an end by a sudden call of 'Markham Crewe!' He moved to the witness chair.

Digby was courteous in his questions and Crewe found the interrogation unobjectionable. He was asked to give a brief résumé of his life and to explain how he came to be in Harrison's employment. Then he told of the finding of the body and his activities resulting therefrom. It was only when he was asked about the Harrison family relations that he felt embarrassed.

'Now this quarrel of which we have heard,' the coroner went on. 'Were you aware of it?'

'Yes.'

'How did you come to know of it?'

'In the same way as the last witness: I heard voices in the lounge.'

'Again I don't want to ask what you heard, but speaking generally, did it support the evidence of the last witness?'

'I only heard a phrase or two. I went away as soon as I discovered what was going on.'

'Naturally. But was what you did hear consistent with the suggested cause of the quarrel?'

'Yes, I think it was.'

'Now, Mr Crewe, I'm going to ask you a more difficult question. As far as your observation went, were the relations between the deceased and the other members of his family good or bad?'

Crewe wondered how he should reply. 'Neither, I think,' he said at last. 'I should not say they were very good, but I should not say they were very bad either.'

'You have heard other—er—disagreements between the deceased and other members of his family?'

'Yes; but not often.'

'Excluding the quarrel of which we have been speaking, what was the last disagreement of which you were aware?'

With his statement to the police probably in Digby's hand at that moment, Crewe could not prevaricate. 'I heard what sounded like another quarrel on the same night,' he replied, 'but of course it might have been a continuation of the same.'

Given this lead, the coroner soon obtained the details. This satisfied him, and he thanked Crewe and told him to stand down.

Captain Collison was then called. He was asked little except to confirm the investigation with the boat and the breaking open of the cabin door.

'When you entered the cabin did you move anything?'

'No. Mr Crewe raised the bed clothes and felt Mr Harrison's heart. He said the body was cold.'

'Did you remain there till the arrival of the police?'

'Yes.'

'And can you state positively that nothing was touched until the police arrived?'

'Yes, I can state so positively.'

'Thank you. Now the doctor, Dr Jellett.'

Jellett stated that he had received a call to the *Cygnet* at 8.20 on the previous morning. He had found the deceased dead in bed in his cabin. It was evident that he had been dead for some hours. The external appearances were like those of death from inhaling carbon dioxide gas, and this suggestion was strengthened in his mind by finding on the table beside the bed a crude apparatus in which this gas appeared to have been generated. He did not however depend on these observations, but with the help of Dr Sinclair he performed an autopsy. As a result he was able to state definitely that the cause of death was carbon dioxide poisoning, and that alone. There was no trace of any other poison, nor of serious disease, nor of any injury.

'Thank you, doctor; that's all very clear. Now you said that the deceased had been dead for some hours. Can you say how long?'

'Not with any degree of accuracy, I'm afraid. The indications vary with the individual, the surroundings, the deceased's health and physical condition, and other factors.'

'But you could make an estimate?'

Dr Jellett could make an estimate, and after a good deal of pressing, he did so. He thought Harrison had been dead from four to six hours when he saw him, which would mean that he died somewhere about three or four o'clock in the morning.

'Isn't there a time in the morning when suicide is most prevalent?'

'That is so: from about four to five o'clock.'

'Now I wish you would tell the jury something about carbon dioxide poisoning—its symptoms and so on.'

Dr Jellett was willing to oblige. Puffing out his chest with some importance, he gave a little lecture.

A mixture of the gas with air of from five to six per cent upwards was dangerous. Incidentally he might mention that the test of the burning candle was quite unreliable, as a candle would burn in an atmosphere dangerous to human life. The gas prevented the normal oxygenisation of the blood in the lungs, with a speed and completeness proportionate to its purity. For this cause it was really more accurate to speak of suffocation from the gas rather than poisoning, though the latter was the popular phrase. The symptoms varied with different persons, but as a general rule they came on insidiously: producing first drowsiness, then sleep, then unconsciousness gliding imperceptibly into death. In some cases there was discomfort and pain, but this was unusual. One symptom was a slow rate of cooling and delayed approach of cadaveric rigidity, and this was one of the reasons why he could not be more definite as to the time of death. He did not think the jury required a more technical explanation, but he was prepared to give it, should the coroner so desire.

The coroner did not so desire, but was satisfied with what he had heard, except on one point.

'Just tell the jury, doctor, whether a victim to this gas can exert himself to escape? I mean, will he realise something is wrong in time to get out of danger?'

'In most cases the answer is no. I don't like to give figures, but in the great majority of instances the victim would be overcome by sleep and would not realise what was happening. Sometimes the converse might be the truth and sometimes there might be a sort of intermediate result. For instance, in one case in which a man and woman were accidentally poisoned, they had evidently realised their danger and had got out of bed, but they had been unable to walk and had fallen to the floor and been overcome.'

This concluded the doctor's evidence, except for one or two unimportant questions asked by jurors. Inspector Pollock took his place. He proved a good witness in that he answered only what he was asked, and that in the fewest possible words. But this very conciseness made his evidence dry, and Crewe was not greatly interested.

As a result of a telephone call the inspector had proceeded to the houseboat *Cygnet*, and there he found the deceased dead in his cabin with Dr Jellett in attendance. He was informed that the door had been broken open, and he had found that it had been secured from within by a push bolt, the keeper of which was torn away from the wood. The only other opening into the cabin was the porthole, a round window closed by thick glass in a heavy brass frame, similar to those in ocean going ships. The frame was closed and fitted tightly, though the screw fastenings were not in place. The porthole in the bathroom adjoining was closed and screwed tight. There was no door to the bathroom other than that from the sleeping cabin. This latter was shut, but not locked.

On the table at the head of the bed were a bakelite bowl or saucer containing chemicals and a decanter shaped bottle half full of liquid. He had these examined by an expert, who was in court. He understood that the chemical was chippings of marble which had been partly acted on by hydrochloric acid—this producing carbon dioxide gas—and the liquid was hydrochloric acid. On the bottle he found well marked fingerprints of the deceased, superimposed over faint ones of the steward, Higgins. There were no prints of any kind on the bowl. This he attributed to the heat generated by the action of the acid on the marble having dried off such prints. In reply to a further question, he said that in his opinion the circumstances precluded anyone but the deceased from having generated the gas.

Some other witnesses were called, but none seemed to Crewe to add to the general knowledge. The technical expert discoursed learnedly on the action of acid upon marble. Jasper Coleman admitted the Higgins version of the quarrel to be substantially correct.

Walpole stated that the deceased had intended to go to Germany on the day after his death, a visit which much interested him and to which he had been looking forward.

This was in connection with a Government loan, and Mr Harrison had been hoping to meet Herr Hitler. Walpole also assured the court that the deceased's finances were perfectly sound and in order, attributing the drop in the stocks to misplaced though natural nervousness on the part of the public. Some evidence of previous quarrels was also taken.

Then the coroner summed up. The jury had, he explained, to satisfy themselves on three points: first, the identity of the deceased; second, the cause of death, and third, if blame were attaching to anyone, and if so, to whom.

It was not a matter for him, the coroner, to decide, but as far as he could see, they would have little difficulty in reaching a decision on all three. They had it in evidence that the remains were those of -Mr Harrison, and no question on the point had been raised. The evidence, he thought, was equally overwhelming that the deceased had died as a result of too much carbon dioxide gas in the air of his cabin. As they had heard, the medical evidence admitted no alternative. And on the third point, the question of blame, he thought they would find their task equally easy. The police statement, it seemed to him, ruled out any possibility but the one: that the deceased had taken his own life. It was not part of their business to state the motive which might have dictated such an action, but evidence of an unhappy home life had been put before them which they might consider might account for it, or perhaps represented the last straw in a series of other worries. However, as he said, that was not their business: they were to confine themselves to the three points he had mentioned. He would now ask them to retire and consider their verdict, unless there was any legal point upon which they wished for advice.

The jury exhibited no desire to hear him further and

retired with the expression of persons bearing matters of weight. But ten minutes was sufficient to dispose of these matters, and they returned with the verdict that the deceased, Andrew Harrison, had committed suicide while temporarily of unsound mind.

As they filed out of the hall, it seemed to Crewe that the greater part of their time and trouble and strain had been wasted: that they had simply taken a tedious roundabout way of reaching a conclusion which had been obvious from the start. A proper enquiry was of course necessary, but he thought that evidence covering the cause of death, the gas generating plant, and the closed cabin, should have been ample, as these three matters settled the verdict beyond any possible question. However difficult it might be to suggest Harrison's motive, the fact that he committed suicide was not, and never had been, in doubt.

Crewe's thoughts turned again to that question of motive as, in silence for the most part, they drove back to the *Cygnet*. Certainly it did look as if there must be serious financial trouble. Though Crewe had not seen as much of Harrison as the others, he had seen enough to make him agree with the view that the man would not have taken such a step for any other reason. Certainly the row with Gloria would not account for it: similar disputes had taken place too often in the past for that. And no other motive had been suggested. It looked as if their financial trouble was only beginning.

Lunch was also a silent meal and after it the party left for Town. Harrison's remains were to be kept in the Henley mortuary till the day of the funeral, when they would be taken to Mount Street. From there the official procession would start.

For Crewe those days before the funeral were among the most hectic he had ever spent. Mrs Harrison had been greatly softened by what had happened, and now treated him as a friend, rather than as a retainer to whom one gave arbitrary instructions. He thus received a free hand to deal with all the correspondence, to meet callers, and to make all the necessary funeral arrangements. So much had he to deal with that he had to get Entrican's help to see him through.

But preoccupied as all of the party were during these days, the matter which outweighed all others in their minds was that which Crewe had foreseen—money. The stocks were still tumbling, and the question was whether this was going to mean complete ruin, or whether the rot could be stopped in time. Kemp and his satellites remained convinced that the property was intrinsically sound, and declared again and again that if only the present crisis could be weathered, all would be well. If confidence, they said, could once be re-established, recovery would be speedy.

Then on the evening of the funeral something happened which gave a completely new turn to their thoughts. After dinner a rather stout blue-eyed man of slightly below middle height called to see Crewe. Instantly Crewe recognised him as the Chief Inspector French he had met at Scotland Yard.

'Good evening, Mr Crewe,' he said politely, 'I have come to make some enquiries into the death of the late Mr Harrison.'

Crewe stared speechless. For a moment he was so overwhelmed with surprise that he could do nothing else. So the matter was not closed. This could only mean one thing— that the authorities did not accept the verdict of suicide!

But if Harrison had not committed suicide—Crewe's brain reeled as he thought of it—there could be only one other explanation of his death. Not accident certainly! It couldn't be—it couldn't be—that they suspected murder?

9

The Chief Inspector

Early on the previous morning Chief Inspector French had lifted the receiver of his desk telephone.

'How are you on with that Mullins case, Carter?' he asked, and paused to listen. 'Then you may hand it over to Kennedy to finish. I'm going to Henley and I shall want you. Arrange with Blair for a car and be ready to join me in fifteen minutes.'

He replaced the receiver, and moving placidly though with surprising speed about the room, he began to collect various articles and papers and to pack them in a despatch case. Then picking up a suitcase from a corner, he opened it and ran rapidly through its contents. By the time he had finished Sergeant Carter appeared.

'Do you want anything along, sir?' asked Carter, pausing at the door.

'Only Old Faithful,' French rejoined, jerking his thumb at the suitcase.

'Right, sir.' Carter picked up the, case. 'Car's ready when you are.'

The two men passed from the room, with its pleasant outlook over the Embankment and across the Thames to the County Council buildings opposite. They traversed some corridors all painted the same dull shade of green and went down four flights of steps to a courtyard. There a car with a plain-clothes driver was waiting. In silence they took their places and the car moved out on to the Embankment.

'Henley, George,' French said as they passed through the gates. 'How will you go?'

'Slough and Maidenhead, I think, sir.'

'Right. Look as slippy as you can.' French wound the window down as far as it would go and lay back on the cushions so as to get the breeze on his hot forehead. It was mid-July and London was steaming. One of those trying spells of damp heat had set in. The air was heavy and oppressive, and any movement threw one into a bath of perspiration. The sun was shining dully through a slight haze, and though it was clear overhead, a line of piled up clouds lay black and threatening on the horizon. People were nervy and irritable, and longed for the relief of the coming storm.

'Lucky pair of beggars, we are, Carter,' French presently remarked, 'getting up the river on a day like this.'

Carter glanced round as much of the sky as he could see between the houses. 'Yes, sir. If we're not drowned before we get there.'

'I wish the storm would come. Clear away this heat.'

'What's the case, sir?' Carter asked after a pause.

French wiped his forehead. 'Harrison. You've seen about it, I suppose?'

'I read the inquest this morning. It seemed pretty straightforward. What's arisen since?'

'I don't know. They're not satisfied about it down there. It seems they wanted the coroner to adjourn, but he decided he knew better and went ahead.'

'Not like a coroner, sir.'

'They're vague about it. If they were as vague to the coroner as they were to me just now over the phone, I don't blame him.'

'They suspect murder?'

'They don't go as far as that. The most they would say to me was that they weren't satisfied with the verdict. Probably all my eye and Betty Martin. But I tell you, Carter,' French swung round in his seat as if stirred to action by his idea, 'if there is anything in it, it'll make a fine old breeze. Harrison was one of the best known men in the world.'

'Good for you, sir, if there's a case.'

'We'll know that better when we're through with it,' French returned dryly. 'But it seems there's more in it than merely suicide or murder. There are pots of money involved.'

Carter raised his eyebrows. 'Swindling?' he asked with an increase of interest.

'I can't tell you that. But the old boy was a multi-millionaire, and it seems his stocks are dropping like blazes. If he committed suicide this is likely to continue, because the canny public can't be persuaded that it wasn't because he saw a crash coming. If the fall continues, it means the ruin of thousands. But if Harrison was murdered it puts a different complexion on things. There'd be no reason to doubt the solvency of the stock then, and it would probably begin to rise at once. So there's a fair amount depending on you and me.'

'Reminds me a bit of that Swedish chap, Kruger.'

French nodded. 'Yes, except that no question of murder was raised in his case. Indeed that affair may be responsible for some of the present trouble. People remember Kruger and it makes them nervous. And quite reasonably. I was stung myself over Swedish matches, and if I had money in Harrison's, I'd see about getting it out before I did anything else.'

Carter grinned. 'I believe you, sir. And so should I if I was lucky enough to have to decide.'

The remark set French thinking. He had lost £500 in that crash, quite a considerable sum for a man in his position. Was he so lucky? He hadn't thought so at the time. And yet was it not better to save and lose £500, than never to be able to save it at all? Yes, he supposed Carter was right.

He felt a good deal of sympathy for all those people who at that moment must be watching the Harrison stock with such intense interest. Intense fear in many cases, he had no doubt. A lot of people put too many of their eggs into the same basket. They saw what they believed was a good thing, and naturally enough they tried to get all they could from it.

Amazing how important people's beliefs were! He had once heard a man arguing that the whole structure of finance was built on faith, or credit, as it was technically called. This man said it didn't matter whether or not money really existed so long as people believed it did. French could not accept that view. He remembered that faith had not put money in the Humbert safe. Yet without faith he could see that modern commerce and finance could not function. It was an interesting question and sometime he must think it out.

He wondered what sort of men he would have to work with at Henley. Though close to Town, he could not remember ever having met any of them. The Chief Constable was well spoken of, but French had not always found people living up to their reputation. However the very circumstances of the call looked as if someone in control was brainy—or perhaps fanciful.

Seeing his chief in a thoughtful mood, Carter had tactfully kept silence. But a movement of French's released his tongue. 'I'm expecting to see my brother-in-law, sir,' he announced. 'I have a sister married to the sergeant at Henley—Speers, his name is. He's a keen man, though I say it myself. And the inspector, Mr Pollock, is well liked.'

'Don't know him,' said French.

'He's been very good to Harry—that's my brother-in-law. Helped him quite a lot when he was sick. Harry'd do anything for him.'

'I'm always interested to meet a paragon. There! Did you see that? That's the first.'

A vivid streak of light had flashed across the southern sky. Even above the noise of the traffic came the crash of the thunder.

'I'm glad to see it. But it's far away still.'

Before they had left the town the sun vanished, inky clouds rolled up and a deluge began. For a few minutes it was so heavy that they had almost to stop, then as quickly as it had come it cleared away, the sun came out again, and the running pavements began quickly to steam.

But what a difference there was in the air! Now fresh and clear and sparkling, as it had been heavy and oppressive and ominous. It seemed to French as if ten years had been taken off his life, and when shortly after they drew up at the police station at Henley, he felt ready to tackle anything that could be put before him.

Inspector Pollock came out to meet them. 'Good day, sir. Good day, sergeant. Very grateful to you for coming so promptly. Will you come to my room?' He ushered them into a plainly furnished office. 'The Chief Constable wants to have a word with you, but he had an appointment in the town. He'll be back in a few minutes.'

'That's all right,' said French. 'We're at your disposal as long as we're here.' His eye twinkled. 'We've no objection to a holiday on the river.'

The inspector, not quite sure how to take this, said the river was not so bad. 'But there's a lot of work when the regatta's on,' he added dubiously.

'Keep you from sleeping all the time,' French smiled. 'How did it go this year?'

They discussed the famous function and then Carter, having selected a propitious moment, asked after his sister and her husband.

'You'll see Speers directly,' answered Pollock. 'He's in on this job, and if it goes to an investigation he'll be at your service if you want him.'

'Is there a doubt about an investigation?' put in French.

'Well, I'm not sure, sir: I suppose there is a doubt. It's the Chief Constable, you know. I went into the thing and I confess I thought it all right. But the C.C. is a bit dissatisfied. He'll tell you. And here he is,' Pollock went on, as an energetic step was heard ascending the stairs.

Major Marsh was a broad-shouldered, square-faced man with a military precision of manner, relieved by a kindly smile. He was indeed not unlike 'The Major', as portrayed in connection with a famous brand of cigarettes. He shook hands with French, nodded to Carter and Pollock, seated himself at the head of the table and opened a file of papers, all as it were in one comprehensive movement.

'We must get down to this thing at once,' he declared as he settled himself, 'for I'm due at Reading as soon as I can get away. How's my friend, Sir Mortimer?'

'Very fit, sir,' French answered. 'He asked to be remembered to you.'

'We did a lot of work together at one time. But I didn't ask you to come down to tell you that. It's this case of Andrew Harrison's death. How much do you know about it?'

'Only what was in the papers, sir.'

'The reports were accurate enough as far as they went,' went on Major Marsh. 'There really is not much to add to them. And it may therefore be,' he paused, turning over the papers before him, 'that you will think I've brought you down here under false pretences.' Again he paused, this time smiling crookedly at French. 'Well, you may be right. But I should like to make clear that I asked for help from the Yard, not because I was satisfied that something was wrong, but because I was not satisfied that everything was right.'

'I understand, sir.'

'What I want you to do is to check up on the facts and see if you are satisfied. If you are, the matter is at an end. If you are not, we can then discuss what further steps should be taken.'

French nodded. 'That's quite clear, sir. But perhaps you'd tell my why you are dissatisfied with the coroner's finding?'

'Of course. It's only fair to say that I've already explained my views to Pollock, and he's not by any means convinced by them. He thinks the verdict is sound.'

'I appreciate the case you make, sir,' Pollock put in hastily, 'but the actual facts of the death seem to me to support the verdict.'

'Of course they do,' the Chief Constable returned. 'I agree with you there. But with me the doubt remains. The reason is this, Chief Inspector.'

Major Marsh again paused, as if to arrange his thoughts. Then he went on more slowly.

'What weighs most strongly with me is that I knew Harrison personally, and that unless my knowledge of psychology is utterly at fault, he never committed suicide. This of course won't appeal to you, but to me it is almost overwhelming. Harrison was a man who thought of very little but his own advantage. And of course he was extraordinarily able. I cannot believe that he would have let things get to such a pass that the only way out for him was suicide. That's my first point.'

'As you say, sir, it's one that I can't check. I never met the man.'

'Of course not. But here's one that you can check: and I hope you will. The man had no motive for suicide. To my mind, it's nonsense to pretend he killed himself because his stocks were dropping. All the evidence we've had goes to prove the stocks were fundamentally sound. But even if they weren't, that wouldn't be enough. Harrison was not the man to sit down and wait for disaster. If he saw his fortune going, he would certainly have realised what he could and cleared out. Under such circumstances I could understand a voluntary disappearance, but never suicide.'

'I understand, sir, the coroner suggested it might have been due to family troubles?'

The major made a gesture of disagreement. 'If suicide because of financial difficulties was absurd, suicide because

126

of family troubles was blithering idiocy. There was no love lost between Harrison and his family. He didn't care two hoots about the lot. In fact if they'd all been taken away and drowned, he'd probably have thought it a welcome relief. Besides, what were the family troubles supposed to consist of? A row with his wife and daughter about the girl's engagement! He wouldn't turn a hair. Particularly when you remember they've been squabbling like that for years. I'm convinced there's nothing in that. And if so, where was the motive?'

'That sounds convincing enough, sir,' French said slowly, adding: 'that is, if you're sure of your facts.'

'I want you to verify them. Well, right or wrong, that is my second point. My third is even stronger. It was mentioned at the inquest, but for some reason which I've given up trying to fathom, nothing was made of it. It is this: Harrison was going to Germany on the afternoon of his death. Not on an ordinary journey such as you or I might make. He was going to see the heads of the German Government upon a very important financial operation; the floating of a large German loan in this country. Now the mere fact that he had arranged to go seems to me to prove he was not contemplating suicide.'

'That is so,' French admitted diplomatically.

'And lastly,' went on the Chief Constable, 'I considered Harrison's life, and it occurred to me that perhaps no living man was more hated. Personally he was objectionable: he was selfish and aggressive and could be extraordinarily rude. And in business he had bettered or cheated vast numbers of people, utterly ruining many. There must at least have been scores who would have been glad of a chance to put him out of the way.' Marsh paused, then added: 'Well, that's the end of my harangue. How does it appeal to you?'

'I'd like to think it over, sir,' French answered. 'You certainly do seem to have made a case for investigation. But it hasn't convinced Inspector Pollock?'

'He hasn't considered it on its merits,' Marsh returned, smiling at his subordinate. 'Oh no, you haven't,' he went on as Pollock attempted a denial. 'You've been obsessed with the details of the death and you can't see how it could have been murder, so you assume it wasn't. I'm not saying you're wrong, remember.'

Though he had only read the details of the death given in the papers, French felt inclined to agree with the inspector. Moreover, apart from these details altogether, the Chief Constable's argument did not greatly appeal to him. Of its four points, he considered there was nothing in the first, third and fourth. As to Harrison not being the man to commit suicide, no one could tell what he himself or anyone else would do, given a sufficient stimulus. Then to a man faced with the dreadful issue of life or death, a visit to Germany would have counted for less than nothing. Lastly, thousands of men are bitterly hated, who are not murdered.

French however realised that if Marsh were correct on his second point, he had undoubtedly established a case for enquiry. No one commits suicide without an overwhelming motive. If Harrison really had none, it did look like the end of the suicide theory.

But had Harrison no motive? Here French thought that the Chief Constable had by no means proved his point. Once again he was building on his estimate of the deceased's character. It was obvious that before a conclusion could be reached, a great deal more would have to be learnt.

He wondered how far Pollock was right in thinking the details of the death precluded anything but suicide. This seemed to him a vital point, and he determined to go into it first thing. If enquiry led him to agree with Pollock, that would end the matter, because nothing that Marsh had put up really upset it. On the other hand, if either accident or murder were possible, Marsh's argument could no longer be disregarded.

'Well,' broke in the Chief Constable's voice. 'What's the decision?'

French came back to his surroundings. 'I'm afraid, sir, I'm not in a position to give any opinion at present. Your second point seems to me very strong. If you are correct in your facts, it would seem at first sight to prove your case. On the other hand I should like to see the houseboat before coming to a conclusion from details.'

Major Marsh nodded. 'That's just what I expected you'd say, Chief Inspector, and it's very satisfactory to me. Now in case you wanted to examine things for yourself, I've managed to stretch a point or two. The cabin has been sealed and we've posted a man to make sure the seal isn't broken. Also I've managed to keep the body here till the funeral, which is tomorrow. If you want to examine it or take prints, you can do so. And of course I needn't say that we'll give you all the help we can: even Pollock, who bears no malice for my having an opinion of my own.' Again Marsh smiled his kindly smile.

Pollock grinned in his turn. 'I'll be glad to do anything to help the Chief Inspector, sir,' he declared.

'Then I must run.' Marsh jumped to his feet and presently the rapid acceleration of his car testified to his haste.

'Well, sir,' Pollock went on when the sounds had died away, 'what would you like to do first? Suppose we go to see the body and then they'll be free to get it up to Town?

Perhaps then you'd like a bite of lunch? After that we could go on to the boat or anywhere else you wished.'

'Fine, inspector, with one exception. If we've time before starting, I'd like to read over the inquest depositions and any notes you may have.'

Pollock took a sheaf of papers from a cupboard. 'Right, sir: they're all here. When I heard you were coming I made up this file.'

French read carefully through all that had yet been officially written on the Harrison case, and then they went to the mortuary, where French took not only finger, but palm prints. Otherwise he found nothing helpful from an inspection of the remains.

'Would you like to see the doctor now or later?' Pollock asked as they turned away.

'Later,' French returned promptly. He had read Jellett's evidence and there were no questions he wished to ask him.

After the bite of lunch which Pollock had recommended they got into French's car and drove downstream along the north bank of the Thames to 'Amalfi'. French was much more interested in this stage of the enquiry. Apart from going on the river, which he always liked, and seeing this wonderful houseboat of which he had heard so much, he had now reached the heart of his problem. What he would learn here would tell him how Harrison had died, and whether he himself was at the beginning of his enquiry or at the end.

The three men walked down past the Colemans' house till they came in sight of the water with the *Cygnet* looming up behind some shrubs. Though French thought he knew what to expect, he was surprised at her size.

'By heck,' he exclaimed, 'she's a big boat, I shouldn't have thought they'd have got her up the river.'

'She's maximum size,' Pollock answered. 'They built her to the extreme limits allowed. She goes through the locks and under the bridges, and no more.'

'Tidy looking craft too.'

Pollock wasn't so sure. 'I was once at Flushing,' he said, 'and I saw some barges going up the Scheldt. They looked like the bow and stem of a ship with about a quarter of a mile of biscuit boxing in between. Not so unlike this affair.'

'I suppose she is a bit like a canal boat,' French admitted. 'Now let's see this cabin.'

Pollock broke the seal and threw open the door. French stepped inside and stood for some time without speaking, looking round and memorising what he saw.

The cabin was of fair size as cabins go: about ten feet by seven, with the longer dimension parallel to the keel. The bed was in the left corner, with its head against the cabin bulkhead and its edge along the outside of the ship. Above it was the porthole, of the same type as in sea-going vessels. At the head of the bed was a table and at the foot an armchair. The bulkhead to the right of the door contained a wardrobe and the door into the bathroom. The furniture was all of French polished mahogany, of simple but charming design.

French looked into the bathroom. It was small, but equally admirably fitted. It also had a porthole, but only the one door—that through which he had entered.

'It was on that table at the head of the bed that the gas was generated,' Pollock pointed out. 'Except for removing the body and the bowl and bottle, nothing has been touched. The photographs of course were taken before that was done.'

French nodded as he began to examine the contents of

the room in detail. 'What have you done about fingerprints?' he asked.

'Nothing, sir, except to dust over the bowl and bottle. As you read, Harrison's prints and a few of Higgins' were on the bottle, but not on the bowl.'

'No others on either?'

'No, sir.'

French first satisfied himself that the door really had been bolted and burst open from without. So no murderer could have left that way. Nor through the bathroom, since the porthole there had been screwed home. He turned to the cabin porthole.

'Hinged at the top, closed, but the bolts not in place,' he remarked. 'What about a man getting through the porthole and drawing the glass shut after him?'

Pollock hesitated. 'That's the Chief's case,' he explained. 'If it was murder, the murderer must have left by the port-hole, because there was no other way. But I can't see how he could have done it.'

'Well, that's a point I want to be clear about,' French returned, dropping into the armchair. 'Sit down on the bed, and let's thrash it out. Now suppose for argument's sake it was murder. First the murderer would want to get in. No difficulty about that, I suppose?'

'No, sir, he could have entered through the door—knocked and got Harrison to open it for him. But if he did, it would seem to involve one thing.'

'Yes? Go ahead.'

'That he was known to Harrison. I mean, it's hard to imagine Harrison letting a stranger in like that.'

'Yes, I think you're probably right there. Very well, the murderer gets in and has a chat with Harrison. Then let's hear the rest of your theory. What was to prevent him from slipping the bolt in the door, starting up his apparatus to make the gas, escaping out of the porthole and letting the glass drop behind him to the closed position?'

'Just that it doesn't seem to me that he could have done any of those things. He might have bolted the door, either when Harrison wasn't looking, or more likely on some excuse that they wouldn't be disturbed in their talk: for I assume he would come prepared with something to talk about. But I don't see how he could have started up the gas without Harrison interfering.'

'Some story about a new chemical process with money in it?'

'Perhaps so, sir: though I doubt it. But I don't think he could ever have got out of the porthole.'

'Just why not?'

'Because Harrison would never have let him. Suppose he started the gas. He would then have to get out of the cabin at once: else he might have been bowled over himself. But it's inconceivable to me that Harrison would have lain there in bed and done nothing. He couldn't but have known something was wrong, and he could so easily have thrown the bowl out of the porthole. If he had been doped, I could understand it all right. But the doctor says he wasn't.'

French made a note to reopen this point with Dr Jellett. 'Yes?' he encouraged Pollock.

'Then, sir, I don't believe, even if all these difficulties had been overcome, that he could have got out of the porthole. He would have had to climb on the bed, and he couldn't have done so without leaving traces on the clothes.'

'I dare say you're right.'

'Look at it this way, sir. Harrison must have been either

conscious or unconscious when he was doing it. If Harrison had been conscious, he wouldn't have let him. If unconscious, the murderer couldn't have smoothed away the traces. So that either way no one could have got out.'

French considered the point, and the more he did so, the sounder it seemed.

'Get into bed, Carter, and cover yourself with the clothes. Lie as like Harrison as possible. And will you, Inspector, climb on the bed as if you were going out.'

They made the test four times, smoothing the clothes each time. In all four quite unmistakable traces were left by Pollock.

'Yes,' French said at last, 'that seems sound enough. And if you're right, the Chief Constable's wrong, and it was suicide.'

'There's still more in it, sir,' Pollock went on. 'You notice the brass ring is closed fully home? Now I've tried it, and you can't close it like that from outside. The hinges are stiff, and if the ring is dropped, it stops short of going home— about half an inch short. And you can't catch hold of it in any way from the outside, as the fixed circle screens it.'

French was more interested still. 'That's a point, certainly,' he said. 'I think I'd like to see that done.'

'Right, sir. I'll ask the captain to give us a boat.'

They went on deck, leaving the local policeman to guard the cabin. French was introduced to Captain Collison, who at once had a boat swung out. Ten minutes later the three police officers were moored outside the porthole.

'You've fingered it all over if you made those tests?' French asked before starting.

'Yes, sir, but only on the outside and after we had tested it over and made sure it bore no prints.'

'Right! Now go ahead and let's see your experiment.'

Pushing with the palms of his hands on the glass, Pollock raised the thick window in its heavy brass ring. Then suddenly he let it fall. As he had foretold, it stopped some half-inch before getting home.

'H'm,' said French. 'Try that again.'

They all tried it in turn, but on no occasion did the ring swing completely into place. And a careful examination showed French that there was no way in which a grip could be got upon it to pull it shut.

That the glass could not be completely closed from the outside seemed decisive evidence. It was the fact that the bolts had not been put in place which had first suggested to Marsh that the murderer might have left by the porthole. Now French saw that this was a faulty deduction. The stiffness of the hinge completely altered the situation. If the glass would keep closed without it, Harrison would have had no need to use the bolts. He would not in fact have done so. Once he had decided on his dreadful deed, he would have carried it out with the least trouble and delay.

French made no comment as they returned on board, but he felt that Pollock had proved his case. He would think it all out once more before he made his report, but now it certainly did seem impossible that the murderer had left the cabin. In other words, there could have been no murderer.

French however, had come down to make an investigation, and make it he would. He examined with the greatest care every inch of the cabin and its furniture, and tested all possible surfaces for fingerprints, photographing his finds. Finally he took the prints of everyone on board, and went over their statements in the hope of gaining some further information.

In this latter he was disappointed. Pollock seemed to have covered the ground exceedingly well. With his mind practically made up, French returned with the others to the police station to consider how much more evidence he must obtain before drafting his report.

10

The Conflicting Evidence

Though it seemed to French a waste of time to interview Dr Jellett, whose evidence he had read in detail, he felt that to omit to do so would scarcely be fair to the Chief Constable. On the way to the police station he therefore turned aside to the doctor's.

'What's all this enquiry about now, Chief Inspector?' Jellett asked at once. 'I understood the affair was over and done with.'

'So I think it is,' French answered. 'The Chief Constable simply asked our people to check the facts over before filing away the papers. No allegation has been made that the coroner's verdict was wrong or anything of that sort.'

This was literally true, though only literally. But the doctor was too old a hand to swallow it. 'Oh come now,' he protested, 'you needn't try to come over me with that stuff. Scotland Yard isn't called unless there's a pretty strong suspicion of foul play. As the doctor concerned, I think I'm entitled to be told if you're trying to upset my evidence.'

'Probably you're right, doctor.' After all it might be wise

to take the man into his confidence. French therefore pledged him to secrecy, and did so.

'I believe murder to be perfectly impossible,' Jellett said decisively, when he had finished. 'To die as Harrison died, he must either have committed suicide or have been unaware that an attempt to murder him was being made. Either he made that gas himself, or he was asleep when someone else did it. But I don't suppose you're going to argue that he slept while someone got in and out of the cabin, whether he went through the door or the porthole?'

'You think that impossible?' French asked.

Jellett snorted. 'Don't you know it is? It doesn't take a doctor to answer that question.'

'I agree,' said French, 'that normally any person would wake if there was someone climbing in and out of a porthole—'

'*On* the bed; *over* the man.'

'I'm not overlooking that, and I agree it would wake anyone under normal conditions. But what about abnormal? What about a whiff of chloroform or some dope earlier in the evening?'

Jellett shook his head. 'No good. I thought of that—long before you did—and at the autopsy I went into it thoroughly. There was no trace of anything of the kind.'

'I take it that can be known definitely?'

'Absolutely.' The doctor spoke testily. 'You may think I swore it without knowing what I was saying, but you'd be wrong.'

French smiled whimsically. 'Sorry, doctor. I didn't mean any harm. I only wanted to be sure.'

Jellett was mollified. 'All right,' he said; 'I know your people's ways. Now since you take up that attitude, I'll tell you something. I needn't, because it has obviously nothing to do with this affair; but I will. There were three marks of a hypodermic in Harrison's left forearm—fairly recent, but much older than a few hours before he died.'

'That's interesting. I suppose you can't say how much?'

'No. Two or three weeks, I should think. Certainly more than a few hours.'

French considered. 'Interesting, but as you say, irrelevant to this affair. Were those the only marks?'

'Yes, the only ones.'

French rose. 'Thank you very much, doctor. That's all I want.'

Once again he had drawn blank. Strongly he felt inclined to give up further enquiry and report that he agreed with the verdict. But as one of the Chief Constable's points had been Harrison's desire to go to Berlin, he thought before doing so he ought to interview Kemp.

'I think that's all I want to see into here,' he therefore told Pollock as they re-entered the police station. 'I'll make some enquiries in Town about that German trip and so on, and then write you or come down and see the C.C. I might just have a look at that bowl and bottle before I go.'

'They're here, sir.'

The bowl proved to be of bakelite, some ten inches in diameter, such as might be used for flowers. A layer of little cubes and chippings was spread thinly over the bottom. The particles looked as if they had lost their sharp edges from the action of acid, but obviously enough acid had not been used to dissolve the lot. French tested the bowl for fingerprints. There were none.

'There couldn't have been any,' Pollock reminded him. 'Dr Jellett said the chemical action would have produced enough heat to dry them off.'

French nodded and turned to the decanter. It was of good quality glass, but small in size and without much cutting or decoration—fortunately for the recording of fingerprints. The prints it bore were reasonably clear, and though French decided they must be enlarged and checked in the usual way, he could see well enough that all of them were either Harrison's or Higgins'. He examined the position of Harrison's with great care, having been caught once or twice in similar cases through failing to do so. But soon he satisfied himself that they were genuine prints made while pouring out the liquid, and not fakes produced by some other person pressing the man's fingers on the glass. The fact that Harrison's prints were superimposed over Higgins' proved that the deceased had been the last to handle the decanter; further evidence, French thought, that no faking had been done.

It was too late when he reached Town to do any more that night, but next day he called upon Kemp. French had a good deal more experience of fine offices than had Crewe, and yet when he first saw Harrison's he was almost as much impressed as had been the younger man. If this building could only have been inspected by those members of the public who were now clamouring to sell their stock, French felt its opulence would have fulfilled its purpose and stopped the rot. Unhappily for the Harrison stockholders, the majority didn't see it, and the few who did knew too much to be affected.

Kemp saw French at once, but he had little to tell him. He was full of the fall of the stocks. He assured French of their soundness with what French believed was genuine conviction. They were still dropping, but less rapidly, and Kemp now believed that actual panic would be avoided and that the firm would escape the complete ruin he had feared.

With regard to Harrison's proposed visit to Berlin, he confirmed Major Marsh's statement on every point. The deceased had been looking forward to the visit with quite unusual keenness, and had spoken of his pleasure in the trip as lately as the afternoon before his death. On that afternoon, moreover, he was in very good spirits, not at all depressed. In fact, to the best of Kemp's knowledge and belief, Harrison had many reasons for wishing to live and none for suicide.

It was not till they reached this stage that Kemp, whose mind was obsessed with his own business, began to question the reason for French's call. Immediately he grew excited.

'You seriously think it might have been murder?' he said eagerly. 'But if you're right, that would save us! Why the mere fact—' He ceased speaking, his mind evidently grappling with a new idea. French watched his changing expression, from curiosity to eagerness, to the dawn of the idea, to a certain slyness. 'That's very interesting,' he said insinuatingly. 'Can you tell me just what leads you to suspect murder?'

French felt slightly dissatisfied with the turn the interview was taking. 'I don't suspect it,' he said bluntly. 'I don't myself question the verdict. I'm simply carrying out a routine job.'

Kemp looked disappointed. 'Ah, quite so,' he agreed without conviction. 'Then is there anything else I can do for you? I don't want to hurry you, but I should like to get back to business as soon as possible.'

Though French had been so downright, he was at that moment more in sympathy with the Chief Constable's doubts than at any time previously. The evidence about

141

Berlin was strong. He thought he might take it as proven, that when Harrison left his office on the day before his death, he had no thought of suicide.

This represented a distinct advance in the investigation and if it were true, a significant fact followed. The conditions in the cabin proved that the man had committed suicide. Something vitally important must therefore have happened to him between the time he left the office and that at which he had gone to bed. Now what could that have been? So far French had only heard of the family row. But he could not believe that that was sufficient. There must surely have been something else.

He wondered whether he had done enough in the case. He had satisfied himself that Harrison had died by his own hand, but he had not disposed of Marsh's criticisms. These, he imagined, could only be met by continuing on his present line of thought; by finding that vitally important something which must have happened after the deceased left his office.

He went back to the offices and asked once more for Kemp.

'Sorry to bother you again, Mr Kemp,' he apologised, 'but I omitted to ask just one question. At what hour did Mr Harrison leave the office on the day before his death?'

'As it happens, I can tell you that,' the manager answered. 'I was in his room till he went, talking indeed about the German visit. I accompanied him to the lift. That was just about four o'clock. Mr Harrison was a hard worker, and usually remained till nearly six, but when he was staying on the river he went early.'

A short enquiry from the lift men and hall porters revealed the concluding stages of the late principal's departure. He had gone down in the lift without a stop to the ground floor. There, discreetly attended by two porters, he had walked out of the building into his car, which was waiting. During all this movement, which French thought must have been like a royal progress, he had met no one. Nor, save the chauffeur, was there anyone in his car.

This had been unexpectedly easy, and French went on to Mount Street to continue the enquiry. On arrival he found that everyone was at the funeral, but in the late afternoon he was able to see the chauffeur. From him he learnt that Harrison had been driven from the office to the *Cygnet*, or as near it as the car could go in the Coleman grounds, and that they had not stopped *en route*, nor had Harrison spoken to anyone during the journey.

As the chauffeur seemed a quite reliable man, it followed that Harrison's upset had taken place aboard the *Cygnet*. It was a nuisance, as this meant that he, French, must interview all who had been there. He would call a halt for dinner and then go back to Mount Street.

When he returned shortly before nine he found all his victims assembled and available for interrogation. From the Henley reports he already knew a good deal about them, and he decided to begin with the two whom he had already met, Crewe and Entrican. Then he would go on to Mrs Harrison, Rupert, Gloria, and Locke, who had accompanied the family to Town.

On the whole the results were satisfactory in the sense that the entire period was covered. When Harrison had arrived on board the *Cygnet* between five and six he had sat on deck with Mrs Harrison, Gloria, Locke and Crewe until it was time to dress for dinner. He had gone to dress no earlier and no later than usual and had turned up punctually for the meal, so presumably his time had been fully occupied in dressing. After dinner he had been continuously in the presence of members of the party, until Jasper Coleman had come aboard and the dispute had broken out. Mrs Harrison admitted having gone to his cabin after the row to see if anything could be done to smooth things down. Though they had disagreed again, they had parted as good friends as at other times. Mrs Harrison said they were then both ready to go to bed, and after she left her husband's cabin he closed the door and she heard the bolt being shot.

The testimonies of all concerned agreed reasonably well, and French believed he had been told the truth. He thought it might be wise to take similar statements from the boat's officers, and he decided to do this in the morning on his way to report to the Chief Constable. As a matter of routine, though he scarcely thought they would be required, he obtained photographs of all concerned.

Though the day had been long and he was tired, French could not get the case out of his mind. When he reached home he took up a novel, intending to read a chapter or two before turning in. But it was no use. He could not concentrate on the story. The fate of Harrison came between him and the pages.

What *had* been Harrison's motive? If the man had no idea of suicide when he left his office, when did the idea enter his mind? Not on the way to the boat. Not during the evening. Surely not after he had gone to bed.

To his own discomfort French had to admit himself puzzled. The Chief Constable's objections were undoubtedly more weighty than he had realised. There did not appear to be any adequate explanation of the suicide.

But if Harrison had not committed suicide, there was

only the one alternative. This was not a case into which accident could enter. The decanter and bowl ruled that out. No, if Harrison had not committed suicide, he had been murdered.

But he, French, had already gone into that. Murder was simply not possible. Harrison had died peacefully. But he could not have done so if he had been murdered. The murderer could not have left the cabin—if he could have left it—without arousing him, and he would then have fought in some way for his life.

It was certainly perplexing. French realised that all he had done so far was to strengthen the Chief Constable's case. It was a disconcerting thought. He couldn't go back to Major Marsh with such a story. He must either find the motive for suicide, or show how Harrison could have been murdered.

Presently he decided that instead of returning to Henley next day he would go to the Yard and spend a few hours reconsidering the whole matter.

He was astonished next morning to find that all the papers were once more full of the affair. Large headlines shouted that the case was not closed, or if it had been, it was re-opened. Fresh developments had taken place. Scotland Yard had been called in. Chief Inspector French and Sergeant Carter had been making enquiries at Henley and in London. And then came the consummation of all this: 'Foul Play Feared.'

It was true that the paper which displayed the latter heading watered it down in its text, admitting that the police had made no such statement. It argued however, that an appeal to the Yard could mean nothing else.

French rubbed his chin as he read the various accounts.

He had been as discreet as usual in his movements and he would stake his life that Carter had been the same. From where then had come this leakage.

It did not take him long to find an explanation. That look he had surprised on Kemp's face? Kemp was fighting for his job and for Harrison's money. Kemp had seen in this story a chance of saving the situation. The run on the stocks was due to the fact that people believed Harrison had committed suicide because they were unsound. If Harrison had been murdered such an argument no longer held. Therefore at all cost get the public to believe he was murdered.

French felt sure his theory was correct. As he looked back over his interview with Kemp, he seemed to see the thought form in the man's mind. He had indeed almost put it into words.

Then a further idea occurred to French, making him sit up and whistle soundlessly. Was Kemp's story true? Had he *invented* the trip to Berlin just to bring about this result? Or rather—he would scarcely state something whose falsity could so easily be demonstrated—had he added to the true fact of the trip, the false garnishing of Harrison's interest in it?

French turned back the pages of his notebook. According to Major Marsh Harrison had himself mentioned the trip, but the statement of his pleasure in it had come from Kemp only.

If Kemp had really invented this addition to his story, it would destroy the second strongest objection to the suicide theory. In fact French was not now sure whether it wasn't the strongest. Motive is notoriously difficult to come by at second or third hand.

For some time French sat weighing the matter. He considered taxing Kemp both with manufacturing this evidence, and with informing the papers of the Yard's action. He had in fact almost decided to do so, when a further fact came to his notice which tended so much in the opposite direction that he felt that till it was cleared up, Kemp's actions mattered very little.

On his desk were the photographs he and Carter had taken of Harrison's cabin, and when he had finished with the newspapers he turned to them. Among other things they showed all the fingerprints he had found. At once he was surprised to see that all of them had been identified—a rather unusual state of affairs. Two prints on the jamb of the door belonged to Mrs Harrison and all the rest without exception were either Harrison's or Higgins'.

At first sight this did not seem to throw any light on his particular problem. If there had been a murderer it was unlikely he would have overlooked so obvious a precaution as to wear gloves. But as French continued his inspection he saw something a good deal more important.

Nowhere was there a smudged space on any print. Nowhere had a gloved palm or finger wiped off part of an impression.

Again and again he had found the marks of gloved hands or fingers when looking at photographs of prints. Why not here?

If not one of the many prints which had been found bore a trace of superimposed gloves, it was legitimate to argue that no gloved fingers had been in the room. French noted places on which a murderer would almost certainly have placed his hands. On many of these there were prints: clear unsmudged prints of Harrison or Higgins. Yes, he felt satisfied no murderer had been in the room. No one but Harrison and his wife and steward.

To suppose that either of these had started up the gas and then climbed out of the porthole was absurd. He doubted whether Mrs Harrison could do it. Higgins had not the intelligence to devise such a scheme. And if either had attempted it, Harrison would never have lain in bed with that peaceful expression. Besides, there was the final clinching point that neither of them could have pulled the porthole shut from the outside.

Here at last was certainty. The absence of gloved or unknown prints was proof. Harrison couldn't have been murdered. Therefore definitely he had committed suicide.

And the motive?

Now that his mind was made up as to the fact, the motive seemed to French suddenly to become of less importance. Admittedly it would be better if he could demonstrate it. It would leave the case, as it were, clean and tidy and complete. But that was theoretical rather than a practical requirement. The Yard paid him to find out the truth: not to satisfy idealistic conditions.

He drew a pad towards him and began to write. An hour later he rang for a stenographer to type his reports, first to Sir Mortimer Ellison and second to Major Marsh. As he handed it over to the young policeman who appeared, he felt with satisfaction that it was a darned good report.

Then suddenly a further point struck him and he once again took up the photographs of the porthole. As he slowly re-examined them the satisfaction became as it were wiped off his face, and an expression of doubt and mystification took its place.

Who had closed the porthole? There were a number of

prints on the brass ring, the wing screws, even the glass. But they were all without exception Higgins'.

Now genuinely puzzled, French looked up Pollock's notes and his own of the interrogation of Higgins. Higgins was absolutely positive that he had left the porthole open: with the glass hooked up to the chain which hung for the purpose from the ceiling. He said Harrison was fond of fresh air, and had more than once regretted not having put a second porthole in the cabin. The glass was found shut, and the stiff hinge proved that it must have been shut from the inside.

Who had shut it?

Not Harrison. If he had done so his prints would have been found. Who then?

Here also there were no smudges or partially wiped prints. Again, who had shut it?

With an ill grace French took the typescript of his report, which was at that moment handed to him, and locked it up in a drawer. Then setting his jaw, he rang for Carter.

'We'll have to go down to this blessed boat again,' he declared grimly. 'Get the car out.'

When a couple of hours later they once again reached Harrison's cabin they had a new and much more intensive orgy of research. Both his conclusions remained amply demonstrated. No one wearing gloves had been in the cabin, and only Higgins could have shut the porthole.

In vain he interrogated Higgins afresh. The man stuck to his story. When he had left the cabin the porthole was open. He had not shut it.

French that evening made a special journey to Mount Street to ask Mrs Harrison if she had noticed the position of the glass when she was in the cabin. She had. She was quite positive it was fully open. Further proof, French saw, was the fact that Crewe had heard the quarrel from the deck, which would have been impossible had the glass been shut.

It was open then when Harrison locked himself in at bedtime. Once again, who had closed it?

11

The Hot Bowl

Thrown once again into a state of doubt as to what had really taken place in Harrison's cabin on that fatal night, French went down next morning to Henley to have one further try at the problem on the ground. For two solid hours he pondered the question of how a murderer might have left the room. He began with the door, working with cords and pins and levers, using every trick of which he had ever heard, trying to bolt the door from the outside. He failed completely and at last had to admit to himself that the thing could not be, and had not been, done.

Then he turned to the porthole. He had already seen the objection that if the murderer had passed out through it, he would have had to climb across the bed and so disturb Harrison. There was of course no difficulty in his getting through the porthole, as such. It was of standard size, which by Board of Trade regulation must be big enough for a large man to pass through. But as French considered the matter further, he saw he had overlooked evidence which conclusively proved that no one had passed through it.

On the fixed brass rim were fingerprints—Higgins' prints. No one could have squeezed out, no matter how slim he was or what precautions he took, without rubbing these marks. And they had not been rubbed.

Nor did it help matters to suppose that Higgins himself was the murderer, for the simple reason that he could not have replaced the prints from the outside. French got a boat to test the point, and he was completely satisfied. The prints were put on by someone standing in the room.

French swore. There had been no murder, because at last beyond doubt or question it was established that no murderer had left the cabin. The death was therefore suicide.

But Harrison had not closed the porthole. Therefore it was not suicide.

It was no good for French to tell himself that this was nonsense, and that what was wrong was his own reasoning. He knew it must be so, but he could not see where his mistake lay.

He began to think of the case from a wider angle. Was there any of it—any part whatever—about which he could get more information? Had every point been adequately covered?

It seemed so. He did not know where to apply for further evidence. Then it occurred to him that the medical testimony had not been checked. He had no reason to doubt Dr Jellett's capability, but it was a fact that the whole of that side of the case depended on his statements and on them alone.

French decided he would put the matter before Dr Livingstone, a specialist to whom in doubtful cases the Yard frequently applied. He didn't believe that it would lead to anything, but it was all that he could think of doing.

He therefore borrowed the bowl and decanter from Pollock, and with notes of Jellett's evidence and his photographs he returned to Town and made an appointment with Livingstone. Some hours later he was shown into the scientist's consulting room.

Livingstone was tall and spare and cadaverous, with heavy expressionless features which belied his great mental ability. He heard French in silence, glanced at the exhibits, and at last spoke—rather disappointingly for an oracle.

'What do you want me to tell you?' he asked.

'Everything,' French returned comprehensively. 'First if Dr Jellett's arguments are sound, and second, if there is anything further that you can think of that he hasn't mentioned.'

Once again Livingstone became lost in thought. 'He seems to be quite all right,' he said presently, 'and I can't think of anything he hasn't mentioned.'

This was not particularly promising. French began to feel desperate. He decided he must ask questions, in the hope of starting some helpful line of thought.

He began about Harrison: the effects of the gas, the question of whether he could have realised an attack was coming and been unable to ward it off, the effect of the gas on the murderer, the possibility of a murderer arranging the bowl to work by delayed action and getting Harrison to bolt the door after him. Everything he could think of French asked. And all without the slightest result.

Then just as he was about to leave a chance question brought out a piece of information which once again reversed all his ideas, and left him definitely accepting a theory which on other grounds seemed untenable.

'About fingerprints on the bowl, doctor,' he was saying. 'It was stated that the action of the acid on the marble would produce enough heat to dry them off. Do you think this is so?'

'I think so, certainly. Quite a lot of heat would be generated.'

'It takes a good deal to dry off all traces of prints. You're sure there'd be enough?'

'I should say so, though I admit I don't exactly know. If it really matters I can try it and see.'

'I'd be obliged if you would. It might be important. You see, if heat didn't take off the prints, something else must. We should know.'

'Do you want an actual temperature reading?'

'Oh, no,' French returned; 'only to see if prints are really dried off.'

Livingstone got up. 'That's easy. I'll do it at once. You slip out and get a similar bowl, and I'll be ready when you come back.'

French had a little difficulty in finding just what he wanted, but he did it at last and bore his treasure back in triumph.

'Come into the lab,' Livingstone called through an open door.

French entered the long well-lit room, with its rows of shelving, its sinks, its gleaming apparatus. The doctor in a white overall was busy with a hammer and small anvil. All about lay bits of broken white stone.

'Here's the marble,' he said, putting down the hammer. 'And here,' pointing to a bottle, 'the hydrochloric acid. Get your prints on the bowl and let me have it.'

French polished his purchase, then pressed his fingers all over the clean surface. He tested one small area with black powder to make sure the prints were satisfactory, then handed it over. Livingstone put in about the same quantity of chippings as was in Harrison's, placed the bowl in a stink cupboard, and poured in some acid.

'No point in our breathing the stuff,' he remarked as he drew down the window of the cupboard. 'I'm not tired of my life, even if you are.'

French reassured him as they watched the acid fizzing and bubbling and the chips slowly growing smaller. The action went on for some little time, the acid gradually becoming used up. Livingstone opened the cupboard.

'Can you lift it?' he asked innocently. 'No, I thought not.'

He smiled as French rubbed his stinging finger. The bowl was really hot: too hot to handle.

'Wait till it cools down,' Livingstone advised, and began to talk about another case on which French had consulted him a short time previously.

Some minutes later French lifted out the bowl, being careful to grasp it by the edges only. Then for the second time he tried his graphite powder. But now there was no result. None of the previous prints remained.

On that particular point here was conclusive evidence. But on the case as a whole it was far otherwise. All it did was to remove a difficulty from the suicide theory. It didn't confirm that theory. It still might or might not be the truth. And Livingstone was unable to tell him anything further.

French felt that his visit had been a washout. Jellett was evidently a sound man. All his statements had been correct. Checking him up had taken most of a day, and French had really learnt nothing.

But though he didn't realise it at the time, Livingstone had given him a new fact. A fact moreover which, when he did realise it, he saw was fundamental. A fact which settled, once and for all, the suicide-murder question.

He returned from Livingstone's to the Yard, tired and disappointed. No news of the case had come in, but his report to Major Marsh was becoming overdue. However he really could not face that at the moment. He would go home, and think of something else. Thank goodness the next day was Sunday. He would have a good rest over the weekend and go fresh to the thing on Monday morning.

On Sunday he took with Mrs French one of those short excursions they so much enjoyed. Healthily tired, he went early to bed, intending to read a chapter or two of his novel before going to sleep. But he didn't read his chapter. Just as he began the great idea flashed into his mind.

That bowl! That hot bowl! There surely was the clue?

He jumped out of bed, and going to his notebook, turned up the description of the cabin furniture. But he did not need his notes to recall the point at issue. That table beside Harrison's bed! It was French polished!

His excitement grew as he considered the point. The bowl was found on the table, on the French polished surface. Surely, *surely*, heat such as must have been generated would have destroyed the polish?

He believed it would, but he was not absolutely sure. The experiment must be tried, and tried at once.

Accordingly next morning saw him starting off for Henley with Sergeant Carter and a melancholy man in tweeds who was the Yard's expert on wood polishes. French had bought still another bowl and had obtained marble chips and acid from Livingstone.

It did not take long to try the experiment, and the result was conclusive. The polish was completely ruined by the heat.

'No French polish nowhere would stand 'eat of that sort,'

the melancholy man explained. 'The old polishes was better than wot we uses now. But not one of them would stand it neither.'

So that was that.

And what followed seemed equally conclusive. No acid had been put in the bowl, and no gas had been generated from it while it stood on the table at the head of Harrison's bed. Its being there was a fake, intended to suggest something which had never happened.

Once again French swore. He had been getting on so well and this line of reasoning had seemed so promising. But where was it leading? Why, to another error. It was suggesting that Harrison had not died from gas at all.

But Harrison had died from gas.

Where, then, had the bowl been when the gas was being generated? And who, *after Harrison's death*, had moved it to the position in which it was found?

Here surely was confusion worse confounded. French felt completely puzzled.

But there was one fundamental matter which was now as clear as day. Whatever else was true or false, there had been no suicide. Harrison had been murdered as certainly as that he was dead.

And murdered in a particularly subtle way. A way, French was sure, long premeditated and worked out with care and ingenuity. But by an ordinary human being—not a superman. That was an oversight, that point about the French polish. The murderer had, so to speak, done well; but he had not done well enough. French reassured himself. What another person could devise, he could discover. Knowing what he knew now, he would certainly get his man.

His first reaction was to go to the police station and share the news with Major Marsh. Then the desire grew to have something more to report at the conference, and he sat down to think.

It seemed clear that with regard to the bowl one of two things must have happened. Either no gas had been generated from it in the cabin at all, it being afterwards introduced, or it had been in some other place in the cabin while the gas was being generated, and was moved to the table after Harrison's death.

He considered these alternatives in order. If no gas had been generated from the bowl in the cabin, it must have come from another source, and the bowl was simply a blind to suggest suicide. What other source?

French knew there were many ways of obtaining carbon dioxide gas. It could be produced chemically, it was sold in capsules for home-made mineral waters, in cylinders for medical purposes, in blocks for refrigeration. That might be left for the moment, and he might concentrate on the question of how it could have been introduced into the cabin.

Here the answer was obvious. Once the obsession of the bowl was removed, it was clear that gas could have been introduced in any quantity through the porthole. Carbon dioxide was heavy. It would sink to the floor and fill up the cabin like water, in spite of the open porthole: certainly to above the level of Harrison's head. Moreover with care and a properly designed apparatus the filling could be done in absolute silence. A soft rubber tube would pass death into the room, death which could be neither felt, seen, heard nor smelt, death drifting down in an invisible cloud. Harrison might be awake and on the alert. It would make no difference. He would be unaware of his danger, and would simply grow drowsy and then pass out. French believed, but was not sure, that alternatively a block used for refrigeration might be lowered into the cabin and left to vaporise. He thought it would do so completely, so that no trace of its presence would be left. On this point however he must get more information.

But if the gas had been introduced by some such method, why the bowl and acid? Equally obviously, to do just what they had. To suggest suicide. To prevent suspicion of murder arising, involving an investigation which might bring out the truth. How nearly the plan had succeeded!

Two difficulties still remained, three indeed. First, how had the bowl and acid been introduced into the cabin? Second, how had Harrison's prints been put on the decanter? and third, how had the porthole been closed?

Now that the major difficulties had been overcome, these quickly yielded to treatment. French was soon able to suggest answers, though of course he had as yet no proof that he was correct.

First, he saw that it would be easy to use from a boat a lever or lazy tongs to lift in the bowl and decanter. A tool shaped like a small hay fork could have been employed to support between two prongs the sides of the bowl or the neck of the decanter, so that these articles could be lowered on to the table and the tool withdrawn. If a slight noise were made, it would not matter. The operation would not have been attempted until Harrison was past objecting.

It was not so easy to answer the second question. How had Harrison's fingerprints been obtained on the decanter?

French felt that this matter of the decanter had not been properly investigated. He sent once more for Higgins and began to question him.

Higgins repeated what he had already stated at the inquest—that there was a set of four of these decanters and that they were kept in the sideboard in the dining saloon. One was filled with whisky, one with brandy, and two were empty. One of these empty ones was missing on the Saturday morning some eight days before the tragedy, when Higgins gave the glasses their weekly clean. How long it was missing before that was not known definitely, but Higgins thought only a very short time, as he believed he would have missed it directly it disappeared.

The decanters of whisky and brandy stood on the top of the sideboard, so that anyone who felt like a drink could help himself. The others were in one of the cupboards. The cupboard however was not locked, and anyone could have taken a decanter unnoticed, by choosing a propitious moment.

Higgins went on to say that his last job every night was to set out on the table in the lounge the decanters of whisky and brandy, together with siphons of soda, a jug of water and glasses. Most of the men—and some of the women—had a drink before going to bed. He usually found four or five used glasses when he cleared up next morning.

None of this seemed very illuminating to French, as apparently anyone who had been on board the *Cygnet* could have obtained the decanter. But the choice of that particular vessel was more suggestive. Obviously the hydrochloric acid had been bought in some other bottle and transferred to the decanter. Why?

It was not difficult to suggest the reason. Nothing else lent itself so well to the obtaining of Harrison's fingerprints. He was a man who liked his drop of liquor. How easy it would be, given the appropriate circumstances, to lift out

160

the decanter by the neck, put a liqueur or some other drink into it and indicate it to Harrison so that he might help himself. A sample to be tested and a request for an opinion might make the thing more plausible. Afterwards the neck would of course be cleaned. Apparently anyone on board could have—and someone of them must have—carried out some such plan. French did not pause to think out the details, but he was satisfied that a scheme on these lines could be devised.

The third question, how the porthole could have been fully closed, held French up for a longer time. He had already gone into the point and had seen that any kind of grip of the rim was impossible from without. But unless all his ideas were wrong, it had been done.

He went to Captain Collison and asked again for the boat. Ten minutes later he was once more moored opposite the porthole. There were two distinct sides to his problem. First, how had the glass been unhooked, and second, how had it been fully closed?

As to the first, no difficulty presented itself. He saw at once that it would be possible to push up the glass, when the chain connection could easily be slipped out. By wearing gloves, by cleaning the glass where touched by fingers, by the use of tools, all traces of such a movement could be avoided.

The second point was the real problem—the point which he had already decided was impossible. How had the ring been pulled tightly home against the brass stop, when the stiff hinges prevented this being done by gravity, and when no purchase for fingers or tools could be got upon it? Here he was baffled for some time, and in the end it was partly by chance that he lit on the solution.

As he moved about in the boat the reflection of the sky struck on the glass at various angles. It was then that he noticed a slight ring-shaped stain some three inches in diameter on its lower segment. At once a wave of satisfaction swept over him.

A sucker! Moisten the edges of a rubber cap, apply them to the glass, exhaust the air, and an adhesion proportionate to the exhaustion becomes available to draw the glass outward!

Here was not only a solution of the immediate problem, but proof—if further proof were required—of the truth of his main theory. It had been difficult to see how the murderer had entered and left the cabin. That difficulty was now overcome. He never had. The murder had been committed from a boat.

French was delighted. Things at last were moving. He had successfully taken two of the three steps necessary to clear up the case. He had proved that in spite of the coroner's verdict murder had been committed, and he had shown how it could have been done. The third step now only remained: to discover who had done it.

Though that was the difficulty in most murder cases, French told himself that in this one it should prove easier than usual. The murderer must have certain obvious peculiarities. He was evidently fully familiar with the *Cygnet*. He had access to the decanters. He had the use of a boat. He was on the river on the night in question. And last, but not least, he must have been Harrison's bitter enemy. There could not, French was sure, be many persons fulfilling all these conditions. A list of them once made, elimination would give him the criminal. French foresaw a speedy arrest.

But however quick he might be, clearing up the case

would still be a matter of days. He could not leave Major Marsh in the dark all that time. Theoretically the enquiry was Marsh's, or even more accurately, Pollock's, and he himself was only an assistant. He decided he would go and see them both and discuss with them the steps to be taken.

Pollock was at the station when he arrived. French realised he must handle him carefully.

'I've got a bit of information, inspector, about this Harrison case, and I want to talk it over with you and the C.C. Is he about?'

'No, sir, he's gone home.'

'Well, I think we should ring him up. You'll see its importance when I tell you that his suspicions were correct.'

Pollock stared. 'You mean—?'

'Yes, it was murder all right. At first I agreed with you. I may tell you,' he declared in a well-simulated burst of confidence, 'that I wrote a report saying it was suicide. It's lying in my desk now. Then I got some information out of one of our scientific consultants that gave me the tip. I saw I was wrong. I held back the report and went into it again.'

Pollock swore, then glanced questioningly at French, who laughed. 'That's all right,' he answered. 'It's how I felt too. Well, what about putting through a call?'

Pollock looked bitterly disappointed and French could read what was passing in his mind. He had to some extent pledged his reputation on the opinion he had given. He had even opposed his superior on the matter. And his superior had been right and he wrong.

French was sorry for him, for Pollock had been decent and helpful. He had himself been in the same position often enough to teach him sympathy.

'There's the phone, sir,' the man said unhappily.

'Ring him yourself,' French returned.

Pollock looked grateful. He rapidly made his call. 'He's coming right in, sir. He'll be here in less than an hour. You'll wait?'

French went on trying to complete his cure. 'I'll wait,' he said, 'and I'll tell you what I'd like to do. I had only a couple of sandwiches for lunch and I'd give a lot for a cup of tea. Come along out with me and we'll have some.'

When about five o'clock the Chief Constable turned up, Pollock had almost returned to normal and French had made a friend. Marsh was also a wise man in dealing with subordinates. He appeared to have forgotten that Pollock had ever dissented from the now current view. Also he was politic to his visitor.

'I congratulate you, if I may, Chief Inspector, on a fine bit of work,' he said when French had finished his story. 'That little matter of the polish on the table is just the kind of point I like. Simple, unexpected, and entirely adequate. I'm fond of the theatre and it would make a fine pivot for a detective play. Well, this is an upset and no mistake. Our acting coroner and his jury are going to get a jar, and I'm afraid so are we. However that's not the point at issue. What we've got to consider now is what we're going to do about it. You'll carry on of course, Chief Inspector? I mean, we only asked you to clear up the preliminary question. Will Sir Mortimer spare you for the larger enquiry?'

'I should think so, sir, if you want me. But of course we'd have to put it up to him. Perhaps you will do that?'

'I'll do it now. Get me the Yard, will you, Pollock?'

A short conversation and the point was amicably settled. Sir Mortimer Ellison answered characteristically that seeing that the County police were paying French's and Carter's salaries, the longer they kept them, the better he would be pleased.

'Then,' went on Marsh, 'we'd better go into committee of ways and means.' Here again he showed himself astute. While apparently taking the lead in the discussion, he contrived every time to leave the initiative with French. The conference ended with French being given a free hand to do what he thought best, but Marsh saved Pollock's face by adding that French would arrange with him what part of any local enquiries he and the Henley men would carry out.

'I'll have to go up and report at the Yard,' French explained to the inspector when Marsh had gone, 'but I'll come back tomorrow and go into the thing with you.'

As far as he was personally concerned, French was well enough pleased with the turn events had taken. It was very hot, and a job along the river was infinitely preferable to the stuffy air of Town. Besides he had had a long spell of his office, and a change out of doors anywhere would have been welcome. Fortunately moreover the case seemed straightforward. It looked as if it would give him work, of which he had never been afraid, but not worry, which he did rather dread.

In a spirit of satisfaction and optimism he returned to Town.

12

The Brown Wool

His interview with Sir Mortimer over, French next day called Carter and set off once again for Henley.

The morning was gloriously fresh and clear, though there was promise of heat later. French registered a vow that if time permitted he would do what he had wanted to do every day since he came down: have a long leisurely swim in the river.

On reaching the *Cygnet* he asked for Collison.

'I've got a bit of news for you, Captain,' he began when they were seated on a shady part of the deck. 'Something that'll surprise you, and that I want you to keep absolutely to yourself.' He glanced round and lowered his voice. 'Mr Harrison didn't commit suicide,' and he went on to summarise his discoveries.

Captain Collison was horrified. Though he had never pretended personal sorrow for Harrison, he seemed to take it as an insult to himself that the murder had been committed on his ship. Evidently in naval circles such things were not done.

'Very distressing,' he exclaimed. 'Why, the boat will be notorious over the entire civilised world.'

'Worse than the *Girl Pat*, I'm afraid,' French returned solemnly. 'It'll be a two- or three-days' wonder. Then,' he shrugged, 'it'll be forgotten. But to reduce public interest and get it forgotten quickly there must be no mystery. We must get the murderer. And that's where I want your help.'

'You may count on it,' Collison said with emphasis. 'A person like that has no right to live. What do you want me to do?'

'Give me your opinion principally. For instance, there's no doubt a boat came alongside that night. Why didn't your watchman see it?'

The captain shrugged. 'There are possible reasons,' he said dryly, 'some of which you might guess.'

'You mean that he might have been asleep? Now that would interest me quite a lot. Can we find out?'

Collison looked at him searchingly. 'Drugged?' he queried. 'I confess I hadn't thought of that. We can ask him.'

French smiled. 'I suppose we can,' he agreed, dry in his turn. 'But can we find the answer?'

Collison considered. 'I think so. It was Peters, and he's a reliable man. I think he'd tell us the truth. But unless he was specially looking out, he could easily miss seeing it.'

'Suppose we hear what he has to say, Captain?' French was impressed by the watchman, when a moment later he appeared. He had a good face and manner and gave his evidence clearly.

But it was entirely negative. He had been awake all night, and though he had not moved much about the deck, he had kept a reasonably sharp look-out. But he had neither heard nor seen anything unusual. He did not believe that any boat had or could have come alongside, as he was sure he would have heard it.

'So then,' said French when the man had disappeared, 'the question arises: How silently could a boat be brought alongside?'

'With care, in absolute silence, I should think.'

'Would any precautions be adopted to save noise? You see what I want. Did the murderer do anything in bringing the boat alongside silently, which might have left a trace?'

'The best way to answer that is to get a boat and do it again. I take it there was only one murderer?'

'I couldn't say that, but let us assume it.'

'Then I'll manage the boat and you and Carter can watch what I do.'

'Splendid!'

'Now first,' Collison went on, 'Peters was stationed on the shore end of the bridge.' He climbed up, followed by French. 'Just look round and see what was within his view. The shore. The fore-deck and roof of the saloon, and the after-deck with the exception of the strip hidden by the saloon. Also craft approaching from all round, until they get close enough to be screened by the ship, which would occur only aft and on the port side.'

'I follow that,' French agreed. 'Then the murderer, if he knew the routine on board, as he must have, would have come up from astern or from the port quarter?'

'I think so. I shall do so at all events.'

Collison called his two deck hands and the small dinghy was swung out. He, French and Carter got into it and slowly dropped downstream.

'Now I'll row. My oars would be muffled of course.'

The captain rowed with skill and precision. Then when

some thirty yards from the *Cygnet* he silently unshipped the oars and laid them along the thwarts.

The dinghy floated smoothly forward, Collison standing in the bows. He had judged his position nicely and she came to rest against the *Cygnet*'s side, some twenty feet forward of Harrison's cabin. Collison passed the end of the painter round one of the deck-rail stanchions, paid out till they drifted down opposite the porthole, and made fast.

'There you are,' he said as if making an offering of the feat to French.

'You,' French returned, 'are an expert, and it's daytime. A landsman couldn't have done that at night?'

Collison shrugged. 'No other way of doing it that I can see.'

As French was turning the matter over in his mind the dinghy bumped suddenly against the ship's side. The bump was neither severe nor noisy, but it was distinct. On a silent night the sound could easily have been heard by a wakeful watchman.

'There,' he said as it did it again, 'that couldn't have been going on that night. The current's evidently doing it. How would you stop it?'

'Fenders. Hang two or three rope fenders along the side, or put a rug or something over the gunwale. Quite easy to stop.'

French considered this. Rope fenders were of course a possibility, but the ordinary man was more likely to have a rug. If however a rug were used, it would be rubbed and scraped along the *Cygnet*'s side . . .

He looked more carefully at the steel plates. They were butt-jointed, with flush surfaces. He ran his finger along one of the joints. Yes, it was certainly rough . . .

He took a lens from his pocket and began to examine the joints at skiff gunwale level for ten feet above and below the porthole. Collison watched him with interest.

'Ah,' said French suddenly, 'what have we here?'

Adhering to a roughness in a vertical joint directly below the porthole was a tiny wisp of something brown and fluffy.

'My case, Carter.'

The suitcase had been left on the *Cygnet*, but Carter quickly swarmed on deck and handed down what was required. With a fine pair of forceps French removed the fluff and dropped it into an envelope.

'If we can get what that came off, it might be a help,' he remarked as he turned back to his search.

Collison seemed surprised. 'Surely there's not enough there to be of any use?' he queried.

'I don't know,' French answered. 'It's astonishing what the microscope will tell you from a thing like this. Enough, I should think, to identify the source.'

'Pretty wonderful to me.'

French minutely inspected the remainder of the joints, but without finding further traces. 'Now,' he said, 'just one other question. Where could the boat have been obtained? Was either of yours in the water?'

Collison shook his head. 'Neither. You see, we couldn't keep them there. They'd float out sideways and perhaps foul something.'

It was clear then that whatever boat had been used had come from a distance. In such cases French usually applied a rough and ready rule. Other things being equal, he began his search nearest to the site of the crime, gradually increasing the distance as he eliminated one source after another. Here the nearest boathouse was that of the Colemans, some hundred yards downstream.

'Have they a boat down there?' he asked Collison, jerking his head towards the boathouse.

'Two, I think. Are you suspicious in that quarter?'

'No, but one must begin somewhere. Well, thank you, Captain, I'm much obliged for your help.'

French saw that as a result of this development there stretched before him one of those long routine enquiries which he so much hated. To find a taxi which had made a certain run, a car which had conveyed a given party, a rifle from which a certain bullet had been fired, or as now, a boat which had done a definite trip—this type of enquiry bored him to distraction. And besides being boring, such investigations not infrequently proved extremely anxious work. His entire case often hung on his success, and usually he experienced the heart sickness of deferred hope.

However there was nothing else for it. He would try at the Colemans' boathouse now. If that failed, he would take the locks at either end of the reach, and having checked up craft passing through, concentrate on all the available boats in between. Sooner or later he would get what he wanted.

He went with Carter to the Colemans' house, only to be told that everyone was out.

'Oh,' he returned, 'that's unfortunate. I wondered if Mr Coleman would allow me to borrow his boat for a few minutes?'

'Oh yes, sir, of course. I'm sure there'd be no objection.'

'Then thank you, I'll take it. Have you the key of the boathouse?'

The maid handed it over and the two men walked down. The boathouse was a picturesque little building of mellow red brick with a roof of old brown tiles. It projected into the water a foot or two beyond the line of the bank, and a neatly mown grass path led to the door. French unlocked the latter and they went in.

It was a larger building than they had imagined from the outside. The water basin was in one corner and an L-shaped concrete stage ran round the other two sides. On racks against the wall were stacked oars, poles, boat cushions and awnings, with a few coils of rope and some fishing tackle. The basin was closed by a portcullis, operated by a small windlass.

In the basin floated two boats, one a light skiff, the other a punt. The punt was unsuitable for the job French had in mind, but the skiff was the very thing. He therefore got into the skiff and settled down to make his examination.

He was careful to touch only rough parts of the wood, so as to avoid smudging possible fingerprints. He paused and considered. Facing the stream, Harrison's cabin was on the port side. Therefore it would be the starboard side of the murderer's boat which would be fended off. He concentrated on the starboard gunwale and the boarding beneath it.

He had an apparatus in his suitcase for jobs of the kind, and Carter passed it down. It was a combined electric torch and lens, so arranged that the light was concentrated on the field. French worked quickly but carefully, passing his instrument along each seam and arris of the wood.

He had scarcely begun when he paused with an exclamation of satisfaction. Caught in a tiny splinter on the edge of the gunwale was a microscopic piece of brown wool. It looked just like that he had found on the side of the *Cygnet*, and he had no doubt whatever they were from the same piece.

'By heck, Carter,' he exclaimed, 'this luck's almost uncanny. If it goes on I'll begin to get frightened. Get out that tweezers and another envelope.'

He transferred his find, labelling the envelope. Then he resumed his search. Not twelve inches along the gunwale was another splinter and another little ball of wool, and before he had gone over all the woodwork he had found a third.

'What does it mean, sir?' asked Carter. 'That young Coleman's our man?'

French shook his head. 'Anyone might have had a key for this place. Get out that powder and we'll have a shot for prints.'

Carter handed down what was wanted, and French blew a spray of grey powder over likely surfaces. The skiff was new and coated with a hard varnish. This held prints well and numbers of them appeared. French gazed at them in perplexity, as one who suffers from a surfeit of riches.

'We'll have the dickens of a time sorting all those out,' he grumbled. 'We'd better have them photographed. Just nip up to the house will you, and phone the Yard.'

Carter, who was kneeling on the bottom of the skiff, did not rise. Instead he pointed to a thwart. 'What's that, sir?'

French bent down. An oval patch was wiped clear right in the middle of a well-defined thumb print. 'You're right, Carter. That's good,' he commended. 'Look round and see if you can find any more.'

They made a systematic search and found more than thirty places where gloved fingers had passed over previous prints.

'Now,' French went on, 'can we get a whole hand?'

But there their run of luck came to an end. Nowhere

could they find an indication of the size and shape of the hand.

'Well, we can't help it. Now go and ring for the photographer. And find the gardener and send him down.'

Carter disappeared and presently there was a knock at the boathouse door. French climbed ashore and opened it. A respectable elderly man whom he had seen about the place was waiting.

'Ah,' French said, 'you're the gardener, aren't you?'

'Yes, sir. Chauffeur really, but gardener between whiles.'

'A nice job,' French declared. 'No worry and all that.' A smile showed in his eyes. 'Are you in charge of the boats also?'

'Yes, sir. I get them ready when they're going out.'

'That's fine for me. Now can you tell me when the skiff was out last?'

The man stopped in thought. 'Last Sunday week afternoon, sir.'

'Last Sunday week? Just how do you remember that?'

'It was the day before Mr 'Arrison was found dead. None of the boats 'ave been out since.'

This was satisfactory information. The last person to have the skiff out was the wearer of the gloves.

'Tell me,' said French, 'is the boathouse always kept locked?'

'Yes, sir, except when there are boats out.'

'I follow. But when a boat's out it's left open?'

'Yes, sir.'

'With the key in the door?'

'That's right.'

Anyone then by watching his opportunity could have got an impression of the key. There was, moreover, now no doubt as to what had taken place. The murderer had obtained a key to the boathouse, had entered and taken out the skiff, committed the murder and replaced the skiff. What more could be find out, while he was there?

As French was considering, Carter returned. 'A man'll be here in a couple of hours, sir. They didn't know who they'd send, but they'll lose no time.'

'Right. I want you to go over both boats and make sure nothing's been dropped in them.'

While Carter, like some huge grey bear, was kneeling in the bottom of the boat, French took his dusting powder to the windlass and tested the handle.

Here was further proof that gloves had been the last to raise the portcullis. Except for the mutilated fragments of prints at each end, the handle was clear.

French next turned to the cushions. These he quickly saw would afford him no help. They could not have been used for fenders, partly because they were too stiff to bend over the skiff's gunwale, and partly because they were covered by some non-woolly fabric like coarse linen. From them he went on to examine the door, the oars and other objects in the house, in each case without result.

'I'll just take a pressing of this key,' French told Carter. 'Then you can give it back.'

French went back on board the *Cygnet*, and fixing a chair in a shady place, sat down to think out his next step. Could he with the information he now had, put his hand on the murderer? And first, as to what he knew about him.

1. The murderer had known Harrison and hated him so much that he had killed him.
2. He had been on the *Cygnet* and knew it intimately.

He had obtained the decanter, and he had approached on the night of the crime in such a way as to keep out of sight of the watchman. He was even able to pick out Harrison's porthole in the dark, which French thought indicated a special investigation for the purposes of the crime.

3. He had known of the Colemans' skiff and how to obtain an impression of the key to the boathouse.
4. He had been in the neighbourhood on the night in question.

With these points French felt he should get a line on the criminal. Comparatively few persons met all four requirements. All he had to do was to make an inclusive list of the possible and eliminate.

What names would he put on the list? All he could think of. They were: Captain Collison; M'Gregor, the engineer; the steward, Higgins; the other members of the crew; Mrs Harrison, Gloria, Rupert, Locke, Crewe, Entrican, Jasper Coleman, Lord Algy Mannering, Miss Morland, Kemp, and last, though not least, an unknown.

Quite a list! Could he divide the names into two classes, the likely and the unlikely? As he looked over them he saw that he could not. Not one of them was likely.

And yet some were less unlikely than others. Collison, M'Gregor, Higgins, the members of the crew, Entrican, Crewe, Lord Algy, Miss Morland and Kemp seemed to him so improbable that for the moment he dismissed them from his mind. That left the Harrison family, Jasper Coleman and Locke. What were the chances of their guilt?

First Coleman. He fulfilled perfectly all four conditions. He had plenty of cause to hate Harrison, not only on his own behalf, but more powerfully, on Gloria's. He knew the *Cygnet* intimately. He would naturally have taken his own boat. He was in the neighbourhood on the fatal night. But there was one snag in the assumption. He did not seem to French the type of man to commit murder. Against this view however there were two considerations. One was that French didn't know him well, the second, that while he might not have murdered for his own happiness, he might for Gloria's.

Locke was equally probable, perhaps more so, as that type of weak and mulish man turns readily enough to murder. His love for Mrs Harrison would supply the necessary motive. Locke must certainly be retained as his second suspect.

With regard to Mrs Harrison, French was more doubtful. She had a motive, but he questioned if she could have carried out the details of the crime. This applied to Gloria also, though she was physically stronger. Rupert could have done it all right, and French marked him third suspect. The others need not be considered till his mind was made up on these three.

His thoughts turned to Entrican. Entrican was away from the boat on the night of Harrison's death. Was this a suspicious point? Probably not. It was likely to be quite in order. On the other hand the absence might be a fake, carried out with the object of establishing an alibi. Entrican had seemed a good deal upset—perhaps more than anyone else. French noted that he would have to find out from Entrican where he was that night, and probably check his statement up.

But Jasper Coleman first. French decided he would stay in Henley and call at the Colemans' after dinner.

13

The Silent Passage

French was much disappointed with the results of his call
on Jasper Coleman. It was not that he had difficulty in
getting the young man's statement. Coleman not only
made it readily, but it proved reasonable. Moreover he
seemed straightforward. What troubled French was that
the story got him no further. It might be true and it might
not, and for the moment he did not see just how he was
to check it.

After the row on the *Cygnet*, so Coleman said, he had
gone ashore. He had been a good deal surprised by
Harrison's outburst, for though he knew he was not looked
upon with favour, he had no idea that the old man's objection to him was so strong. The whole scene, he made no
attempt to deny, had left him feeling very sore. He was
undecided as to whether, considering his comparative
poverty, he should not give Gloria up. He did not therefore
go home at once, but went for a walk to think out his
problem. He left the *Cygnet*, so far as he could remember,
about half-past ten and walked till midnight. By this time

he had decided that Gloria must herself settle about the future, and that he would do whatever she wanted. On arriving home he went straight to bed and fell asleep almost at once. Next morning he woke at his usual time, feeling quite normal. He had intended to go to Town and to ring Gloria up later. He would have done so only for Crewe's coming over with the news of Harrison's death.

French asked a few questions, then said good night and got into the car for the journey home. All he had heard was plausible and might well be true. On the other hand he had learnt nothing which would have prevented Jasper from slipping out of the house in the middle of the night, murdering Harrison, and returning unnoticed.

As they ran swiftly through the darkening evening French continued turning the affair over in his mind. If there was nothing to prove Jasper's guilt, no more was there anything to demonstrate his innocence.

But stay. Was there not?

It occurred to French that his thinking had become muddled. What exactly was his theory?

Undoubtedly that if Coleman had murdered Harrison, it was because of the quarrel and his threatened loss of Gloria.

But now French saw that that was absurd. The murder was too well thought out to have been devised on the spur of the moment. Whatever else was doubtful, its premeditation was a certainty. More than that. Even if Jasper had been a super-genius, he could not have got together the apparatus in the time. Apart from the disappearance of the decanter several days before the quarrel, the gas could not have been provided without pre-arrangement. Therefore if Jasper were guilty, it was not because of the quarrel.

But if it were not because of the quarrel, French's case

against him broke down, for he could suggest no other motive.

Of course it was possible that Jasper had realised for longer than he said that Harrison would cut off Gloria's money if she married him, and had planned the murder earlier. But French did not think this likely. If so, the man would never have allowed the quarrel to break out. He would have realised its danger as an indication of motive. No, if he had been going to kill Harrison, he would have kept out of his way beforehand.

These arguments French found strong. And to them was added the convincing fact of Jasper's personality. The more French saw of him, the less like a murderer he seemed. Although his innocence was not actually proven, the probabilities were strongly against his guilt.

French's thoughts passed on to Locke. Had he information which would enable him to reach a similar conclusion about Locke? He had already taken a statement from the man in Mount Street. Would a second interrogation be of any use?

At this stage in the enquiry he doubted it. With a torch he looked up his notebook to see again what Locke had said.

His statement, French now remembered, had been as clear and as probable as Jasper's. There was not about Locke the seemingly transparent honesty of Jasper, but there was nothing in his bearing to suggest that he was lying.

He had said that the evening in question had been delightfully cool after a very hot day (a statement confirmed on all hands) and for this reason he and Rupert had gone for a walk. That was about ten o'clock. They had walked for more than an hour, returning to the *Cygnet* some time after eleven. When they arrived they found that everyone had gone to bed, and they quickly followed suit. They had known nothing of the quarrel, which must have taken place while they were out. Locke had gone to sleep soon and had not waked till the morning. He had heard nothing unusual during the night, and the first intimation he had received that anything was wrong was when Crewe had come to his cabin with the news of Harrison's death.

All the other relevant testimony had backed up Locke's story. Rupert agreed about the walk and their ignorance of the quarrel. Crewe had confirmed taking the news to Locke and the latter's evident amazement thereat. The watchman had seen Locke return with Rupert, and swore that after it no one had gone ashore. It was difficult therefore to see how Locke could have taken out the Colemans' skiff.

There was moreover no evidence of motive. Admittedly Locke was in love with Mrs Harrison, but this had been going on for several years, and there were no indications of any change in the situation. French decided to suspend judgement about Locke until he had considered the other possibles.

The first of these he had already decided must be Entrican. In his preliminary interrogation, as soon as he had found that Entrican was ashore on the night of the murder, French had asked him no more questions. Now he must settle the point of whether that absence was real or faked.

Next morning therefore after a brief report-progress visit to the Yard, he set off with Carter for the house in Mount Street. Entrican was there and saw them at once.

'I'm on a routine job, Mr Entrican,' French explained. 'I have to report where everyone connected with the household was at the time of Mr Harrison's death. We do it in all cases of the kind. Now I understood you to say that you

181

were in Town that night, and I therefore put your story into the category of the less urgent and left it over. But now I must get it for completeness' sake.'

Entrican looked uneasy. 'I'll tell you anything I can,' he said doubtfully, 'though I don't quite see why you want to know it.'

French put on a knowing smile. 'To keep my job, sir. Our people like routine, and so we give it to them. Of course you can refuse to answer. In fact I suppose technically I should warn you that anything you say may be used in evidence.'

This appeared to startle Entrican. He was now obviously very uneasy indeed. 'Does that mean you're accusing me of anything?' he asked.

'Certainly not, sir. But information that we couldn't use in court would be little use to us.'

'I've nothing to say that could be wanted in court.'

'If that's so, nothing will be brought into court,' French returned sweetly. 'Yes, please?'

Entrican made a gesture of resignation. 'Oh, well,' he said, 'have it your own way. I went to Town to meet a lady, and I met her, and that's all there's to it.'

'Yes, sir: that's all right. A newly arrived Australian cousin?'

Entrican looked a trifle sheepish. 'Well, no, admitted. 'I did say that, but it wasn't exactly true.'

'I see. Who was the lady?'

'That's none of your business.'

'I'm afraid it is. Was she a Londoner?'

'She lived in London, yes.'

French spoke more sternly. 'Now, sir, you would be well advised to say who she was. That's not a threat, but you understand that all statements have to be checked.'

Entrican snorted. 'Well, I object. I tell you it had nothing to do with the case.'

French shrugged. 'If you won't,' he said lightly, 'you won't. I can't force you. You might however tell me what you did in more detail. You left here—when?'

Entrican seemed surprised at his easy victory. 'About five or later,' he answered suspiciously.

'Yes? And then?'

'Then I went up—by bus. The cars were engaged!'

'I see. Had you changed then?'

'No.'

'You did change, did you?'

'Of course I changed.'

'Where?'

Entrican looked increasingly uneasy and annoyed. 'At the Piccadilly Palace, if that's any help to you,' he said ungraciously.

'Quite.' French noted the name and went on imperturbably. 'And where did you meet the lady?'

'Again no business of yours.'

'Very well.' French was bland. 'Where did you spend the night?'

Entrican didn't answer and French went on: 'If it was with the lady, say so,' he invited. 'You must see that to make a mystery out of it merely suggests you've something to hide.'

Entrican swore. 'Curse you!' he exclaimed savagely. 'Can't you mind your own infernal business? I didn't spend the night with her. If you must know, I went up intending to, but she couldn't come with me. Said her husband was coming home and she must go back. You can see now why I'm not giving her name.'

French nodded. 'Of course, sir. That's all right. But there can now be no objection to telling me where you stayed.'

'At the Piccadilly Palace.'

'When did you reach it?'

Entrican thought. 'About half-past ten,' he replied sulkily. 'I put her into a taxi and went there straight.'

'And didn't leave till the morning?'

'Well, what do you think? Do you want to know the time I began to undress?'

French grinned. 'That's all right. You mustn't mind. We have to ask these questions and no harm is meant.'

Relief showed in Entrican's eyes. 'I've had a pretty rotten time,' he apologised. 'This means I'll be out of a job in a week or two.'

'A man like you will have no trouble in getting another.'

'Not one that suits me so well.'

If this story were true, Entrican's absence was genuine and not a faked alibi. French felt inclined to believe it. Certainly it covered all the facts. The intrigue with the married woman would explain the lie about the friend from Australia. The fear of the affair coming out and causing the loss of one of the plums of the secretarial world would account for the man's agitation. Again, his motive would be to keep Harrison alive, and so retain his job in being. And lastly, he would never have said he spent the night at the Piccadilly Palace if he had not done so, as he would know how easily the statement could be checked.

So obvious did this last point seem, that French hesitated about the need for checking it. However his training asserted itself and he decided he must leave the matter complete.

He therefore went with Carter to the hotel. It was a large modern building with over a thousand rooms and a bathroom to each. In the reception office were four young women. French tackled the first.

'I wonder if you remember the man,' he went on. 'Here's his photograph, and here,' he put forward Entrican's signed statement, 'is his signature.'

Neither the first nor the second young lady remembered him, but the third did. 'Yes,' she said at once. 'I've seen that man recently. I don't remember exactly when, but he has certainly been here.'

The hotel was one of those with an inclusive charge for bed and breakfast. The records showed that Entrican had occupied his room and had had his breakfast before paying his bill next morning. But there was one unusual item on the bill: a charge for a glass which he had broken in his bedroom.

'What were the circumstances of that?' French asked.

None of the young women remembered. 'The chambermaid must have reported it,' said one. 'We can send for her, if you like.'

French wondered if it were necessary. Then he decided he should know everything possible.

The matter had now moved outside the sphere of the reception clerks, and French was conducted to the office of the under manager. There the chambermaid presently joined him. She proved a capable looking woman, whom he felt would tell a reliable story. She remembered the incident and was sure of her facts.

'Yes, sir, that's the man,' she said, picking Entrican's photograph from a number of others. 'I didn't see him arrive, but he rang for me about eleven. He was in his dressing gown. He had knocked his glass into the bath and broken it. He wanted another. I took him another and notified the office.'

'Did you see him next morning?'

'Yes, sir. I saw him leaving. He remembered me and said good morning. He was a very pleasant gentleman, sir. He was carrying his suitcase, a red shade of brown. I noticed that because the visitors generally leave their suitcases for the porters.'

French nodded. He had noticed that red suitcase in Entrican's room at Mount Street. He wondered about the incident of the glass. Was it suspicious? Was it done to prove Entrican was actually in the bedroom?

On the whole he thought not. He had a look at the bedroom and saw that it would be quite an easy thing to knock the glass into the bath, as the latter was just beside the shelf upon which it stood. Then Entrican had got through the business of replacing it as quickly as possible. If he had wished to impress his personality on the chambermaid, he would certainly have talked to her. Thirdly, he made no attempt to see her in the morning: from her own statement their meeting was accidental. And lastly, he had made no attempt to impress himself on anyone else.

French now believed that not one of his three most likely suspects was guilty, and he turned to his second list. The case against each of these possibles would now have to be gone into similarly.

He wondered if he might eliminate all who had been on the *Cygnet* on the fatal night? If the watchman were correct, none of these people could have gone ashore to get the Coleman boat, as he swore he would have seen them. French felt he could not accept the statement without further investigation. He determined to go down once more to Henley and make a few tests.

He telephoned to Captain Collison making an appointment

for nine o'clock, and shortly after that hour found himself seated with the captain in a sheltered corner on the deck, cigars in their hands and whiskies and sodas on the table between them.

'You see the point,' he explained. 'The watchman said no one could have gone ashore during the night unseen by him. If he was correct, no one on the ship that night could be guilty of the murder, because he couldn't have got the boat. Question is, was he correct?'

'If you knew that,' Collison said dryly, 'it would save you some trouble.'

French smiled. 'You're dead right, captain.'

'I've thought over that point of someone leaving the ship,' went on Collison. 'Has it occurred to you that an athletic man might have dropped out of a porthole and swum ashore?'

'Yes, I've thought of that. Curiously enough the question came up in another case I had some time ago. A rope ladder could have been hooked on to the porthole. But I found it would be impossible for anyone to get aboard again without dripping a lot of water over the cabin. And Higgins hadn't seen any.'

'A rope over the stern?'

'Perhaps. But not if your watchman was correct.'

Captain Collison shook his head. 'I'm not so sure. His evidence was that no one crossed the gangway. That's different from seeing a man at the stern.'

'The man at the stern would have to climb the rail. He'd be in full view. However, we needn't worry about that. I want to test the gangway. If I can go ashore and return unseen, it doesn't matter about these other possibilities.'

'You'll not do it.'

'You think not? Well, I won't bet.'

'Can I help you?'

'Yes. Get the same watchman and warn him that you've heard an attempt is to be made tonight, and that he must keep his eyes skinned.'

'It'll be convincing—if it comes off,' Collison agreed as he sent for the watchman. 'Look here,' he went on as the man appeared, 'keep this to yourself, see?'

The man saluted quickly, and Collison proceeded with bland mendacity. 'The chief inspector has just come down to warn me that he fears an attack on the ship tonight. Some papers that some people think are on board. They're not, but that doesn't matter. Now you fairly keep your eyes skinned. I'll give you a flex and bulb, and if you see anything don't make a sound, but press the bulb. We'll do the rest. But if you hear a call come and lend a hand. Understand?'

French chuckled as the man disappeared. 'Nothing like doing the thing in style,' he declared. 'But you're not giving me much of a chance.'

'I thought you wanted a test.'

'That's just the point,' French returned dryly. He was apologetic about asking the captain to sit up, but Collison said he was bored stiff with nothing to do, and even this would be a relief.

'If someone did go ashore that night, I estimate it would be about two in the morning. But we'll not wait for that. I'll try earlier, soon after midnight.'

Soon it began to get chilly and the two men moved into the saloon. The night was perfect for the test, all the factors being weighted against French. It was calm and fine, with a clear sky and a nearly full moon. There would be no real darkness. At the time of Harrison's death it had been dark.

There had been only the thinnest crescent moon, and a light wind had raised tiny waves whose lapping would have drowned other slight sounds.

In due course the watchman was posted with his flex and bulb and the deck and cabin lights were turned out. French and Collison sat smoking and chatting. The captain seemed glad of someone to speak to, and began going over some of his naval experiences. He told a story well, and the time passed quickly. Presently French looked at his watch.

'Half-past twelve,' he announced. 'I'll have a shot now.'

'Right. I'll slip up to my cabin and look out for you.'

French had brought a small outfit. He put on old rubber-soled shoes and a long dark brown cloak fitted with a hood and mask. As he moved up the after companion he felt it would be a sharp eyed watchman who would see him.

'If only I don't cut across some light ashore,' he thought as he reached the deck and stood for a moment taking his bearings.

It was very still. The air was scarcely moving and save for an occasional little gurgle the river was flowing silently past. One felt rather than heard it. In the distance was the faint hum of a car and across the river a dog barked spasmodically.

French moved forward. He walked upright and easily, but placed his feet carefully to avoid kicking anything. On the deck all was straightforward, but when he reached the gangway he tested it carefully lest it should move under his weight. It did not, and he reached the bank unnoticed.

This had really solved his problem. However he decided to continue the test lest, once again, he crossed a light. He walked to the boathouse, returned, crept on board and went below, following the alleyway to Collison's cabin.

'See anything, captain?' he demanded softly.

'You haven't been?' returned Collison. 'I'll swear you never crossed the gangway.'

'Been to the boathouse. Come along, captain: we'll both go this time.'

They made a second successful test, Collison wearing an old black waterproof. But at a third attempt in their ordinary clothes they were seen.

'It doesn't matter,' French declared. 'It's been conclusive. If we could get ashore in the moonlight on a silent night like this and after warning the watchman, there'd have been no trouble then.'

A cabin had been prepared for French, and presently he turned in. But he could not sleep. This discovery was a blow to him. It meant that the case was like so many others he had had: there was no royal road to success. He could not at one stroke eliminate a whole bunch of suspects. The case of each would have to be gone into separately. Unless he got some other discriminatory clue, he would have to include everyone on the ship that night as a potential murderer.

And as far as Locke was concerned, this point could no longer be taken as confirmatory evidence of innocence. French sighed as he thought of the work which stretched out before him.

14

The Forked Stick

There now began for French a period of weariness and discouragement. One after another he took the persons on his second list of suspects, went into each case thoroughly, and registered nothing in the slightest degree helpful.

After several days of tedious work he had been able to prove that all the people on the ship on the night in question, as well as the Colemans, Entrican, Kemp, Walpole, the latter's assistant, Stowe, Moffat, Blanche Morland and Lord Algy Mannering *could* have committed the murder. In addition so might an unlimited number of unknowns, provided these had been able to obtain a key to the Colemans' boathouse.

But in no single case could French get proof that any one of these persons *had* committed it. He remained just as far as ever from certainty.

As well as these personal investigations, he was of course running many other lines of research. The local police had been scouring the country for traces of any person or car seen in the neighbourhood about the estimated time of the crime. The sources from which the marble, hydrochloric acid and bowl had been obtained were being tirelessly sought. An intensive search was in progress for the coat or rug or cushion which had been used on the skiff's gunwale. But here again nothing useful was discovered.

A hopeful line of enquiry was that connected with Harrison himself. French made a careful examination of the deceased's private papers, discussed with various people his movements during the few days prior to his death, and interrogated persons in whose company he had been seen. But once again all this labour was profitless.

Then a phrase dropped by Kemp set French working in a new direction, or rather in an old one which he had provisionally abandoned.

He was chatting rather desultorily with Kemp in the latter's office, discussing among other things the public reaction to the financial crisis. In answer to a question Kemp admitted that a number of people believed that Harrison had disappeared intentionally on his way back from France, with the definite object of depressing his stock and swindling its holders. Among these he happened to mention Locke's name.

French pricked up his ears. 'Locke,' he said.

'I didn't know he was interested.'

'He's not interested in the sense of holding Harrison stock. But he's a friend of the family—or of some of its members.'

'I expect a lot of people thought Mr Harrison was swindling. How did you come to know Locke's opinion?'

Kemp was not expansive, but his reserve gave way under French's suave but insistent questioning. Locke apparently as the result of too many whiskies and sodas, had made his accusation to Kemp himself. He had declared his belief that Harrison had sold before he went to France, and re-bought during the slump.

'And had he?' French asked.

'No,' returned Kemp, 'he hadn't. Not a halfpenny worth was sold before he left. But he didn't lose by the affair either. In fact his action was typical of the man.'

'How do you mean?'

'I mean that when he saw disaster coming, he was able to turn it into a triumph. While you and I would be getting the facts of a situation into our heads, he'd have grasped the whole bearings and worked out a scheme to turn it to his own advantage.'

'Any secret what he did?'

Kemp hesitated. 'No, I suppose not,' he said rather unwillingly, 'but keep it to yourself. You remember the story he published? He said he hadn't discovered what was happening to his stock till he got ashore from that yacht about midday. It was probably true that he didn't know till he got ashore but it wasn't true that he got ashore about midday. He really got in about eight that morning. He read a newspaper over his breakfast, and there he saw what was happening. His first impulse was to publish the fact that he was all right, but he quickly saw something worth two of that. He rang me up secretly and told me to buy—his own stuff. I bought all that morning: hundreds of thousands of pounds worth, at a continually dropping price: far more, I may tell you now, than we could have paid for offhand. Then about midday when he thought I had bought enough, he authorised me to announce his return. The stock rose and we sold some of it to pay for the rest. Altogether we must have netted over £100,000.'

'And you're satisfied there was no element of design in that?'

'If you mean, was the disappearance a swindle, I'm satisfied. If it had been, he would have sold at the higher price before he went, and then re-bought at the lower before his return.'

French wondered. He did not feel so certain. Harrison could scarcely have sold stock before leaving, because that would have been to provide proof of the swindle. As it was, what Kemp admitted he had done was suspiciously near a swindle. And for the matter of that what Kemp himself had done was suspiciously near aiding and abetting. French was surprised that Kemp did not seem to realise the point.

The mention of Locke had brought the man back to French's mind. He felt he had dismissed him from his calculations too quickly. Well, he was at a loose end and would rectify the mistake without further delay.

The first step was to pick up as much information about him as possible. He began by looking up what was publicly known of his career in various books of reference. At once he noted a significant fact. Before going into the brewing industry, in which he now held a position of some importance, Locke had qualified as a chemical engineer. He thus knew not only how CO_2 gas might be made, but also where the necessary chemicals could be unobtrusively obtained. A chance conversation brought out the further fact that he was a yachtsman. He could therefore have handled the skiff with silence and despatch.

All this was suggestive. Locke unquestionably had opportunity to commit the crime, and his relations with Mrs Harrison supplied the motive. Not only was he genuinely in love with her, but if he were to marry her his financial future would be assured. Though able—it appeared that he held some really clever patents—he was by no means rich;

then he would be a wealthy man. He certainly had a completely adequate motive.

All the same, as French had already seen, this motive was largely discounted by the fact that Locke's attachment had been of long standing. All the evidence was to the effect that he had been devoted to Mrs Harrison for years, and there was no suggestion that the situation had in any way changed. If he had waited all that time without taking action, why should he do so now?

French obtained from Higgins another statement which he thought: also tended in the direction of Locke's innocence. Higgins, French felt, must have been a veritable Peeping Tom. Though he denied it indignantly, French believed he had habitually listened behind doors and above portholes and put eager eyes to intriguing keyholes.

Higgins said that some week or more before the tragedy—he could not remember the exact date—he heard Locke and Harrison talking in the lounge after the others had gone to bed. He would, he was careful to explain, have been in bed himself at the time, had it not been that he was feeling exceedingly unwell—something he had eaten had disagreed with him. He thought a small glass of brandy would do him good, and it was when he was going for this that he heard the voices.

'What were they saying?' French asked.

Higgins indicated in a rather stately manner that he never overheard conversation to which he was not an invited listener. But French cut him short.

'Keep that for someone who's likely to believe it,' he advised curtly. 'You certainly wouldn't have mentioned this conversation if you hadn't known what it was about. Repeat what you heard, and don't be more of an ass than you can help.'

Higgins collapsed at the unexpected tone, as French knew he would. Mildly he proceeded with his story.

It appeared that Locke and Harrison were discussing investments in an exceedingly amiable manner. Locke was asking for inside information about certain stocks which he had heard were shaky. He wanted to know whether or not to sell. Higgins hadn't heard the names of the stocks nor, according to his own story, had he waited to hear Harrison's reply.

This statement, French realised with annoyance, was like so many more in this exasperating case. It suggested an idea, but stopped short of proving it. It suggested that Locke was sufficiently good friends with Harrison to eliminate the possibility of murder, but it did not actually put this beyond doubt. It was a weight on the credit side of the balance: no more.

On the whole French thought his preliminary opinion was correct and that he must look elsewhere for his man. He saw Locke, who unhesitatingly confirmed the conversation, without however adding anything of interest. French decided he could not yet come to a final conclusion on the matter. Some other evidence must first be obtained.

But from where? He did not know. And try as he would, he could make no further advance. A large number of persons *could* have murdered Harrison, a certain number had the necessary motive—and there the affair stopped.

The case when he took it over had seemed easy. Complacently he had told himself that he had only to note the possibles and elimination would do the rest. He had made his list, but elimination had failed him. Here he was after over a week's work, not a whit nearer a solution than when he started.

For the first time in the case serious uneasiness began to creep into his mind. Was this one of those apparently simple affairs which turn out so appallingly difficult? Nothing to go on! Or rather plenty to go on, but not the one or two things that mattered. For the first time in the case doubt of his ultimate success reared its ugly head.

Then an idea occurred to him.

His thoughts had gone back to the placing of the decanter and bowl on the table by the head of Harrison's bed. They had, he believed, been passed in from the boat through the porthole by means of some instrument like a lazy tongs or hay fork. Suddenly he wondered if he could find the implement?

Where might it be? Certainly not in the murderer's possession. To keep it would be too dangerous. Doubtless he got rid of it at the first opportunity. Where?

The nearer to the *Cygnet* the better, for the same reason. Was there any obvious place near the *Cygnet* where it might be hidden?

Where but in the bed of Old Father Thames? Could the murderer simply have dropped it out of the boat on his way back? French thought it not unlikely.

As he pondered the idea, certain other points occurred to him. The murderer would not throw it far from the boat. He would slip it silently overboard, avoiding a splash.

If so, it would have been sunk somewhere on the course which the boat followed on its return to the Colemans' boathouse. What would that have been?

French believed that the murderer would have hugged the shore. To go out into the stream would be to court observation, either by passing between the watchman and a light or from some passing boat.

If this reasoning were correct, the implement must be lying on the river bed inside an area of, say, three hundred feet by fifty.

French sat whistling softly. Were the chances of success sufficient to warrant the expense of a search? Because dragging wouldn't do. It would mean a diver.

Presently he came to a decision, went in to see Sir Mortimer Ellison, obtained his approval, rang up a firm of divers and made the necessary arrangements.

It proved a terribly slow job. The diver walked backwards and forwards between the bank and a line some thirty paces out, raking every foot of the bottom. He began downstream, in the unrealised hope that the mud would float away from where he was working. Each passage to and fro was within three feet of the last, and an elaborate arrangement of ropes between the shore and an anchored boat was required to keep him in place. The work was tiring and he had to come up for frequent rests. By evening the job was scarcely half done.

Next morning they started again with fifty per cent of their chances gone. French was worried. The cost was going to be greater than he had anticipated, and now the reasoning which had led to the search seemed depressingly weak.

It was therefore with immense relief that he saw on the very first trip the diver's arm appear and wave above the surface a long handle with a couple of prongs at each end, one pair wide apart, the other closer together.

It was obvious that the prongs would fit beneath the sides of the bowl and round the neck of the decanter respectively. With such a tool it would be easy to pass these articles in through the porthole, manoeuvre them over the table, and silently withdraw the prongs.

French was more than delighted. Not only was his theory proven, but he had obtained an invaluable clue. He had only to trace the purchase of the tool to be led straight to his man.

But that he had done well was no reason why he should not do better. He decided to continue the search in the hope of further luck.

The diver resumed his weary marchings, working gradually nearer the *Cygnet*. Then just two hours after his first find, he made his second.

This was even more satisfactory: a cast-iron cylinder with a release valve and rubber tube connection fixed to the top.

French could scarcely believe in his good fortune. Carbon dioxide gas he knew was sold in these cylinders, and what was more to the point, each of them bore a serial number, so that its progress from the manufacturer to the retailer could be traced. And the retailer, facing a line of French's suspects, should be able instantly to say with which of them he had dealt.

Here was the sort of clue for which all detectives sought— and found so seldom. A direct path stretched from that iron bottle to the murderer of Harrison. All he had to do was to follow it—to reach the triumphant end of his case!

Enthusiastically French took his precious cylinder to the Yard and set his best man to clean it. 'Mind you do it carefully,' he adjured him, 'I don't want that number scraped out.'

But unhappily an unexpected development robbed him of his reward. Even in the short time during which the metal had been lying on the bed of the river, rust had deeply corroded it. Not only the number, but the manufacturer's name was illegible.

To French it was a bitter disappointment. He thought

that a royal road to success had been provided him, and he found once again that no such thing existed. Success in this case as in others was to be had only by care and hard work. Well, he might give up his momentary dream and settle down to it.

He therefore thought out and put into train a number of enquiries. What firms manufactured these cylinders? To what wholesalers did they send them? To what retailers were they passed on? Could any cases of sales of single cylinders to strangers be traced? And similarly with the pronged lifting tool. Where could it have been obtained?

These enquiries French delegated. And once they were under way he himself was out of a job. Slowly his depression returned. And as the days began to pass without apparent result, he grew once again moody and pessimistic.

Then one afternoon he amazed Carter—they were at Henley—by shutting down work early and going for a swim, and a little later in the evening he surprised his wife with tickets for 'the funniest show in town'. He felt stale, and believed a change of thought might freshen him.

He slept well, and next morning felt in much better form. Arrived at the Yard, he quickly polished off certain routine matters, and then taking up for the hundredth time the dossier of the case, he set himself to go over the facts once again, pondering each in turn, slowly weighing its possible causes and consequences in the hope of stumbling on some new point of attack.

He had not been long at work when a new idea did come. That disappearance of Harrison's! Had he not been taking too much for granted? He had been considering it as an independent happening, unconnected with murder. Was this justified?

He gazed blankly at the dull green painted wall in front of his desk, as he turned the idea over in his mind. He had considered two possibilities: Harrison inspecting the invention and Harrison disappearing to depress his stocks. Either of these might still be true, but was there not a third possibility? Might not Harrison have been kidnapped?

If so, the motive would be obvious. Suppose someone else wished to depress Harrison's stock? Suppose someone else had put out the rumours and kidnapped and released Harrison, so as to make his pile from its fluctuation?

So far so good, but a difficulty immediately arose. If Harrison had been kidnapped, why did he not say so? Why did he not go to the Yard and have the guilty party punished. Why did he make up the elaborate story of the invention?

There might, French thought, be an answer to this. On a journey from Paris to London Harrison could never have been kidnapped by force. If he had been kidnapped at all, it could only have been by some trick.

And Harrison might not have been willing to admit he had been tricked. It might have hurt his self-esteem more to let people know he had been fooled than to pocket the indignity secretly.

But if Harrison had been kidnapped, there might be a very direct connection with the murders. Suppose he had identified his abductors? Suppose he had said nothing in public, but in secret had turned the tables on them? Suppose he was blackmailing them, making them disgorge their gains? Would this not explain the whole affair?

It certainly looked like it. It was at least the first theory he had formed which covered the fact. Whether its details were correct or not, French felt more and more certain that the murder had arisen out of the abduction, and that the same party or parties were responsible for both.

Of course he would have to check it all, but if he were right it would enable him to eliminate a number of people from suspicion. Who on his list of possibles were necessarily innocent of the abduction? Who were elsewhere than Dover when Harrison passed through?

He turned once again to the dossier: Crewe, Entrican and Hearn were at Mount Street during that whole day. Mrs Harrison was also there at both lunch and tea. Gloria and Rupert were out during the day, but turned up for dinner. That didn't exclude them, but it would be easy to learn where they were. There his knowledge ended. He had no note of the whereabouts of the other suspects. But he could find out and must.

There ensued another day or two of interviews and checking of statements; uninteresting routine work which bored him stiff. And the result of it was disappointing. Only in the case of three more suspects was he able to satisfy himself. The rest remained as doubtful as before.

The three were Gloria, Rupert and Locke. Gloria was at a garden party near Reading, Rupert at the rehearsal of a new play, and Locke in York.

Tentatively then French felt he might eliminate Crewe, Entrican, the three Harrisons, Hearn, and Locke. But that left him with a long list of possibles, and for the moment he did not see how he was to reduce it further.

Then gradually it was borne into his mind that there was an obvious way after all, and he wondered how he could have been stupid enough to miss it. If he could not work from his suspects to the abduction, he must reverse the process. He must begin with the abduction, and find out who was guilty of it. Of course there was a preliminary. He must first make sure that the affair really was an abduction. So he would learn whether to proceed with this line of research, or drop it for something else.

Greatly cheered at having once more a definite programme, French turned to his notes on the disappearance. The *Westminster Guardian* people had been the first to hear of it, but they hadn't given much away as to the source of their information. He should begin by clearing this up.

An application to the editor was indicated, and half an hour later he was writing his name and business on a form in the vestibule of the *Guardian* building. Ten minutes wait and he was in the editor's room. Mr Garfield proved a small, precise and dapper man with a small, precise and dapper manner, and little external indication of the great gifts of mind and character which had brought him to the top of his profession.

'I won't waste your time with preliminaries, sir,' said French, knowing his man. 'We're going into the disappearance of the late Mr Andrew Harrison. Your people were the first to hear of it. I want to ask for all the information you can give me.'

For answer Mr Garfield picked up his desk telephone. 'You should see Mr Holloway,' he explained. 'He's our news editor and dealt directly with the affair.'

In a moment Holloway came in, long, loose and lanky, a complete contrast to his chief. Introductions followed.

'There's no mystery about the thing so far as we're concerned,' Holloway said, sprawling astride a chair. 'We were rung up. The caller asked for me, and when I heard what his message was about, I took it personally. I didn't know the voice and the speaker would give no name. He said he was calling up from a booth on the street near Dover Marine Station, and that he had just seen something which he thought might interest us.

'He had come to the station to meet a lady off the boat and put her into the train. He met her and saw her into a carriage. As he was standing at her door he saw Harrison walking to the train, a porter carrying his suitcase. The porter put the suitcase into the next compartment, and Harrison got in. Presently, however, he got out again, carrying his suitcase himself. He walked up the train as if he was looking for someone. But the speaker happened to notice him presently crossing the platform and going into the gentlemen's lavatory. Still he thought nothing of the matter and continued talking with his friend till the train started.

'The speaker had already forgotten the matter, but then a trifling incident occurred which caused him to remember it. He felt his shoelace loose, and in tightening it he broke it. This meant unlacing the shoe to bring the lace to a more central position. He did so, but it delayed him for two or three minutes, and when he had finished the station had cleared of passengers.

'Just then he noticed a man leave the lavatory. There was something about him both strange and familiar. He looked more closely and saw it was Harrison, but Harrison in different clothes, a different hat, and glasses. In other words, he had disguised himself. He was still carrying the suitcase. He looked quickly round and in a stealthy way hurried out, walking quickly away in the direction of the town. The speaker realised it wasn't his business, and made no attempt to follow him. He said he was ringing up because he thought we'd be interested.'

'I expect you were too,' said French. 'Rather altruistic of the speaker, wasn't it? What did he get out of it when he didn't give his name?'

'I asked him that, and he turned out not so altruistic as you suggest. He had a grudge against Harrison, who he said had once done him down. Now he thought that if Harrison was trying any tricks he'd put a spoke in his wheel.'

French smiled. 'There's a reason for everything,' he observed, 'if you can only find it. Well, that's a very interesting statement. What did you do?'

'I confess I was intrigued. I had heard rumours about the Harrison stock and I knew it was going down. The obvious idea occurred to me that Harrison was expecting a crash and was clearing out. But at once I saw difficulties. If so, I asked myself, why had he returned from France to England? It would surely be easier to disappear in Paris than in Dover. Then I thought, perhaps he had had a wireless on the boat or a letter on landing?

'However I needn't trouble you with my thoughts: only with what I did. The first thing was obviously to find out if the story was true. I rang up Harrison's office, and was told he had been in Paris and was expected back by the service in question. I asked where he had stayed in Paris and I got the hotel on the phone and found he had left for England by that service that morning. So it seemed O.K. so far.

'I then rang up the station master at Dover Marine and asked him could he trace Harrison or a man of his description having left the station as had been described. He replied presently that he could not, but I realised that this didn't invalidate the story, as there was no reason why Harrison should have been noticed.'

French grinned. 'You're lost on a newspaper,' he declared. 'You should come over and help us at the Yard.'

'If you can't do better than I did, you'll want all the help that's going,' Holloway retorted dryly, while his chief looked pained that anything could be considered more important than newspaper work. 'By the time I had an answer to these questions the train was in, and I had then to find out if Harrison had arrived by it. I rang up his office and his home—several times—and at last it became clear, firstly, that he hadn't come, and secondly, that no one knew what had become of him.

'This seemed so important that I thought we should have a conference to decide on our action. I therefore consulted Mr Garfield. We came to the conclusion that the story was our scoop and that we must print. We did so, and it turned out that we were the only paper that had the news.'

'Mrs Harrison came to me that night,' put in Garfield. 'She admitted she didn't know where her husband was, and wanted me to hold up the news of his disappearance. I should have liked to oblige her, but of course I couldn't. My first duty was to the paper.'

French thought the whole story was very suggestive. It looked as if he had been wrong about the kidnapping. Harrison, if this tale were true, had disappeared voluntarily and had made up the yarn about the invention. French spent a considerable time wondering whether he should check up on the story, or whether since there had been no kidnapping, it really interested him.

Then it occurred to him that once again he was putting the cart before the horse. It was wrong to say: Since there was no kidnapping this story did not interest him. The real argument was: If this story be true, there was no kidnapping.

The story therefore interested him very much indeed. He must know certainly whether it was the truth or an invention.

It wouldn't be difficult to imagine a motive for putting out such a story. Harrison's disappearance wouldn't have much effect in depressing his stocks unless it were known. And mere knowledge of the fact would scarcely be enough. Some hint of underhand dealing would be required. Indeed the maximum effect would probably be caused by just such a story as had been told.

Did this not mean that Harrison had been kidnapped after all? Who so likely as the kidnappers to put out the story?

Then French saw that it wasn't quite so simple as that. The story would be equally useful if Harrison had disappeared voluntarily. If he had, why should he not have put it out himself?

French swore. Out of all these contradictory considerations there emerged only one unquestionable fact—that he must investigate in detail the whole episode. There was at least a sporting chance that in this direction might lie the vital clue he was seeking.

15

The Austin 20

Visits to Henley had proved a welcome change to French from the monotony of his office at Scotland Yard. But he had not looked forward to being at Henley with anything like the pleasure he felt as on the following morning he stepped into the 9.40 from Victoria to Dover. He loved the sea, and though he preferred to be on its bosom, a visit to its shores was by no means to be despised.

His thoughts went back to that day nearly a year and a half earlier when he had just left Victoria for Dover. Then he was starting on the wonder journey of his life: a cruise to the Eastern Mediterranean. And though the trip had proved shorter than he had hoped, and instead of going to Istanbul and Troy and all sorts of other thrilling Eastern resorts he had got no further than Athens, that speedy end was due to a wholly satisfactory cause: that by then he had solved his problem and established his case.

French wondered if ever again he would have so pleasant a case. How he wished he could be sent to Canada, as Dew was to take Crippen, or to South America, like Hollingworth

208

about the Panter swindles! Well, perhaps some day he would. And in the meantime here he was going to Dover—at least a jolly sight better than staying at the Yard.

The journey over, he waited till the passengers had disappeared and then introduced himself to the station master.

'I understand that the *Westminster Guardian* people rang you up at the time,' he went on when he had explained his business, 'but since then the affair has grown more serious. I may tell you, strictly between ourselves, that Harrison didn't commit suicide: he was murdered. We think the murder and the preliminary disappearance are connected, so you'll see just how serious it is.'

The station master, duly impressed, promised secrecy and his best help.

'What do you want me to do?' he continued. 'I've already made enquiries into the matter, but without success.'

'All I want is that you should facilitate my enquiries,' French returned. 'I should like to begin interviewing all the members of the staff who were about the platform when the boat train left.'

'That can be done easily. It's a matter of looking up the various rosters. I'll have a list made.'

A tedious investigation followed. One by one French questioned platform porters, steamer porters, ticket examiners and other men who had been on duty when the train left. The great difficulty was of course the length of time which had elapsed since the affair had happened. However he was very thorough, and did not pass from any individual till he was satisfied he had learnt all the man knew.

But the sum total of his information was small. He found the porter who had carried Harrison's suitcase from the ship to the train, but he could not get any information about the telegram. Indeed, before he had finished he inclined to the view that there hadn't been any telegram, and that Harrison's statement about it was false. No one, moreover, appeared to have seen the financier leave either the train or the station.

This was most unsatisfactory. All the same French felt more than ever convinced that his progress in the case depended on his tracing Harrison's movements. He therefore set to work on a new line. If the station officials had not seen Harrison, perhaps some of the passengers had.

He sent an advertisement to the papers asking all those who had travelled on the service kindly to communicate with New Scotland Yard. He knew that only a small proportion of those who had done so would reply. Yet the plan seemed his best hope and was certainly worth trying.

As a matter of fact it worked well. A couple of days later a list of some thirty persons had been compiled. To each was sent a letter, asking if he had seen Harrison at Dover. One man replied that he had.

This was a Mr George Armstrong, an artist who had rooms in Chelsea. Early on the following day French called to see him.

'I knew Mr Harrison slightly,' he was told. 'He had wanted to have Mrs Harrison's portrait painted, and someone gave him my name. He approached me, and though in the end I refused the commission, we had a number of interviews about it. I saw him twice on the journey. I saw him first at the Gare du Nord in Paris: in fact we had a word or two on the platform. I didn't see him at Calais, but I did at Dover. I had chosen my seat in the train and was standing on the platform beside it when he went past. I watched him get into his compartment, which was close by.'

'Had he any luggage?' French asked, as a check on general accuracy.

'One small suitcase.'

'Yes, sir?'

'Harrison had only settled down when a man stepped up to the door and spoke to him. He was dressed in a plain uniform like a bank porter or a commissionaire of some kind. I didn't know the uniform. Harrison got out immediately. Both of them looked serious, as if discussing bad news. The man took the suitcase and they went off towards the station exit. That was all I saw of them. I watched, but so far as I know, Harrison did not come back.'

'Can you describe this uniformed man?'

Armstrong thought for some moments. 'Tallish and thin, with a clean-shaven face, dark hair and spectacles, I think. I'm not very sure, I'm afraid.'

'No special marks on his face: cuts or moles or deep wrinkles?'

'Not that I noticed.'

Here was a mystifying story. If true, and French thought it was, it falsified that told to the *Westminster Guardian* on the telephone. Once again in French's mind the balance of probability swayed. This story seemed to back up the kidnapping theory. Was the message of the uniformed man, he wondered, a trick to get Harrison from the train and into someone's power?

If so, something else appeared to follow. If the uniformed man had induced Harrison to go with him, he would scarcely have left his victim to telephone to the *Guardian*. Therefore someone else had telephoned, and as it was absurd to suppose that the message and the kidnapping were disconnected, it meant that there were at least two people concerned. A conspiracy and perhaps a gang was what French must look for.

As Harrison had gone in the direction of the station entrance, a cast from there was indicated. French walked along the high-level footway and down the steps into a narrow twisted street of private houses. Once again he felt baffled. There were here no shops, no cab rank, no traffic, no group of loungers, in fact no stand from which departing passengers might have been observed.

With Carter he called systematically at all the houses within view. Unhappily, his efforts were foredoomed to disappointment. There was nothing to have attracted attention to Harrison, and no one had seen him.

Then he remembered that a further line of enquiry remained to him. Of the thirty passengers who said they had crossed by the service in question, one lived near Dover and had driven home from the Marine Station. This lady had not seen Harrison, so French had not called on her. Now he wondered if she could have noticed the two men.

He had her address and in a few minutes was in a taxi driving to her house. She lived in a small cottage off the coast road, about halfway to Folkestone. Fortunately she was at home. But there his luck seemed to have run out.

'No,' she said, 'I didn't see anyone like either of those you describe. I don't think I should have in any, case, as they probably left before I appeared. Being in no hurry I waited on board till the crowd had gone ashore, and I think I was last through the customs.'

French, disappointed, was about to leave, when a further idea occurred to him. If she had been so late coming ashore, it was possible that Harrison had left the station before her. In this case would her chauffeur have not been waiting for her when he did so? Might he not have noticed something?

'Could I speak to your chauffeur, madam?' he asked.

'No,' she returned with a slight smile, 'because unhappily I haven't a car.'

'Then how did you come from the steamer?'

'In a taxi.'

'I didn't see any at the station. How did you get it?'

'I wrote beforehand to the Birkenshaw Garage, Queen Street.'

Half an hour later French was with the garage proprietor.

'Yes,' Mr Birkenshaw said after referring to his records, 'I remember the case. Mrs Marsham runs an account and we had a card from her from Paris: I remember it because it had a good view of the Seine flooding up on to one of the bridges. She asked us to have a car to meet the boat on that date.'

'Can you tell me who drove?'

'Yes, if you wait a moment.'

The driver, it appeared, was John Lemon, a young man to whom the proprietor gave an excellent character. 'Sharp as a weasel,' he declared. 'But very reliable. If there was anything to be seen, he'll have seen it.'

Lemon unfortunately was out on a job, but after some half hour he appeared. French took to him at once: one of the best type of the younger generation.

'Yes, sir,' he said, 'I saw the men you mean. They got into a car and drove away.'

'That's good,' French returned with immense satisfaction. 'Tell me about them: the more detail, the better.'

'I was down there a minute or two early,' the young man went on. 'You have to be there by the time the boat's moored, because your fare may come off among the first.

But it happened I was down a minute or two earlier than that. I had just got the car turned and ready when another car drove Up. The driver was like you describe; tall and thin with dark hair and spectacles and in a uniform. He left the car and went into the station. Then after a while he came out again with another man, like the other you describe. They got in and drove away.'

'That's good,' French repeated cheerily. 'Was there any luggage?'

'One small suitcase. The driver was carrying it and he took it with him in front.'

'Then the second man didn't sit with the driver?'

'No, sir: he got in behind.'

'I see. Did you happen to notice the car?'

'Yes, sir, I did in a way. I'm interested in cars, you see, and I hadn't anything else to look at. It was an old Austin 20—a real good car in its day, but now badly out of date. I noticed it particularly because I remember thinking it must have changed hands. The man who could have afforded that car when it was new, would likely have had another since. I mean, I was sort of amusing myself guessing about it.'

French smiled. 'That's what we at the Yard do for a livelihood,' he told him. 'I'm afraid I don't know what an Austin 20's like. Can you describe it?'

'It's a big car, a seven-seater: two in front, three in the back, and two tip-up seats facing the back. Some of them have glass partitions between the front and back seats and some of them haven't. This one had.'

'Covered, I suppose?'

'Oh yes, sir. And before the days of sunshine roofs.'

'Colour of body?'

'Black, sir.'

French nodded. 'Did you happen to notice the registration?'

'Surrey letters, but I don't remember the number.'

'You don't remember the actual letters?'

'No, sir: only that it was Surrey.'

'I'm not complaining. I wish all our constables did as well. Now that uniform. What sort was it?'

'I couldn't rightly say, sir. It wasn't any of the services. I don't think. More like those Cruelty to Children men. That sort of thing.'

'The colour?'

'Blue. Blue cloth bound with dark braid round the edge, if you understand. A long coat.'

'And a cap?'

'Yes, sir: a round peaked cap like a station master's only without the gold braid.'

French's next steps were obvious. With Lemon's help he got out as detailed a description of the car and its passengers as he could, and this he telephoned to the Yard for insertion in the 'Wanted' column of next day's *Police Gazette*. He gave a copy to the police at Dover, and he telephoned it to Folkestone, Deal, Sandwich, Canterbury and other adjoining places, so that local enquiries might begin at once. Then he rang up the Surrey County Motor Taxation office at Kingston, and asked that a list be got out of all the black Austin 20s of the model in question. This was promised for the next afternoon.

The Surrey people were as good as their word, and when French called at the Kingston office he was handed the required list. 'You're lucky it was such an old model,' the officer told him. 'A modern Austin would have probably have run into hundreds, but there are only eighteen of these old crocks left in the county.'

The next step was to ring up the local police in each case. It was not long before he had replies. Twelve of the cars had been elsewhere than Dover on the clay in question. Two owners had lent theirs during the period and further enquiries were being made. One had sold his some three weeks prior to the critical date. Three owners were from home and were being traced.

Of these cases there could be no doubt as to which was the most promising. Obviously that which had recently been sold. If a car was required for an irregular purpose, the natural practice would be to buy an old car, do the job, and resell. Without waiting for the returns to be completed, French decided to act on this assumption.

The sale had been made to Henderson's Garage Ltd in Hammersmith Broadway, and there next morning he betook himself. It proved a large concern, but when he put his questions he found that records were efficiently kept, and he was quickly answered.

'Yes, we bought that old Austin 20 in part exchange for a new one,' the manager explained. 'It wasn't worth a great deal and we gave its full value. We make it in the commission on the new one, you understand.'

French nodded. 'Can you tell me where the old one was on the afternoon of the 26th of May last?'

The card index flicked over. 'No,' the manager returned, 'I can't. We sold it again a week before that date. We had it in fact less than a fortnight. We hadn't even overhauled it. The purchaser said he wanted it for immediate use, and if it was in fair running order he'd take it and get the overhaul done later.'

'I follow. Who bought it?'

Again the cards were consulted. 'Mr Stanley Allison, 6 The Crescent, Basingstoke.'

'Did Mr Allison come for it himself?'

'You've beaten me there,' the manager returned, closing his index. 'We don't record such facts. Nor,' he smiled in a watery way, 'if you want his description, do we keep photographs of our clients.'

'I'd like his description all the same,' French insisted. 'Can you put me on to whoever dealt with him?'

'Yes, I can do that.' Once again the cards came into play. 'Mr Medway,' the manager said, and spoke on his desk telephone. An alert looking young man speedily appeared.

'I'm not sure that I can remember much about the affair,' Medway pointed out when they had retired to his office. 'We sell great numbers of cars, and there was nothing to fix this particular sale in my mind.'

'The age of the model,' French suggested. 'It was unusually old, wasn't it?'

'That is so. I remember the car. I'm not so sure about the purchaser.'

'Tell me what you can.'

'The man came in and said he was a market gardener living near Basingstoke. He was looking for a second-hand car with a roomy back. He wanted it for his men to carry garden produce to the local market. He didn't care what it was, so long as it was in reasonably good order and cheap. I showed him two or three: an old Daimler, a large Morris and one or two others. Then he said he'd prefer one with a partition behind the driver. He explained that in delivering flowers, the wind the car made tended to injure the blooms, I and as the drivers would never shut their windows, he'd like the back of the car protected. Then I thought of the Austin, which was the only old car I had with such a screen. He wasn't keen on it; said it looked too shabby to do his business credit. But he tried it out on the road. It went better than he had expected, and he decided to have it. He paid the money and took it away then and there.'

'That interests me quite a lot,' said French. 'Do you think you can now describe the man?'

It appeared that recalling the sale brought the purchaser back also into Medway's mind. 'Yes,' he answered, 'I do remember him now. He was a tallish man, rather slight, clean shaven and with glasses and dark hair. He seemed a smart fellow, and I remember thinking he looked more like an engineer or scientist than a gardener.'

French was delighted. It looked as if he were on the right track. It did not take him long to make a further telephone call to the chief officer of police in Basingstoke.

The answer which came to his enquiry caused French to chuckle with satisfaction. There was no Crescent in Basingstoke, and no market gardener of the name of Stanley Allison was known to the police.

16

The Rowcress Doctor

French believed that he had now sufficient evidence to enable him to reconstruct what had taken place.

Some two or more persons had wished to increase their nest eggs by manipulating Harrison's stock. For this purpose they had decided that Harrison must vanish and reappear. Their method was to kidnap him at Dover. A car would be required, and as it would be dangerous to use their own, they had bought one for the purpose. Having watched Harrison take his seat in the train, they had approached him with some confidence story. It must have been a good story, for he had swallowed it and gone with them. They had then somehow rendered him helpless until it suited them to release him. As a result, the stock had accommodatingly moved first down and then up.

Assuming this reconstruction were correct, French believed he could go a step further. Their scheme completed, the conspirators would be left with a car on their hands. It might prove an embarrassing possession and their first care would unquestionably be to get rid of it. How?

There seemed only two ways. It could be abandoned or it could be sold. Both unhappily were dangerous. But there could be no doubt as to which was the safer. To abandon the car would be to broadcast the fact that it had been used illegally. On the other hand its sale would be normal and unsuspicious.

That they had sold it French felt certain. Could he trace the sale?

Here it occurred to him that there was an obvious way of doing so. The purchaser—if there were one—would have notified the Surrey registration authorities of the transfer of the licence. Kingston should be able to give him his information.

A telephone query produced a speedy reply. The car had changed hands three times within a few weeks, and its latest owner appeared to be Messrs Thompson, Garage Proprietors, Bristol.

French at once put through another call, this time to the police in Bristol. In a couple of hours there was a reply. 'The car's there all right,' the super told him. 'It was sold by a tallish dark-haired man who gave his name as James Hamilton, of "Waverley", Dollond Road, Swindon. But from what you've told me, I'll bet long odds there's no such place. However that's a matter for you. I've had the car locked up in case you wish to see it.'

'I'll come first thing in the morning,' said French, and rang off.

Thompson's garage was as large or larger than that near Hammersmith Broadway. French took this in each case as evidence of design. The larger the concern, the smaller individual transactions would bulk and the less chance there would be of the Austin 20 deal being remembered. He saw the assistant who had negotiated the purchase, and was satisfied from his description that the seller was the same man who had bought it, and who had accosted Harrison at Dover Station. This opinion was supported by a message from the police at Swindon, which stated that there was no Dollond Road In the town.

The next item was an inspection of the car. It was unlikely that anything had been left behind by the kidnappers which would prove a clue to their identity, but it was not impossible. When police scrutiny consisted only of using the eyes, assisted perhaps by a lens, it was easier for a criminal to guard against it. All he had to do was to see that nothing had been forgotten and to rub the surfaces over with a cloth. Now things were weighted a little more against him. Since the authorities took to using the microscope on dust recovered by vacuum extractors and of photographing objects with various unusual rays, information could be gleaned which had formerly been unobtainable.

But when French began the examination, his unaided senses immediately told him two interesting facts. The first, which was given him by his nose when he opened the rear door, was doubtful. So faintly that it might be due to imagination, he thought he recognised the characteristic smell of ether or chloroform.

If so, here was the very thing he had been hoping to find! He had not forgotten the three puncture marks on Harrison's left forearm. Their suggestion had been obvious: that a hypodermic had been used to keep the man asleep. The difficulty of using the instrument on an unwilling subject had however given French pause. But did not this suggestion of ether offer the solution? If Harrison had first been gassed, the hypodermic could easily have prolonged his coma for the required period.

The second discovery delighted French still more. Through the bottom of the partition separating the front seat from the back of the car a hole some three-quarters of an inch in diameter had been drilled. Moreover the metal on the inside surface of this hole was partly bright and partly rusted, showing that the drilling was recent. For what purpose, French asked himself, could that hole have been drilled but to pass in gas, probably through a rubber tube?

Greatly pleased, he continued his search, but without further success. So far as he could see, he had learnt everything possible from the car.

One other consideration also delighted him. That criminals tended to repeat their methods was a commonplace, and if gas had been used in this car it suggested a connection between the kidnapping and the murder. It supported his belief that the same party or parties were guilty of both. No longer could he doubt that he was on the right track.

He saw the local police doctor and had his theory satisfactorily vetted. But though the criminals' procedure was growing clearer, he was no nearer finding their identity. Nor could he think of any steps which he had omitted to take. It was with feelings divided evenly between satisfaction and misgiving that he returned to Town.

But on reaching the Yard next morning he found that one of his lines of enquiry had borne fruit: not perhaps very luscious or well-grown fruit, but indubitably fruit. The attempt to trace the movements of the car had had some success. A doctor had been found who had seen it.

He lived in a little hamlet called Rowcress, some dozen miles west of Folkestone. Three hours later French was in his consulting room.

'I don't know that I can add much to what I have already

told the local constable,' the doctor said. 'He called on me with a description of a car and asked me had I seen it during a certain period. I asked him why he thought I might know of it, and he said he was questioning anyone who might have been out at night. As a matter of fact I was out at night and I think I did see it. At least I saw a car of the same make and apparent age, though I didn't observe its number.'

'Tell me all about it, sir.'

It appeared that about three o'clock on the morning of the day on which Harrison returned to Town the doctor received a sick call. It was to a house only a couple of hundred yards from his own, and as he had little to carry, he decided to walk rather than take out his car. The road lay parallel to the main railway between Folkestone and London, some hundred yards from it. About halfway to his patient's was Rowcress Station, and an approach road branched off to it from that he was traversing. Close to the road the car was parked.

The night was clear with a moon, and he could see objects in fair detail. He noticed the car, and as a former partner had one of a similar make, he was sure of its type. It showed its parking lights only, and there appeared to be no one in it.

He duly paid his call, and on his return journey he saw the car again. It was in sight as he approached, standing in the same place. But before he reached it, three men appeared walking quickly from the direction of the station. They got in and drove off. That was about half-past three.

'I suppose you couldn't describe the men?' French demanded.

The doctor could not, and seemed to consider the question

unreasonable. 'It was only moonlight,' he pointed out. 'I saw the three figures and I could see that they were men, but that was all. They were perhaps fifty yards away from me.'

'In which direction did they go?'

'Towards Ashford: it's only about four miles.'

'The London direction?'

'Yes.'

French's next step was obvious. Were the men coming from the station, and if so, what had been their business there?

The station master proved as ready as the doctor to give his help, though the interview opened unpropitiously enough. 'No, sir,' he replied to French's question, 'no one could have seen the three men you speak of, because no one was here. The station is closed at night.'

'But there are night trains? I thought that at least a signalman would be on duty?'

'No, the station is closed from nine in the evening till seven next morning. The box is what we call switched out and all signals are left standing off.'

'A pity from my point of view. And were there no traces of visitors during the night? Nothing displaced or anything of that kind?'

The station master shook his head. Then suddenly an idea seemed to strike him. 'You're asking about Friday, the 28th of May? That's a long time ago. Now there was an unusual thing happened somewhere about that time, but I can't remember if it was the same morning. I don't know if any of the men remember.'

'What was the incident?' French asked.

'One morning about that date when the early signalman was coming on duty—at seven a.m.—he crossed the up

224

platform as usual to get to the box. You see where it is? As he passed a man came out of the shelter. He said, "When is there a train out of this damned hole?" The signalman was a bit taken back, but he answered civilly—or says he did.' A crooked smile twisted the station master's somewhat gnarled features. 'He asked where the man wanted to go, and the man said, "Anywhere I can get a wash and some breakfast." The first stopping train each way passes shortly before eight, and the signalman told him he could have his choice of Ashford or Folkestone. He took a first single to Ashford and left at 7.50.'

'Rather unusual surely?' French commented. 'If the station was locked, how did he get in?'

'The signalman didn't ask him, and until after the train left I didn't know that he wasn't just an ordinary passenger. But there would have been no difficulty about that. He had only to climb the wire paling and walk across the rails and up on the platform.'

'Can you describe him?'

The station master shook his head. 'I issued him a ticket and saw him into the train,' he answered, 'but except that he was carrying a suitcase I didn't pay any special attention to him. But you can see the signalman if you like.'

French said there was nothing he would like better and a few minutes later the man appeared.

'It's about the passenger who wanted a train out of this damned hole,' French began encouragingly.

The signalman glanced at him keenly for a moment, then apparently satisfied, allowed a slow smile to creep over his saturnine features. 'I'm not surprised questions are being asked about him, sir,' he said. 'I've often wondered what he was up to.'

'What do you think?'

'He'd been having a night of it, or more than a night I would say from his beard.'

'His beard?'

'He had missed his shave, I'd say, more than once. Yes, sir, he was a bad case. Sleeping it off, I would say, and not very wide awake at that.'

'Describe him, will you?'

The signalman was evidently an observer, and as he clumsily covered the points he had noticed, the suspicion which had early leapt into French's mind became a certainty. This irascible traveller could have been none other than Harrison.

A few other questions made the matter clear. There were evidently at least three conspirators in the thing. They had arrived at Rowcress about three in the morning, intending to leave the presumably helpless body of their victim in some place where he could sleep off his drug. They had not driven the car to the station door, and French wondered why. Then he saw that there was a good reason. As the station was closed, a police patrol, seeing it there, might have become suspicious, while its presence on the road could be accounted for by a visit to an adjoining house.

The three men had evidently carried their victim to the shelter on the up platform, doubtless choosing it because all the rooms with doors were locked. By seven o'clock the effects of the drug had worn off enough to allow Harrison to speak to the signalman, though he was still far from normal.

All this was very satisfactory, but French now hesitated as to whether he should first follow up Harrison or the car. Then he saw that Ashford probably represented the first stage in both quests, and he repeated Harrison's question with a real desire for information.

He had not much to say to the police at Ashford. They already had a detailed description of the car, and it was unlikely that the fact that it had been in their neighbourhood on the night in question would produce any fresh evidence. However the superintendent promised to have another enquiry made, and French drifted off for some lunch.

As he hurried over his belated snack, he kept turning over in his mind what Harrison had probably done. And at once the signalman's story gave him the hint. A barber's and an hotel.

A question to the waitress told him the nearest barber's shop, and when he had there drawn blank, a similar question gave him a number of other addresses. At the fourth of these his luck turned.

A man—undoubtedly Harrison—had come in shortly after the shop opened at eight o'clock, and had had a shave. His beard was long, and he had explained this by saying he had had a fall and had been knocked out for a couple of days. The barber had been respectfully sympathetic, but in his own mind had formed a conclusion similar to the signalman's.

At the barber's French obtained the address of his next call. Harrison had asked for an hotel where he could breakfast.

French had more difficulty at the Willington Arms than at either Rowcress Station or the barber's shop. For a long time he could get no response, then after many hints and promptings a waiter gave him some news. A man, evidently Harrison, had walked into the dining-room about half-past eight in the morning. At that time there happened to be no one in the office, and he had demanded, not very pleasantly, whether there was no one in the damned place who could attend to visitors. He said he had been up all night, and wanted a room with a bath where he could change. The waiter found the manageress and the matter was arranged. Some half an hour later the man had come down for breakfast. He had asked the waiter for a paper, and the latter had brought him the *Westminster Guardian.*

Harrison had seemed in a very bad temper. He had ordered ham and eggs and coffee, but the waiter noticed that he had eaten little, while drinking cup after cup of coffee. The waiter had also watched him reading his paper and had been much intrigued. Harrison had glanced at the paper without opening it and had immediately seemed overwhelmed with astonishment. He had simply gaped at its front page with its title, *Westminster Guardian,* printed in the familiar Old English lettering. Had it been a news page this would not have seemed so extraordinary, but as everyone knows, there is nothing on the *Guardian* front page except small advertisements. Harrison after remaining spellbound for some seconds, had at last turned to the main news page, and then he had seemed more amazed than ever. For a time he had completely forgotten his breakfast. After the surprise he had had a period of deep thought, and then other breakfasters had come in, and the waiter had been unable to watch him any longer. But he had noticed his expression when he called for his bill. He was then smiling as if in anticipation of some pleasure.

All this was extremely satisfactory to French. He felt sure he understood what had taken place. Harrison had been put to sleep on the Wednesday afternoon. He had wakened up on the Friday morning. He had bought the paper, and the first thing he had seen was the date. It was a day further on than he had believed! No wonder he had seemed amazed.

He had then opened the paper and read about his own disappearance. No wonder again that his amazement grew.

Under these circumstances his next step would be exactly what had been observed. He would settle down to puzzle the affair out. No doubt he would quickly find the explanation. He would see that he had been trapped and drugged, and the fall of his stock would supply him with the reason.

But he had ended up smiling. Why? Surely because he had seen how to turn the affair to his own advantage.

From all this an obvious deduction followed. Harrison's action supplied the final proof that his disappearance had been involuntary. Otherwise there would not have been that surprise.

This was an important step forward. If French could assume—and he believed he could—that the kidnappers and the murderers were the same persons, he should be able to get on to them through the stock. Who had benefitted? If he could only find that out he believed he would be well on his way to solving his problem.

Further inquiries at the hotel revealed still another confirmatory fact. At five minutes past nine Harrison had made a trunk call, and the sum charged on the transaction was that for a call to London. Kemp, French remembered, sat down to his work at precisely nine each morning. The fact that Harrison had waited till five minutes past nine seemed too significant to be an accident.

17

The Histrionic Constable

French returned to London that evening well pleased with his day's work. Bit by bit the actions of the criminals were becoming revealed, and a long experience told him that just in this way were cases cleared up and the guilty brought to justice. A few more days of similar progress, and his job would be done.

But just at this point the rosy vision faded. Yesterday's discoveries had been due to the finding of the doctor. But that episode had been worked to a finish, and it had not led to a further step forward. Once again he was at a standstill.

How to find the three men who had driven off from Rowcress in the car? That was the question the answer to which had so far eluded him. What did he know about them?

Extraordinarily little. Beyond the facts that they had been at Rowcress at three o'clock in the morning of the 28th of May, and had probably made well on the fall and rise of the Harrison stocks: nothing. If one of them were the man who had met Harrison at Dover, he had his description. He should be easy enough to find, and yet French had already employed all the obvious methods without success.

He puzzled over the affair all the way up to Town, without obtaining any light. But just as he was leaving the Yard for his home an idea flashed suddenly into his mind, and he saw that he had had a clue all the time, until now overlooked.

Late though it was, he went back to his room and sat down to think the thing out. If his idea were really as good as it seemed, it should give him all he wanted.

Harrison had gone to Paris on the Sunday and had intended to return on the Tuesday following. But for some unknown reason he had changed his plans and come a day later. How had the conspirators learnt of this change?

In order to carry out the kidnapping, they must have known the date of his return and the service by which he was travelling. How?

Here certainly was food for thought. There seemed two obvious possibilities. Either Harrison's change of plans had been brought about by the kidnappers themselves, or they must have learnt of it through his telegram to London.

French took the second alternative first. To whom had the man telegraphed? He looked back through the dossier. To Kemp only. He had told Kemp to let his household know, and Kemp had rung up Entrican. But of course a host of other people must also have been told: many of the office staff, the entire household, probably several outsiders.

No, on closer inspection this was not such a promising line. French went round to see Kemp and Entrican, but only to find that by lunch time the news was common property.

What then about the other possibility: that the gang had

delayed Harrison in Paris? French felt he must know the cause of the change of plans. A visit to Paris seemed indicated, and he went in to consult Sir Mortimer Ellison on the point.

He was delighted to find the A.C. in favour of the journey. 'It may be a wash out of course,' Sir Mortimer admitted. 'Harrison may have stayed on perfectly legitimate grounds or,' a twinkle showed in his eyes, 'you may not be able to find out his reason. On the other hand, if your men kept him there, you may get right onto them.'

It was late when French reached Paris: too late to do anything that night. But early next morning he called at the hotel which Harrison usually patronised. There he had little difficulty in learning the man's movements. He had stayed frequently and was well known to the staff, and the fact of his disappearance and subsequent murder had called the attention of all concerned to his last visit. Owing to this French was able to obtain much more detailed information than would otherwise have been possible.

Harrison had reached the hotel on the Sunday evening at a time which showed he had gone direct from the Gare du Nord. He had been given his usual suite and had said he was leaving by the 8.20 service on the Tuesday morning. He had been out, it was believed, most of Monday, but that evening two men had called and had dined with him in his private sitting-room. They had remained till the small hours, Harrison coming down with them when they were leaving. He had then given notice that he should not be called early on the following morning, as he was staying one day longer in Paris. Next morning after breakfast he had sent a telegram to London. He had filled in a form in the hotel and handed it in at the office to be despatched. The clerk remembered its approximate contents—once again it had been fixed on her mind by the disappearance. It said: 'Staying a day longer. Return by same service tomorrow,' or words to that effect. It was addressed, the young lady believed, to Harrison's London office. Shortly after breakfast Harrison had gone out, and had remained out till the evening. He had dined alone and next morning had left by the 8.20 service.

This telegram, French noted, checked up with that received by Kemp, so at the outset one point was cleared up—that Harrison had sent it himself.

The next thing was to trace the two men who had called on that Monday evening. Here French had no difficulty at all. One was a financier well known to the hotel staff, a M. Picoux, who lived in the Avenue de Ségur. A telephone call fixed up an early interview, and an hour later French was seated with the gentleman in his office.

'I have sometimes been surprised that no one enquired about that last visit Mr Harrison paid to me and my partner,' M. Picoux declared when French had explained his business. 'Of course we discussed a matter which could not possibly have had any bearing on his disappearance or death, so I supposed that was the reason.'

He went on to explain the business. He was the senior partner of a firm of financiers, and his firm believed the French Government was about to issue a large loan in connection with which he thought he and Harrison might do profitable business. Harrison had written him that he was coming to Paris, fixing up a meeting for that Monday evening. Harrison had not visited his office, as they wished to keep the entire matter private. During their meeting Harrison had been impressed with the proposals, but he wished to go into them further, and so had remained over in Paris for another day. Harrison had spent the whole of it with M. Picoux in interviewing other financiers, and they had reached a satisfactory agreement.

This was really all that French wanted to know. If Harrison had remained in Paris on his own business and at his own desire, the visit no longer interested him.

There were just two points to be cleared up before French left for home. Firstly, could this suave and well-dressed Frenchman or his friends themselves have had anything to do with the disappearance? Secondly, had they unwittingly told anyone else who might?

A few enquiries however set the matter at rest. M. Picoux's reputation was such that no assumption of his having been involved in such a crime remained tenable. Moreover all concerned declared that they had not mentioned Harrison's change of plan to anyone.

The intimation to the conspirators had therefore been given through Kemp. French found himself driven back to this extremely unpromising avenue.

He pondered the problem during his journey back to London, and by the time he reached Victoria he had evolved a plan which he thought might possibly obtain for him some further information, though he was far from sanguine on the point.

Next morning he sent for a young constable who had recently been drafted to the Yard, and who French had discovered had been a shining light in an amateur dramatic society. He had seen some of their shows, and had been impressed by the young man's prowess in ingenuous and youthful parts. French determined to turn this gift to account.

'I want you, Jackson,' he explained, 'to call on these men

in this order,' and he handed him a list beginning with Kemp and Entrican and including all the likely names he could think of. 'Go and ask them anything you like. Ask them if they had ever seen Harrison in grey herringbone pattern overcoat, if you can't think of anything better. Then let yourself be pumped. You're young and innocent and want to make yourself a big fellow by showing off what you know. See?'

The young fellow grinned. 'That won't be hard, sir,' he declared.

'Well, see you do it naturally. Don't try any actors' tricks and give the show away. Tell them I sent you to ask the question, and let out that I think Harrison was kidnapped, and that I've got a clue to the kidnappers. And when they ask you what the clue is, as they will if you're any good, say that someone had told the kidnappers about Harrison staying a day longer in France. Say, "Mr French thinks he's on to the party who did that, and that it'll give him all he wants." Then note their reactions. See what I'm driving at?'

The young man grinned as if the job was one after his own heart. Highly pleased, he took himself off.

He was back within a hundred minutes.

'I didn't expect you so soon,' French greeted him. 'What have you been up to?'

'I think I've got what you want, sir. I came to report and to ask you whether I should stop or carry on further.'

'Well?'

'I saw Mr Kemp at his office and asked him about the coat and also what tobacco Mr Harrison used, and I gradually let out what you told me. He seemed surprised, though a bit bored, and I left, believing he knew nothing of the affair. Then I went to Mount Street and saw Mr Entrican.

He took the thing quite differently. He wasn't surprised and he wasn't bored, but he was frightened. He was just absolutely scared stiff. It seemed pretty clear that he had either passed on the news himself, or knew who had, so that was why I came to ask if you wanted me to carry on.'

'No,' French decided. 'You've done all right. That'll do in the meantime.'

French had to admit that this news surprised him. Entrican! Could Entrican really be guilty? He had an alibi for the night of the murder, and when French had gone into it it had seemed watertight. But admittedly that investigation had been preliminary and not so thorough as he would have liked.

He thought some further details about Entrican's reception of the news might be desirable. He therefore called Carter and set off to Mount Street. Hearn opened the door.

'I find, Mr Hearn,' French began with a regrettable lapse from veracity, 'that I have mislaid my notebook containing your evidence. I wonder if you'd mind repeating it so that I may get it down again?'

Thus approached, Hearn was naturally out to help. French led him through the events of that morning, upon which he had refreshed his memory before starting.

'Now during the forenoon you said Mr Entrican had a phone message,' he went on. 'Can you fix the time of that more accurately?'

Hearn had given it as about half-past eleven, and this time he repeated, now mentioning what he had not before referred to, that he had a cup of coffee each morning at that hour, and the call came just while he was drinking it. 'What happened then? Did the telephone upset Mr Entrican?'

'Yes, sir, it did,' the butler returned with some surprise. 'It seemed to be bad news, and I almost asked him if anything was wrong. But he said nothing and went back to his room.'

'He didn't tell you what was in the message?'

'Not then, sir. In a minute or two, less than five, I should think, he came down again and went out. I was in the hall as he passed through, and it was then that he told me.'

'What did he say?'

'Simply that the message was to say that Mr Harrison wouldn't be home till the following day.'

French nodded, while he thought rapidly. 'I think that's all I want about that,' he said slowly, adding carelessly, 'And was Mr Entrican long out?'

'No, sir, he came back in about fifteen minutes.'

'And didn't go out again?'

'Not till after tea.'

To prevent Hearn guessing the object of his enquiries, French continued asking about the later events of the day. 'That,' he concluded, 'will let me get my report written up correctly. I'm sorry to have troubled you with the stuff twice.'

What Hearn had told him seemed significant. Entrican had received the message, been greatly upset thereat, and had promptly left the house for some fifteen minutes. Why had he done so?

If French were on the right track, only one answer was possible: to advise his associates. Suppose he had advised them, what channel would he have used? Would he call on them or telephone or telegraph?

Then another point struck French. The boat from Calais on the 8.20 service reached Dover about 1.20. Even if the abductors lived in London they must have left before 11.30. Therefore a personal call might be ruled out.

A telephone or telegraph message was more likely. In either case Entrican would probably have left the house to send it, so as to reduce the chances of discovery.

There was nothing for it but to try for both, and success at this distance of time was scarcely to be hoped for. French thought a telegram on the whole more probable, as the conspirators were unlikely to have a telephone number in Dover. A telegram would have the advantage that it could be sent to a post office or hotel, where it would lie till it was called for. Of course, this meant that such a call had been pre-arranged.

On the other hand a telegram had the drawback that it left a more complete record. Well, French could but try.

He went to all the telegraph offices which Entrican could have reached in fifteen or twenty minutes, and saw the postmasters. An order from the Home Office is theoretically necessary before a postal official will disclose information of this kind. But usually a postmaster, if carefully approached, will allow a senior detective of the Yard to see his records, on the understanding that if anything is used, the necessary authorisation will be procured. It was so in this case. French was shown the file of telegrams. Luckily those for the date in question had not yet been destroyed.

A very brief search only was necessary. On his first call French delightedly found a message. 'To Kealing, Ambrose Hotel, Folkestone. Appointment postponed twenty-four hours. Barton.' French had brought with him a sample of Entrican's writing. He rapidly compared it with that of the message. They were the same.

'I shall certainly want that,' he said to the postmaster. 'If I may take it along, I'll let you have the order in due course.'

Rejoiced to be once again on what he believed was a hot scent, French set off with Carter for the Ambrose Hotel at Folkestone. A town so near Dover might well have been chosen as a place of call for possible late news.

At first, however, he thought his visit was going to be in vain. No one remembered the receipt of the telegram or to whom it had been given. The manager admitted that it must have been received and given to someone, or otherwise it would either remain, or have been opened and returned to the Post Office, and this letter had not been done.

French then tried another line. Had three men—perhaps a greater or less number, but probably three—called at the hotel, perhaps for an early lunch, more likely for a drink, on that 26th of May? Or had they called to enquire for letters or telegrams, or on any other business whatever? But again his questions produced only shakings of heads and declarations of ignorance. Nor did the Austin 20 help. No one had noticed it.

As a last resort French produced his bunch of photographs. These included everyone who had come into the case, as well as a number of others of a similar type. He handed them round: to the reception clerk, the hall porter, the head waiter, other waiters . . .

His hopes were falling rapidly, then a barmaid halted over a photograph, and they began as quickly to rise.

'I've seen that man fairly recently,' she said holding out one of the photographs. 'I don't know when or where, but I have seen him.'

French took the card and then experienced a sudden surprise. It was that of Sir Richard Moffatt.

Moffatt and his friend Stowe had not figured prominently in the case. French had noted their existence, had interviewed them, had heard their stories and the information was all in the dossier, but nothing had occurred to cause the slightest suspicion to fall on them. And this girl's statement didn't of course arouse suspicion. Anyone might call at the Ambrose Hotel in Folkestone; or the barmaid might have seen Moffatt elsewhere.

French selected Stowe's photograph and put it with three others of a similar type. 'Ever see any of those?' he asked, and awaited the reply with real excitement.

The girl peered at the four cards, wrinkling her pretty forehead in an admirable display of thought and concentration. Then she made a little gesture.

'Yes; you're right! I do remember. This one,' she pointed to Stowe, 'was with the other. I remember it all now. Three of them came in some time before lunch for a drink. And I remember now, they asked if there was any letter or telegram for them: I forgot the name they gave. I told them to try at the office, and one of them went away and I think he got a telegram, for he told something to the others. I remember they were pleasant spoken people. They had their drinks, bade me good morning and went out.'

'Thank you,' said French, 'that's very helpful to me. Now I hate to bother you, but if you could identify the third man, it would help me still further.'

He had, however, got all the help she could give him. Either the third man's photograph was not in his collection, or she had forgotten him too completely to identify it.

Stowe and Moffatt! Was it possible that he had so completely missed the truth? Well, better late than never. He believed this new hint would give him what he wanted.

18

The Tooting Shed

When next morning French reached the Yard, he turned to
the dossier of the case to refresh his memory as to what
his routine enquiries had already told him about his new
suspects.

Stowe and Moffatt were partners of a firm of financiers
doing business of a similar kind to Harrison's, but on a
much smaller scale. They had assisted him in certain
ventures, 'playing jackal to his lion', as it had been put by
one informant. There might well be, French thought, a
motive for what had taken place in their business relations.
If so, it should not be difficult to find.

Stowe was married and had a family and lived in a
detached house with a small amount of ground in Hampstead.
Moffatt was unmarried and had a flat in a large new block
near Esher. Both were obviously well to do, though neither
appeared exactly rich.

They were on visiting terms with the Harrisons, dining
with them fairly frequently, and entertaining them, though
less often. At most of these dinners business appeared to

have been discussed. French indeed imagined from what he had heard that they seldom met when business was not discussed.

So much the dossier told him. Not having suspected either of them, he had not followed up these routine enquiries.

Now however all that was changed. He must find out all he could about them, and he leant back in his chair and began to consider how he should do it.

At once he saw that it would be unwise to let them know they were suspected. He must work away secretly till he had enough evidence to make an arrest.

To obtain information about the households he decided to adopt a time-honoured subterfuge. Young Constable Jackson had done well when he sent him to Kemp and Entrican. He would try him again.

'Go and make friends with the servants,' he told him. 'I'll fix up with the local people for you to be on the beat in the neighbourhood. Scrape acquaintance, particularly if there's a good-looking girl there. Take her to the pictures. You know the dope.'

Jackson grinned as usual. French looked at him with some misgiving. There seemed more genuine pleasure in his expression than he altogether approved. French hoped the interviews would be turned to the best advantage.

He felt he could not bank on Jackson only. The man might find out something useful, but on the other hand, he might not. French determined to adopt another time-honoured expedient himself. He sent a man to Stowe's office with instructions to shadow him home and thus find out what time he arrived. Then on the next night he himself called at Stowe's house some half-hour before this time.

'I'm a chief inspector from Scotland Yard,' he explained,

showing his card, 'and I want to get some information from Mr Stowe. Has he come home yet?'

When told, as he expected, that the master of the house would not be back for half an hour, he hesitated, then asked might he come in and wait. Apparently there were visitors in the drawing-room, and the table was being laid in the dining-room. To his great satisfaction he was shown into Stowe's study, a cheerful book-lined room on the first floor with a bright fire and extremely easy chairs. The maid handed him a paper and said she would tell Mr Stowe directly he came in.

Here was luck such as he had hoped for, but scarcely expected. He had tried this trick a great many times, and he had found it only came off about once in every five.

He heard the maid's footsteps retreating down the stairs, and he felt sure that if anyone came up he would be adequately warned. He therefore put down his paper, silently crept across the room to Stowe's desk and very gently raised the lid.

For a successful business man it was not very tidy. Letters, bills, memoranda and various other papers were heaped on a mass on a blotting pad with an engagement block down each side. Notebooks relating to financial matters were stacked at the back. In front was a whole battery of pens and pencils.

French worked at his utmost speed in going over the papers. From time to time he entered a name or address in his notebook, particularly if the business with that person or place was not made clear by the context. Thus from the engagement block on the blotting pad he copied down six addresses and twice as many names. Then, the half-hour being up, he softly replaced the disturbed papers, closed the desk, and returned to his chair.

His precaution was justified. He had scarcely been seated when heavy steps ascended the stairs, and Stowe entered.

French had met him when making his preliminary interrogation, and Stowe was civil enough. He was sorry to have kept the chief inspector, and what could he do for him?

'I'll tell you, sir, if you can give a moment,' French answered. 'We've been considering whether the fact that the late Mr Harrison remained an extra day in Paris just before his disappearance could have had anything to do with his death. I was sent to Paris, and I learnt that that business was in connection with a suggested French Government loan, but I could not find out whether Mr Harrison proceeded further with the matter. You told me, sir, that your firm was associated with Mr Harrison's in certain matters, and I wondered if this were one of them. If so, I came to ask if you could tell me something about it?'

Stowe shook his head. 'I'm sorry I can't tell you anything,' he returned. 'I didn't even know why Mr Harrison stayed that extra day in France. He certainly never mentioned the matter to me.'

'I knew, sir, that that might be the case. However there was the chance and I thought I ought to take it. You can't put me on to anyone who might know?'

Stowe could not, and French with apologies for the trouble he had given, took his leave.

His bag consisted of fourteen names and nine addresses, as well as notes of certain disconnected sums of money. Probably there was nothing worthwhile in the whole lot. Certainly he had seen nothing in the slightest degree suspicious.

With the help of the local police he soon found who lived at the nine addresses. He heard first about those in Town, of which there were five. These were, a solicitor, a jobbing gardener, a firm of house agents, an elderly well-to-do widow, and a bank manager. None seemed very promising, but all had to be interviewed. The calls on the solicitor and gardener produced no result, but at the house agents French got more than he could have hoped. Their office was in Tooting, and thither he took his way.

He asked for the head of the firm, and was shown into the office of a Mr Morton. There he produced his chief inspector's card, and pledged Morton to secrecy.

'This matter is not in any way connected with either yourself or your firm, Mr Morton,' he went on. 'It's just a deal that I want to investigate. Do you recognise that man?' and he handed over Stowe's photograph.

Morton looked at the card for some moments. 'Yes, I do,' he answered doubtfully, 'but I'm hanged if I can remember where I saw him.'

'A client perhaps?'

'Very likely. Let's see: perhaps one of my staff could help us.' He rang a bell. 'Ah, Hawes, look at this photo. Who is it?'

The young man who entered examined the portrait in his turn. 'It's that man, sir, who hired the shed in Brighteagle Street,' he said at once. 'I'm afraid I don't remember his name. But I went to the shed with him for his inspection and I remember him quite well.'

'Fine,' French declared encouragingly. 'You remember where the shed was, then?'

'Oh yes, sir. I took him there.'

'If you know the property,' Morton broke in curtly, evidently disapproving of French's intrusion, 'you can get the name from the cards. Go and turn it up.'

The card index revealed not only Stowe's name—which French was delighted to find was Mr Victor Cunninghame, with an address in Essex—but also the entire transaction in which he had been an actor.

It appeared that he had called on the 12th of May previously to ask if Messrs Morton had a shed or garage in the nearby area to let for a month or six weeks. He was, he explained, moving into new premises and the garage accommodation was not ready. He wished to keep two lorries and a car.

It chanced that Morton had a shed which he thought might suit, and the clerk, Hawes, was sent to show it to him. Cunninghame expressed himself as satisfied, and then and there took the place for a month, with the option of extension for a second month on the same terms if a long term letting had not meantime been made. He had returned to the office, signed the agreement and paid over the rent in advance, in notes. At the end of the month he had sent back the key with a note to say that his own premises were ready and he was giving up the shed. A man had been instructed to make sure the premises had been left in good order, and on receipt of his satisfactory report, the matter had been considered closed.

'That's a great help to me,' French declared, scarcely believing his good fortune. The hire of the shed must surely have been connected with the Harrison affair, but even if not, it would lead to something interesting, as Stowe had made the deal under an alias.

'Would you now please add to your kindness,' he went on. 'I should like to see this shed, and if Mr Hawes could let me have the key for a day or two, I should be very grateful.'

'Something wrong?' Morton enquired with interest.

'I don't know, but I suspect something for the simple reason that Cunninghame is not your client's name.'

'Well, go and see the shed, and if there's anything else we can do, let me know.'

French thanked the manager and left the office with Hawes.

'It's only a couple of blocks away,' the latter explained. 'We don't want a car.'

They set out through the drab streets of the poorer parts of Tooting, between dreadful rows of small working-class houses, relieved by occasional newsagents, tobacconists and public-houses. Presently Hawes stopped at a large doorway wedged in between two decaying houses, and unlocking it, they entered the shed.

It was a small, empty structure with an earthen floor, some twenty feet wide by forty long. A narrow skylight stretching along the major axis gave a poor light. French stood looking round.

'Now,' he said, 'if you leave me the key I'll return it to you in an hour or two.'

Hawes looked disappointed that he was not to see a great detective actually at work. However he could do nothing but agree, and French and Carter were left alone.

The earthenware floor was hard and dry and bore no identifiable prints, but only vague marks of car wheels. The two men examined the whole place with the greatest care. But entirely without result. At the end of a couple of hours they had to admit that no traces of previous occupants remained.

'Hard luck that,' said French. 'They got the shed to keep the car in: I'm as sure of that as that I'm alive. But we can't prove it. I must admit I hoped for a bit of wheel track or something we could swear to.'

The shed had yielded nothing: what about its surroundings? French began the much more tedious job of making enquiries from all the adjoining neighbours.

Seven houses they tried without success, but at the eighth they obtained some really valuable news.

It appeared that the father of the family was at home, recovering after an accident. He was a taximan, and being bored with his convalescence, he had given pretty close attention to any of the affairs of his neighbours which presented themselves. Among these was the letting of the shed immediately opposite his house. From his bed he had seen the clerk Hawes arrive with Stowe and leave again after a few minutes. He had been surprised not to see further manifestations of a let, but for several days no one had entered the shed. Then one evening shortly before dusk an old Austin 20 had appeared and had been driven in. The shed was unlocked by the driver, a tall young man with glasses and dark hair, and after a few minutes he had left on foot. The invalid had noted the car's number at the time, but unfortunately he could not now remember it.

For a week or more nothing happened, then about ten one morning the same man appeared, went into the shed and brought out the car. It must have been returned at some time when the taximan was asleep, for the next thing he saw was it being taken out in an exactly similar way at the same time on the following morning. Late that afternoon it returned, and on this occasion as well as the driver there were two other men. The three left the shed together some hour later.

During the next day there was a mild activity about the

shed. The dark-haired young man spent a considerable amount of time in it. He entered fairly early in the morning and stayed for perhaps half an hour. He repeated the visit about midday and again in the afternoon. Then quite late he reappeared with the other two men and after some delay the car was driven out with all of them in it. The taximan had missed its return, but three or four days later the dark-haired man had come alone and taken it out. That was the last he had seen of car or men.

All this interested French extremely. It now looked as if in that shed across the road Harrison had spent the most notorious day of his life. All the movements to and fro fitted in perfectly with this assumption, and would fit in with nothing else that French could imagine.

He wondered why the conspirators had driven Harrison all that long way up to Town and down again to Ashford? Then he saw that there might be good enough reasons for it. First, the party had to be at their businesses in London on the day after the abduction and they would certainly travel in their own car more secretly than in any other way. Then again if Harrison vanished at Dover and reappeared within a few miles, the police would naturally look for the hiding place there rather than in London. French doubted whether, had he been in Stowe & Co.'s place, he would have done as they had, but he saw that a case for their action might be made.

All this was admirable as far as it went, but unless it went a good deal further it was not going to be much use to French. Proof, not theory, was what he wanted. How was he going to get it?

It was not an easy problem and French gave it a lot of thought. Then at last he came to the conclusion that his best chance was from the party themselves. Could he bluff them into giving something away? Some little phrase which would show they knew more than they had admitted, and which couldn't afterwards be explained away? Some plan of that kind might give him what he wanted.

He turned to consider the characters of the three men. Which of them would be most likely to yield to such treatment?

Stowe, he could tell from his appearance and manner, was of strong character. Moffatt was not, he judged, such a leader, but he was no fool or chicken either. Entrican, French felt, was his man. Entrican was comparatively weak and fearful, and he felt sure, could be scared into some admission.

He determined to try Entrican, particularly as the man must already be panic-stricken as a result of Constable Jackson's revelations.

The same excuse he had used with Stowe could be employed to see Entrican. An hour later French and two helpers reached Mount Street. Leaving the helpers with their car in a side street, he asked for the secretary.

Entrican grew very uneasy on seeing his visitor. But French was polite in an offhand way. The vital question would have greater weight if it were unexpected. Therefore let the approach be reassuring.

He put his inquiry about Harrison's delay in France on the day before his disappearance. As he talked Entrican's relief obviously grew. He was only too anxious, he said, to help the chief inspector in any way he could, but of this matter he really knew nothing. Harrison hadn't mentioned it to him.

French accepted his statement and made as if to go, yet

lingered discussing the affair in a conversational way. He was confiding and allowed himself to be pumped. Then at last he thought the moment propitious.

'I can tell you in confidence,' he went on, 'for I know you won't repeat it, that we're just at the end of the case. We know practically everything that was done. It was quite a pretty conspiracy. The parties bought a second-hand Austin 20 and fitted it up so that they could flood the back compartment with ether and chloroform. They inveigled Harrison into the car at Dover, and while driving innocently along were gassing him. Then they gave him a hypodermic, took him to a certain shed in Tooting, kept him there for twenty-four hours and placed him, still unconscious, in a shelter on the platform of a small station near Ashford. We know everything except the identity of the men, and we're on the way to learn that.'

There was no question now of Entrican's frame of mind. He was panic-stricken; almost crazy with fear. French was careful to hide his satisfaction, and contentedly went on with the good work.

'Yes, they were a clever gang,' he declared reminiscently, 'but they just weren't clever enough. They made one big mistake. One of them sent a wire to the Ambrose Hotel in Folkestone, telling those in the car that Harrison had put off his return for twenty-four hours. Now we've only to find out who that was, to get the whole lot. And I'm expecting the information every minute. We have a squad going through all the messages sent during the morning of that day. As you doubtless know, messages are kept for some months. Probably the names may be false, but when we get a message about postponing operations for twenty-four hours, the handwriting will give us the rest. And of course we've got a connection between the abduction and the murder. You take my word for it, the whole lot'll hang inside of ten weeks.'

An entirely unforeseen difficulty now arose. Entrican's fear grew to such a pitch that French felt that if he didn't remark it, the man would guess his trick. He thought first of pretending that Entrican was ill, then of feigning illness himself. But in the end he took refuge in an old stand-by: his notebook. As he finished speaking he avoided looking at Entrican, but drew out the book and spent some time searching for imaginary items. Then when Entrican had somewhat recovered he replaced the book in his pocket, saying: 'Well, I see. I've covered everything I had to ask you about. I suppose you can't put me on to anyone who knew Mr Harrison's business on that day he stayed in Paris?'

Entrican busied himself in getting out whisky and soda, and was thus able to hide his face. But French refused a drink, and with thanks bowed himself out. He walked smartly away, but on rounding the corner drew up to his two assistants.

'I want you to watch the house,' he explained. 'I don't think you'll have long to wait. Carter and I'll sit here in the car, and you, Jones, go to the corner and give us the office if he comes out.'

But French seemed to have for once made a mistake. For two hours they waited, till he had all but decided to return to the Yard, leaving the others to carry on.

There was just one danger in the plan he had adopted. If Entrican was very weak and imaginative, he might commit suicide. French did not think for a moment that he would do so, but if he were guilty of the murder there was the possibility. He was therefore agreeably reassured when about five o'clock Jones signed that the man had left the house.

Carter had started up the engine every few minutes, to keep it hot and ensure a quick get away in case of need. Now a touch on the starter was alone required, and in a few seconds they had picked up Jones and were moving along Mount Street in pursuit. But the chase did not long remain so easy. In a few yards Entrican picked up a cruising taxi and it took all Carter's skill to keep the vehicle in sight.

They turned west into Park Lane, south to Piccadilly, round the elbow of the Green Park to Constitution Hill, past the front of Buckingham Palace and down Birdcage Walk.

'Looks like going home,' exclaimed Carter as they passed into Great George Street and across the end of Parliament Street to Bridge Street.

French did not reply, but when the quarry turned north along Victoria Embankment, he whistled. A few yards more and Entrican's taxi entered the gate of Scotland Yard.

'Drive past,' said French quickly. 'There's no need for him to know we've been shadowing him.'

A few yards further on French got out, and moving carefully back, entered the building by a private door. He beckoned a constable.

'If a man named Entrican has asked for me, have him shown to my room in half an hour.'

A little wait, French thought, would do the man no harm. He was well aware that solitary reflection in the atmosphere of the Yard had a salutary effect on the evildoer.

When at last Entrican was shown in, it was to find a very different French than he had up to then met. Instead of a genial and courteous greeting, he received an unsmiling stare and a curt request to state his business. He was no longer dealing with a frail human being, but with the inexorable might of the British realm.

'I rang you up to ask for an interview,' Entrican said hesitatingly.

'Yes. What is it?'

Entrican twitched. He was pitiably nervous. For a moment it seemed as if he would break off the interview and leave the room. But French knew he wouldn't.

'I want,' he went on presently, 'to make a statement.' He hesitated again. 'A confession really in a way.'

19

The Dover Episode

French looked at him coldly before replying. 'You should be careful about that,' he said judicially. 'Any statement you make will be taken down and may be given in evidence in court. It is my duty to warn you of that officially, but I may add unofficially that before making statements it's often wise to consult a solicitor.'

All this, while true and even kindly, had the effect for which French was striving. Entrican's nervousness increased. A sweat broke out on his forehead.

'No, really,' he returned, 'I want to tell you the whole truth. You frightened me this afternoon because I thought you might suspect me of something I hadn't done. I want to tell you exactly what happened. I have done wrong. I admit it, and I suppose I shall suffer for it. But I haven't done what you appear to think I had.'

French pressed a button on his desk. 'We'd better have a witness,' he said gravely, and when a constable entered, he went on: 'This man will take down anything you may care to say. You still wish to go on?'

'Yes, I do wish it.'

'Very well. You'll be asked to sign the statement. Begin it,' he turned to the constable, '"I, Henry Entrican, make the following statement of my own free will and desire and without any pressure having been brought on me to do so, and after having been warned that I am not bound to make any statement and that what I say will be taken down and may be used as evidence in any further proceedings." You agree to that?'

Entrican nodded. He seemed almost beyond speech.

French's severe manner relaxed and he became more his old pleasant self.

'Very well,' he said. 'Take your own time and tell me what you want me to know. Smoke if you wish to.'

Entrican moved uneasily on his chair, then took out his case and with trembling hands lit a cigarette. He seemed to find it impossible to begin. French did not help him.

'I have to confess,' he burst out suddenly after one or two false starts, 'that I was a party to the abduction of Mr Harrison. I had nothing to do with the actual affair, but I knew it was being done, and it was I who sent that telegram to the Ambrose Hotel at Folkestone.'

French gravely inclined his head, but without speaking.

'But,' went on Entrican desperately, 'that's all I did that was wrong. As far as the murder was concerned I knew nothing about it. I know nothing about it now. I don't even know who did it. Of that,' he spoke with the utmost earnestness, 'I am entirely innocent.'

This was almost word for word what French expected to hear. Whether Entrican were guilty or innocent, he would say the same thing. Unless some proof of the statement were forthcoming, it got them very little further on.

'I cannot advise you,' French returned, 'but it seems to me you have said so much that you must tell your whole story in detail. Would you care to do that now, or to wait for the advice of a solicitor?'

Though French knew that he was strictly correct in taking up this attitude, he believed also that nothing was more calculated to press Entrican on to a full confession. He was therefore not surprised to hear the man say that he must get the thing off his chest, and that as he was going to tell the truth and the truth only, he didn't want anyone's help.

'Very well. Go ahead.'

At first Entrican's statement was a little incoherent, but as he continued he seemed to recover confidence. 'I must begin,' he said, 'at the beginning and that was when I started gambling. I needn't go into that in detail, but I gambled over poker and other games until I lost a lot of money and got hard up. It's an old story of course, but it was new to me. Gradually my difficulties grew greater until at last I simply didn't know what to do or where to turn. I know I was weak, but I just couldn't stop.

'It mayn't sound much just to speak of like this, but when you're really facing the ruin of your whole life it's a different thing. It's more important than anything else. I was in such a state that I would have taken almost any way out that presented itself.

'Then a way did present itself. I knew it wasn't right. But it seemed a lot the lesser evil and I agreed to adopt it.

'Among those I had played with were two men; I think you know them, James Stowe and Sir Richard Moffatt. They were partners in the same sort of business as Mr Harrison, and I came across them first in connection with my job. As it chanced I lost a lot of money to Stowe. I also lost to Moffatt, though a smaller amount. However the amounts didn't matter, as I couldn't pay either. I now think,' he hesitated, 'no, perhaps I shouldn't say that. All I can stand over is that gambling brought me completely into their power.'

Whether Entrican's hesitation was genuine or assumed, French was not sure. But in either case his meaning was as clear as day. He suspected, or pretended to suspect, that he had been cheated.

'Then one evening matters came to a head. Stowe approached me for payment. He was quite polite about it. He said he'd had some bad losses himself, and must find five thousand pounds immediately. My debt was nothing like this: I owed him seven hundred odd. But he said he could only meet his own difficulties if all that was owing him were paid, and mine was an essential part of the debt. In short he said he must have the money. He said he deeply sympathised with me, but that it was a matter of his going under or of me, and if I could not produce the cash, he would have to go to Harrison. I said that wouldn't help him, that Harrison wouldn't pay, but he thought otherwise.

'Then Moffatt came up and said he had had bad luck too. He swore he was at the end of his resources and must have his money. I owed him a little less than three hundred, but I could no more pay three hundred than seven. After a miserable interview they gave me a week to find the thousand.

'I may tell you, Mr French, that if I'd had more nerve I'd have committed suicide. But I just couldn't bring myself to it. Always I thought something might happen to help me. And if the worst came to the worst I determined I'd realise all I had and go abroad and try to make a fresh start.

'At the end of the week we had another interview, and then Stowe put up what he called a way out for us all. There was a way, he said, by which we could make a lot of money: a very large sum for each of us. Moreover it would hurt no one, and though it was, or part of it was, illegal, it was not immoral. We could carry it through and still feel that we had done nothing very bad.

'Well, you seem to know what the scheme was. In a word it was to depress the Harrison stock, buy as much as possible, wait till the stock recovered, and sell. They estimated that with the resources they could muster, a profit of over a hundred thousand would be possible. They would not of course buy the stock outright. Before they had to pay it would have risen enough to sell at a great profit. I needn't go into the technical part of it. No doubt you understand how these things are done?'

Again French nodded without speaking. He was by no means well up in the methods of financier crooks, but he could find someone else to explain them.

'This seemed to me an admirable idea. If it was not wholly straight, it was being done on a smaller scale every day and no one thought anything but enviously of those who did it. I was delighted until I asked how it was to be done and discovered what you seem to know.

'Stowe had thought the whole thing out. There was to be a regular campaign. Rumours were first to be started that all was not well with the stock. No statements would be made, but questions would be asked. An influential foreign financier, for example, would be drawn aside, and under promise of secrecy, would be asked if the stock was all right. "I've heard rumours, my dear So-and-so, and as I have myself a fairly large holding, I've been a bit anxious.

I'm so relieved to hear that you think there's nothing in them." That sort of thing repeated in widely different places by different people—Stowe had a good many in his power who would do this for him—would soon produce a result. Each person consulted would himself mention it to others, and soon the rumours would grow and their source would be forgotten. Those rumours were bound to have an effect and the stock would fall.

'But Stowe was sure it wouldn't fall enough for our purpose. There would have to be an actual slump. And then he put forward the second step. Harrison was to disappear. At the same time the rumour that he had absconded with what was left of his money was to be started. If this happened, the stocks would simply collapse. Then if Harrison were to return, whether he said he had been the victim of an outrage or not, the stocks would bound up again. Then we would make our pile.

'This was all right except for the abduction of Harrison, and there I drew the line. I said I wouldn't have anything to do with it. Stowe said he had never intended that I should. He himself would handle that part of it. All I would have to do was to keep them posted about Harrison's movements, so that they could make their own arrangements. They made it clear that no more would be expected of me and that I should not even know how the abduction was done. Most solemnly they assured me that no harm of any kind would be done to Harrison, and I believed them, as his safe return was necessary for success. I was to get one-tenth of the profits and the others three-tenths each.'

For the first time French mentally registered a disagreement. Entrican was wrong in this. If Harrison had been proved to have been murdered, it would have produced the same result to his stocks. However he saw how a plausible ruffian like Stowe might overbear a weak man like Entrican.

'That's about the whole of the story. I spread no rumours: they agreed that in my position it would be inadvisable. But the stock began to fall and I knew they had been at work. Then I heard the rumours. At last Stowe came to me and asked for full details of Harrison's movements. I gave them to him for a fortnight. Presently he said they had decided to act when Harrison was returning from Paris. I was to know nothing about it, but they arranged that if I learned of any hitch or last-minute alteration I was to wire to that hotel in Folkestone, using assumed names. When I heard from Kemp that Harrison was staying that extra day I did send a wire: though how you got on to it I don't know.

'There's just one thing more to be said, though it's the most important of all. It was your remark that if you knew the abductors, you would know the murderers. That's not true.' Entrican's voice grew more earnest than ever. 'I know nothing whatever about the murder. I don't even suspect anyone.' He hesitated and hung his head. 'I admit I did suspect Stowe or Moffatt at first. But in talk with them I soon came to see that I was wrong. They were as much puzzled about the affair as I.'

The voice ceased, and for a time French did not reply. This story was plausible—indeed likely. Every word of it might be true. And Entrican's manner was reasonably natural. On this latter point French would not have cared to bank a lot, but at least there was nothing suspicious in the way the man had spoken.

On the other hand if Entrican were guilty, this was just the kind of tale he would tell. He had admitted only what he saw French already knew: what he could no longer keep hidden. Was this merely the attempt usual under such circumstances, to shift the major responsibility on to someone else's shoulders?

'Did you hear the details of how the kidnapping was carried out?' French asked presently.

Once again Entrican spoke unwillingly. 'Yes, I insisted on being told what was to be done, to satisfy myself that no real harm was intended.'

'Then you can answer some questions. Who drove the car and accosted Harrison at Dover Station?'

Entrican hesitated, obviously unwilling to reply.

'You may as well answer,' French went on. 'We know so much that we'll find him in a few hours in any case. I don't say it'll do much for you, but to help the police at least won't do you any harm.'

'A man called Peter Jepton, a friend of Stowe's.'

'His address?'

'I don't know. I've only met him through Stowe.'

'Very well. Now how did Jepton get Harrison to agree to go off with him?'

'He was made up as a porter at a hospital. He said that Mrs Harrison had been motoring near Folkestone and had had a collision and was in the Folkestone Hospital, dangerously injured. He said he had been sent by the hospital authorities to drive Harrison over.'

'Harrison evidently believed it.'

'They chose that story for another reason. The ether and chloroform mixture had a smell. They had a little gas in the car when Harrison got in, so that he might smell it at once and not when it came on later. Jepton apologised for it, saying they had had to carry an accident case in the car earlier in the day. It was cold and raining, and Harrison

262

didn't try to lower the windows. As a matter of fact, they were wedged, and if he had remarked on it, he would have been told they were out of order. Also, Harrison was asked not to smoke, on the ground that the smell would be offensive to subsequent patients. As you probably know, ether and chloroform make an explosive mixture.'

'How,' French went on slowly, as he assimilated this information, 'did Stowe know the amount of this gas to give? And who gave the hypodermics?'

Again Entrican seemed overwhelmed at the extent of French's knowledge. 'Jepton had partly trained for medicine,' he explained. 'His father died leaving hiin too badly off to finish his course, and he had to go into business.'

'Why did they drive Harrison to Town instead of to some place near the coast?'

'They all wanted to be at business next day. If Harrison had been left say in Dover or Folkestone, one of them would have had to remain with him. As it was they were away one day only, for liberating him was done at night.'

'I follow.' French considered. 'A message was sent to the *Westminster Guardian*. Do you know anything about that?'

'Yes, that was part of Stowe's scheme, and Stowe was to send it himself. I don't know if he did so, but I imagine he must have. He thought that a mere disappearance would not be enough. There must be something definitely suspicious about it, and Stowe invented that story of Harrison going to the lavatory and changing his clothes to suggest a flight.'

'It was well thought out at all events. Well now, is that all about the abduction?' French considered again. 'Yes, I think so. Now turn to another point. How did the scheme succeed?'

'I don't follow you.'

'I mean, what did you make out of it?'

French was surprised to find that for the first time Entrican hedged. The question was clearly most unwelcome. French could not see why. The really serious matters had already been dealt with. Concealing his re-awakened interest, he determined to continue to probe the matter till he was satisfied that no further secrets lay hidden beneath it.

'Not very much,' Entrican declared. 'The fall and rise again were not so great as Stowe had anticipated.'

'Well, you can surely tell me more than that? You know I'll have to check it all up, so it will save me trouble and won't make any difference to you.'

Entrican grew more and more uncomfortable, and French correspondingly keener.

'As a matter of fact, I can't answer that question, for the thing hasn't been settled up yet. I don't think it was very much.'

'Did you have any talk with Stowe about it?'

'Oh yes, I did. But as I say, nothing was settled as to how much I was to get. All I know is that he was disappointed himself.'

'Then he has the money—much or little?'

Entrican hesitated. 'I suppose so,' he said doubtfully.

French wondered what all this was leading to. It now seemed quite clear that the man was lying, whatever he might have been doing before. He shook his head and once again grew stern.

'Come now, Mr Entrican,' he said, 'that won't do. You can't expect me to believe that you don't know all about it. Listen to me,' he held up his hand as Entrican began another denial, 'I'm going to know everything about this matter. If you don't tell what you know now, I'll find it out elsewhere. I know so much that nothing can prevent me learning the rest. Now if you keep something back, it'll also be my business to find out why you've done so, because you must have a reason. I didn't ask you for this statement, but remember that partial statement is worse than none.'

Entrican did not reply. He was evidently thinking deeply. French kept silence for a little and then went on: 'I wish to remind you of the warning I gave you, and if you would like professional advice before deciding to answer or to keep silence, you are entitled to have it. It is however only fair to point out what suspicions that will raise: now that you've gone so far.'

That did it. French could see the fear in the man's eyes. He made a gesture of despair, then burst out: 'Yes, I was trying to hide that! I know the circumstances looks badly, but it's the truth. And the whole of what I'm telling you is the truth.'

French shrugged. 'As you like,' he said indifferently.

Sweat again shone on the man's head, and again he surreptitiously wiped it off. 'I see I must tell you,' he went on. 'I would rather not, because I can't help seeing how badly it must look. But I can't help it. You've got me cornered.'

'If you're innocent to tell the whole truth is your best policy.'

'I know: I believe you're right. I'll tell you everything. The truth is that Stowe got very little out of it because Harrison discovered what had been done and blackmailed him for the return of practically all he made.'

French all but whistled. Was the man mad? Handing over

265

a motive for murder, complete, cut and dried and entirely adequate! No wonder he hadn't wished to reveal that particular item! But French felt his own conscience was clear. He had kept most scrupulously to the judges' rules. And after all, from his own point of view, Entrican had done the wise thing. If he, French, had found this out otherwise, nothing could have persuaded him that he was other than guilty.

He nodded, striving to appear unimpressed. 'That's more likely,' he approved. 'How exactly did Harrison make the discovery?'

'He woke while they were giving him the hypodermic. He was too drowsy to make any actual move, but he saw Stowe and Moffatt. I don't think he knew Jepton, but of that I'm not sure.'

'I see. And what, did he do?'

'He told Stowe afterwards that when he got to Ashford and saw the morning paper, he was amazed because it was a day too late. Then when he saw how his stock had fallen he realised the whole thing. He at first intended to go straight to the police, then it occurred to him that Stowe must have made a pile out of it, and that if he could get the money it would punish Stowe and repay himself at the same time. So he said nothing, but gave out a tale that he had been on a yacht.'

Here was the answer to another of French's puzzles. Why, he had wondered, if Harrison had been kidnapped, had he concealed the fact? Simply to get Stowe & Co.'s money! If he had had them sent to jail, he would have forfeited that!

How fully Kemp's opinion of the man had been justified! Kemp had said that he would back Harrison to turn any circumstances to his own advantage. Here a fraud had been committed upon him, or upon his stockholders as the case might be, and he had scooped the profits for himself! And not only that, he had seen how to commit practically the same fraud, and to make another pile in that way. He had made, so Kemp had said, over £100,000 by buying and selling himself. How much had he got from Stowe? French put the question to Entrican.

'Stowe said he had made £118,000. Harrison had estimated this, though he hadn't known the exact figure. But he knew it must be above a hundred thousand. He said he would take the hundred thousand and leave Stowe the rest, whatever it was, for his trouble. I got about eighteen hundred.'

'I don't think you did so badly,' French declared dryly.

Eighteen hundred for Entrican, and prison looming in front of him, if not worse. Over two hundred thousand for Harrison, and death what he actually achieved. And what for Stowe and his two friends? No doubt between five and six thousand each. *And* in all probability the condemned cell and the scaffold. Truly the ways of transgressors were not easy.

But French could do his moralising later. He considered if there was anything he had omitted to ask his visitor. Then he saw that there was.

'Now,' he went on, 'that night: of yours in Town, the night Mr Harrison was murdered. You gave me a detailed account of how you spent that night. Do you still stick to your former statement, or would you like to modify it in the light of what you have now told me?'

It was a shot more or less in the dark, but French knew that he would have to re-test the alibi, and if further light could be thrown on it, so much the better. But Entrican now seemed broken and without further fight in him, and it produced more than he could reasonably have expected.

'No, Chief Inspector,' the man replied, 'that story was only partially true. I see I needn't try to keep anything back, so I'll tell you. I didn't dine that evening with a lady: I was at Stowe's. Stowe rang me up that afternoon. We had a short code for speaking over the telephone, so that if by chance we were overheard, no one would be any the wiser. If he talked, for instance, about the flowers in his garden, it meant that he wanted to see me that night at dinner at his house. On that day before Harrison's—death, he rang me up and gave that message. I dined at his house with Moffatt and Jepton. Mrs Stowe was from home.'

'I see. Was that to talk business?'

'Yes. Harrison had found out then and offered his terms. That was on the previous Monday, when Stowe and Moffatt dined on the *Cygnet*. He had then given Stowe a week to think the matter over, so we had to settle something by the following day. We had had one or two consultations, and this meeting was to take a final decision.'

'And did you take the decision?'

'Yes, we decided to pay up. After all we had eighteen thousand among us. It not only paid our debts, but left us a bit over. I thought we got out of it well, and so did everyone except Stowe. He was annoyed at having been outwitted, though he came round to our view before we parted.'

'And what did you do then?'

'Just what I already told you. I went to the Piccadilly Palace Hotel and stayed the night. I could have gone back to Henley, but I hadn't known how long I should be detained at Stowe's and so had asked for the night's leave.'

French whistled gently as he thought over all this. Now he really did appear to have the whole story: all except the chief item. But he could not expect Entrican to tell of that crucial point. Who had committed the murder? Was it Entrican? Or Stowe? Or one of the other members of the conspiracy? Or a combination of them?

On the face of it, Stowe, though this was not in any way proven. Stowe certainly had the strongest motive. In addition to the loss of some £30,000, he had his wounded self-love. Entrican had lost some £10,000, and that of course was a strong enough motive. But as he truly said, he had got out of his difficulties and had £800 as well. French was sure that escape from his troubles would have counted with him more than this unexpected windfall. The others apparently had to face a loss of the same amount as Stowe.

Would they have saved it by the murder? Had they in point of fact saved it? This was one of the many points French had still to find out. In any case, was it theirs legally? Or would the law take it from them? And if it took it from them, what would it do with it?

French was thankful these questions were not for him. But he had his own. The first was pressing: should he arrest Entrican? If he did so, it would tell the others what was on the cards. If not, Entrican would do the telling. Which would be the better?

He temporised in the end. 'Now before you go, Mr Entrican,' he said, 'I shall want you to sign your statement. I'm afraid I shall have to ask you to wait in another room till it's typed. Show Mr Entrican to a waiting room, constable, and then get on with that typing at once.'

By the time the signing was completed he had made up

his mind. Again he temporised. Entrican would be 'detained' till he was able to make some further enquiries. And he would himself get his questions in to Stowe and the others before they heard the news.

20

The Faulty Alibi

French had now two principal lines of enquiry stretching out before him: the activities firstly of Jepton, and secondly of Stowe and Moffatt, for these last French had got into the habit of classing together.

First then, Jepton. What was his address, and was he the man who had driven the Austin 20? These questions settled, French would turn to that other: Had Jepton taken part in the murder?

How was the address to be obtained? French did not wish to ask Stowe. It was important that the man should remain unprepared for his own interrogation.

He thought the address might be had in a simpler way. Stowe and Moffatt were men of position. It was unlikely that they would associate with a nobody. Jepton's name would almost certainly be in a directory.

A search immediately embarrassed him, not by scarcity, but by riches. There were many Peter Jeptons in London alone. Well, that was a problem of a very familiar type.

He sent for a junior and instructed him to find out if any

of those mentioned suited the description of the driver of the Dover car. If he found such a man he was not to let him know he was the subject of enquiries, but to report to French.

Then he went to see Stowe at his office. But here he had no luck. Both Stowe and Moffatt were in Denmark, though expected back in a couple of days.

However, it turned out that he was not to be idle after all. He had scarcely regained his room when he had a phone from the young constable. The very first Peter Jepton on his list answered the description. He had a flat in a large block in Sutherland Avenue off Maida Vale. The constable had ascertained also—from the porter—that he had some business in the City to which he went every day. He was supposed to be well enough to do, though evidently not lavish in the matter of tips. He kept late hours and was believed to 'see life' in the evenings. He had an NJ sports car, registration number AIZ–0004 and powerful in everything except the silencer.

All this seemed promising to French. After a few moments' thought he made two further telephone calls. First he rang up the local Maida Vale police and got them to undertake some arrangements. Then he spoke to the garage at Hammersmith at which the Austin 20 had been sold.

As a result of these arrangements an interesting meeting took place at nine o'clock that night at the police station. French arrived there a little before the time and had a chat with the officer in charge.

'Yes,' the officer said, 'he'll be here all right. I sent a letter as you suggested.' He handed over a carbon and French read:

Peter Jepton, Esq.,
The Cantamary Building,
Sutherland Avenue.

SIR,—As you are doubtless aware, a fatal accident took place in Edgware Road on the evening of the 14th inst., and we are informed that your car, No. AIZ–0004, was standing at the place at the time.

I should be obliged if you would make it convenient to call at 9 p.m. tonight in order to give us any information on the matter which you may possess.

Yours faithfully,
    J. G. HARGREAVES,
    Supt.

'That'll bring him, you think?'

'Yes, I sent it with a constable. He'll be here.'

'Well, my man from the garage will be here too. Where will you put him?'

'Down in our store off the staircase. There's a good light on the stairs and he should see anyone coming up. He'll be hidden himself of course. I've fixed up half a dozen other people.'

As he spoke the man who had sold the Austin 20 was shown in. French introduced him and explained what he wanted him to do. The man was quite keen to act, and took up his position behind the open door of the store with every sign of enjoyment. Presently a constable came to say that Jepton had arrived

and French himself went into retreat in a small ante-room, the door of which was left slightly ajar. He could hear what went on, as well as seeing between the hinges a narrow vertical section of the room.

'Let him wait,' said the super, and rang up Jepton's number. There was no reply and he got the porter at the Cantamary Building. 'I asked Mr Jepton to step round here tonight in connection with a motor accident case. If he has not left, will you please tell him we have got the information we required, and that he needn't come. You might apologise from us for the trouble we gave him.' He turned to the constable.

'Now get those other people upstairs and let Jepton follow.'

A number of men as like Jepton as could be found had been asked to call at the station, and at irregular intervals these were sent up past the waiting garage attendant. Jepton followed them and entered the room. The super stood up. 'I've just been ringing you up, sir,' he declared politely. 'I'm sorry to say that you were sent for in error, and I've just been ringing up to try to stop your coming and to offer you our apologies for having troubled you. Will you sit down for a moment and let me explain?'

Jepton was inclined to take a high hand, but French could see the relief in his face, and he evidently could not bring himself to be unpleasant.

The superintendent told a smooth yarn about a report coming in of the accident and the sports car, and of a typist's error which had just been discovered in the car registration. 'It should have been AOZ, not AIZ,' he declared, adding: 'I have reprimanded the typist severely, and I trust you will accept this apology and not ask for further disciplinary measures to be taken against him.'

Jepton had some sarcastic remarks to make, but he was soon got rid of, and French with some eagerness went to question the garage hand.

'That was 'im, that last was,' the man declared promptly. 'I'd swear to 'im anywhere. 'E's the man wot bought the Austin and took 'er away.'

The station sergeant had been instructed to detain Jepton in talk for a few moments, and as soon as the garage man had been thanked and sent home from a side door, the super put his head into the charge-room.

'Mr Jepton there still?' he asked. 'I wonder, sir, if you would come back for a moment? There is a question we want to ask you.'

Rather unwillingly Jepton returned. The super indicated French. 'A chief inspector from Scotland Yard, sir. He would like to ask you a question or two.'

'Yes, Mr Jepton,' French added. 'Will you sit down?'

That Jepton had suddenly grown nervous he could see at a glance. But his manner remained unpleasant as he answered: 'What is it now?'

'It's this, sir,' French said gravely, and both he and the super watched the other unblinkingly. 'I'm in charge of the case about the late Mr Harrison, and I have here a statement which I should like to read to you. After that I should like your comments, though it is my duty to warn you that you need not make any unless you like,' and he went on to give the usual official caution.

Jepton attempted to bluff, but fear showed in his eyes, and French with a thrill of satisfaction realised that at last he was on the right track. He took an official looking paper from his pocket and pretended to refresh his memory.

'It is alleged,' he went on, 'that Mr James Stowe, Sir Richard Moffatt, Mr Henry Entrican and yourself entered into a conspiracy to kidnap—and actually did kidnap—the late Mr Andrew Harrison, with the object of fraudulently depressing his stocks so that you might make money. The method,' French tapped his paper, 'is given in detail. The purchase of the Austin 20, the story of Mrs Harrison's alleged accident, the ether and chloroform in the car, the hypodermic injections, the shed in Tooting, and so on: I needn't weary you with the full story. All I want to ask you is: bearing in mind the warning I gave you, have you anything to say on the matter?'

Jepton evidently found it difficult to speak. He made more than one effort, then burst out in a hoarse voice. 'It's a lie! The whole thing's a damned lie! I don't even know what you're talking about. I never heard of those men you mention. If there's any truth at all in your story, you've got hold of the wrong man.'

'I hardly think so,' French returned. 'Do you deny, for instance, calling at the Ambrose Hotel in Folkestone on your way to Dover?'

'Of course I deny it.'

'And if I brought witnesses into court who swore they had seen you there on that occasion, it would be a lie?'

'Yes, I told you so. A complete lie.'

'But if the garage man at Henderson's garage at Hammersmith, and the other garage officials at the Vulcan Garage at Bristol, and a passenger who was in the next compartment to Mr Harrison when he was called away by the spurious hospital porter, and the driver of the hired car who was waiting for his fate off the steamer at Dover, and the convalescent taximan who lived opposite the shed in Tooting—if all these and certain others were to swear to you, you surely wouldn't still deny it?'

Jepton gazed vacantly before him in amazement and consternation. He was clearly so much taken aback that he did not know what line to take. French changed his tone.

'Come now, Jepton, don't be a fool. The game's up, and you know it. From what I've said you must see that we know all about the abduction. However, that's not what I want to talk to you about. It's a much more serious matter. You know that the late Mr Harrison was murdered by filling up his cabin with carbonic acid gas through the porthole?'

The colour slowly faded from Jepton's cheeks. He sat gazing speechlessly at French, clearly unable to reply.

'Now,' French went on, 'I'm not making any accusation, but if you care to make any statement about your movements on the night of the murder I shall be glad to listen. As I said, you needn't do so. Or, if you prefer, you may send for a solicitor and consult him before answering.'

'For some moments there was silence, while Jepton made strenuous efforts for self-control. Then at last he spoke, in a low hoarse voice.

'I admit the abduction,' he said slowly. 'You evidently know all about it. And you're right. I took part in it. But you're utterly and absolutely wrong if you try to connect the abduction with the murder. I'm innocent of that, and I'm as certain as I'm alive that the others are too.' The colour began to creep back into his face. 'You gave me a bad fright, and I don't know what right you had to do it. Luckily for me, I can prove my innocence. God help the poor devils you get your claws into who can't.'

'You have no grievance whatever,' French returned mildly. 'I didn't accuse you of the murder. I asked you if you cared to make a statement about it. Now you say you can prove your innocence. That's exactly what I wanted to know. If you can give me proof, the matter of the murder is at an end so far as you're concerned: though the abduction is not.'

The last phrase brought Jepton back to earth. He forgot his righteous indignation. 'I can prove I am innocent of the murder,' he answered, 'because on that night I slept in the Princes Street Station Hotel in Edinburgh.'

French nodded. 'That's all right. That will be enquired into and if found to be true will be entirely satisfactory. But it would be better if you would give me the names of some other people whom you saw in Edinburgh. If possible on the evening before and the morning after.'

Jepton eagerly agreed, and French took his detailed statement. 'I'm sorry,' French went on, 'we shall have to detain you here until the question of a charge for the abduction is decided. You'll not be uncomfortable, and you can get anything you like to pay for. A decision will be reached as soon as possible.'

Ten minutes later French was speaking to the chief officer of the Edinburgh police and arranging for a series of enquires to be made which would definitely establish or break down Jepton's alibi.

When he returned after lunch next day a reply was waiting for him. A detailed investigation had been made and the fact that Jepton had passed the night in Edinburgh had been established beyond question. So far as the murder was concerned, then, Jepton was definitely innocent.

French felt he could not continue to detain the man on the lesser charge, but he was so anxious to prevent a warning being conveyed to Stowe or Moffatt that he stretched his conscience a little and kept the Edinburgh reply to himself. After all it was only for another night. His remaining two suspects would be back on the following morning, and he would see them at once. Jepton could then be released, and probably Entrican also.

Next morning a polite though urgent summons brought Stowe and Moffatt to the Yard. French took Stowe first. He conducted the interview very much as he had that with Jepton on the previous evening. Producing his paper he pretended to read from it the details of the kidnapping. Stowe took it differently from Jepton. Motionless, his face an inscrutable mask, he sat listening. He heard French to the end, nodded slightly and remained silent.

'Do you care to make any statement on the subject?' asked French at last.

'No,' Stowe returned. 'Why should I?'

'You realise that there will probably be a charge against you gentlemen?'

'No, I don't. Why should there be?'

'Well, perhaps you are not aware that abduction is contrary to English law?'

'That doesn't interest me. I had nothing to do with any abduction.'

French shook his head. 'I'm afraid, Mr Stowe, you won't get any British judge or jury to agree with that. Remember I can prove in court all I told you.'

'I don't care if you can prove it in Hades. It doesn't affect me.'

'Perhaps you'd care to explain that?'

'There's nothing to explain about it. People are only kidnapped or abducted when they are taken into custody against their will. If they arrange with their so-called captors to put over a little play acting, they have every right to do so.'

'Is your statement then that the late Mr Harrison entered into a conspiracy with you to fake an abduction?'

'I object to your offensive choice of words, but otherwise that is my statement. Now it's my turn to ask a question. What business of yours is it? And if you still think it is your business, what do you propose to do about it?'

'What proof can you offer that Harrison was party to the affair?'

'I'm not bound to offer any proof. It's your job to get what proof you want. If Harrison was not party to it, why did he keep it dark and give out that tale about the yacht? Again, if you investigate a little further than you've gone, you'll find that Harrison made the same use of it that we did. You didn't know he made a cool hundred thousand for himself out of it?'

'Did you have an interview with Harrison in his cabin on the *Cygnet* on the Monday before his death?'

'What's that got to do with it? As a matter of fact, Moffatt and I did meet him.'

'Do you deny that at that meeting he charged you with the abduction and threatened that unless you paid him a hundred thousand out of what you had made—leaving some eighteen thousand for you to divide up among you—he would proceed against you?'

'Of course I deny it. See here, Chief Inspector, just what are you getting at?'

'It happens that interview was overheard. If a witness were to swear in court that Harrison was blackmailing you to the extent of a hundred thousand, you would deny it?'

'Of course I'd deny it. I'm getting tired of this. Will you soon have finished?'

French shrugged. 'Very well, it'll be a matter for the jury

280

to decide between you. But that really isn't what I wanted to speak to you about. It's—'

'Then what in Hades are you wasting time for?' Stowe broke in offensively.

'It's something much more serious,' went on French imperturbably. 'You are aware of course that Mr Harrison was murdered by filling up his cabin through the porthole with carbonic acid gas. Now having repeated my warning, would you care to say where you were that night?'

For a moment Stowe did not reply. 'Does that mean,' he then asked quietly, 'that you're accusing me of murdering him?'

'No, sir,' French answered, 'it does not. You can see for yourself that the circumstances are suspicious. I am giving you the chance to dispel that suspicion. You can take it or leave it as you think best.'

This time Stowe did not reply for quite a long time. He was evidently thinking intently. Then at last he seemed to come to a decision. 'I see your point,' he said, still in that slow steady voice. 'I admit there's something in it. If I don't satisfy you of my innocence of the murder, you'll make a lot of trouble.' His tone grew sarcastic. 'Well, I suppose I can't blame you. You're blundering on trying to do your best. You want me to tell you where I was that night? Well, I can do so. I was at home: at my house.'

'Any proof of that?'

'Only the proof that anyone can give for such a statement. For heaven's sake, Chief Inspector, use your brains. What sort of proof do you expect me to give? That I had a dozen policemen in my room all night?'

'Now, sir, none of that will help you. I asked you if you could give any proof that you were at home that night. Can you?'

As the man did not reply French continued. 'Let's take the night in detail. Had you anyone in for dinner?'

Stowe looked decidedly evil: venomous, French thought. But after a moment's thought he said, 'Yes, Moffatt, Jepton and Entrican. Any objection?'

'About what time did they leave?'

'Jepton and Entrican together about ten, I think: I don't really remember. Moffatt stayed on after them till eleven or later.'

'Very well, when Sir Richard Moffatt left who remained in the house with you?'

'Only the servants; the parlour maid and cook. Mrs Stowe was from home.'

'Did the servants know if you were in or out?'

'How could I tell you that? If they were awake they would have heard me going upstairs, and I answered their knock in the morning. You'd better ask them.'

'That's already been attended to, sir,' French replied mendaciously.

Was he mistaken, or did there flicker a momentary expression of fear in Stowe's eyes? If there did, it was instantly gone. But French felt a sudden quickening of interest, and registered a vow that when he did question the servants, it would be properly done.

He asked Stowe to wait and turned his attention to Moffatt. But Moffatt told the same story. Whether it was the truth or whether the two men had made it up together, French did not know. Moffatt said he had left Stowe's a few minutes after eleven and gone straight home to Esher. He couldn't say whether anyone had heard him coming in, but he thought it unlikely.

Moffatt was asked to wait in his turn, and French went

out to interview the servants in both houses. He could not risk their being put on their guard, and in so serious a case he knew he had a perfect right to detain the employers while enquiries were being made.

With Carter he drove to Hampstead. Stowe's house was small, but stood in its own tiny piece of ground. The door was opened by a maid of a good type; decent and reliable looking.

'Is Mrs Stowe at home?' French asked.

'No, sir, she's gone out. Who shall I say?'

Though it did not matter very much, French was pleased. 'I'm an inspector of police from Scotland Yard,' he told her. 'I wanted to ask a question of Mrs Stowe, but I expect you can give me the information. May we come in for a moment?'

She hesitated, and he smiled.

'You'd like to be sure I am what I profess,' he said pleasantly. 'Well, you're very wise to be careful. Have you ever seen a police card?'

'Yes, sir: my father was in the force.'

'Ah, then you'll recognise this.' He handed her his own card, and without a word she led them into a sitting-room.

'It's about the events on a certain evening some four weeks ago. I've already been with Mr Stowe about it and he can't remember. Perhaps you can. On that evening Mrs Stowe was from home and Mr Stowe had three men to dinner: Sir Richard Moffatt, Mr Jepton and Mr Entrican. Does that bring the evening to your memory?'

'Yes, I remember the evening you mean.'

'Good,' French's manner was easy and encouraging. 'Now can you tell me the time at which everyone left?'

The woman shook her head. She was sorry, but she really couldn't remember.

French settled down to probe. Had she seen them going out? Had she heard them? Had she been in the sitting-room after they had gone? Had she seen Stowe going up to bed? Or heard him? Every detail that French could think of he asked about. Often he had been surprised how successfully systematic questioning brought forgotten facts into the memory.

On this occasion it worked better than he could have expected. But it was only a chance word that revealed the invaluable information. She had at last remembered that Jepton and Entrican had left early, because shortly after ten she had gone to the study to enquire if Stowe wanted anything more, as she wished to go to bed. Then he and Moffatt were alone.

'And did you hear Sir Richard go?' French asked.

It was in reply to this that the word was dropped. 'Yes,' she answered, 'they went out shortly after.' French thought it was a slip, but when he asked about it, he found it wasn't. 'They' was the word she had intended to use.

'You mean,' French went on, 'that Mr Stowe went out with Sir Richard?'

'Yes, he must have done. I heard their voices in the hall and the door shutting and then silence. If Mr Stowe hadn't gone too, I'd have heard him going up to bed.'

This seemed to French extremely interesting, but it was not till he asked his next question that he really grasped the significance of the reply. 'I suppose you didn't hear him come in again?'

'It just happens I did, sir. Your asking all those questions brings it back to me. I wasn't feeling too well that night and I didn't sleep. I heard Mr Stowe coming in and going up to bed.'

'About what time was that?'

'It was very late, or early, rather. It was close on five. I remember thinking he wouldn't be going to business that morning.'

With an immense effort French controlled himself.

'No,' he said with an easy smile: 'I suppose if you play all night you can't work all day. And did he go to business?'

'He did, and it surprised me. He got up at his usual time and went off as if he'd had the whole night in bed.'

French continued with his questions to prevent the woman suspecting the value of what she had told him, but when he was once clear of the house he let his imagination have its way. Here at last was the answer to his problem, the solution of the mystery! Stowe—and probably Moffatt also—had been out between the approximate hours of eleven and five on the night of Harrison's murder. To have taken a car, gone from Hampstead to Henley, got out the Coleman boat, pumped the gas into the cabin, replaced the boat, cleared all the apparatus away and returned to Town, would have taken—he must go into that, but he imagined anything from four to six hours. At last he had found something that worked in.

'We'll go down to Esher and see if we can get a similar line on Moffatt,' French concluded. 'The two beauties can just wait at the Yard.'

The visit to Sir Richard's flat was not, however, so profitable. There no one remembered the night, and no one could tell when the man came in and went out. He had a key and he could have let himself in at any time and slipped quietly up to bed unheard.

This testimony, though not helpful, at least was not destructive to French's theory. Moffatt could have been with Stowe.

French wondered if he now had enough evidence to justify an arrest. Admittedly he had not enough for court. Alternatively he could detain the men for about a week. Surely by that time he would have obtained the proof he required.

He had no longer any doubt as to what had happened. If Stowe were out on legitimate business, he wouldn't have lied about it.

But how to get the proof? The whole affair had been so well covered up that this seemed almost impossible. And unless he saw how to obtain it, he'd have to let the men go. A search warrant could be had of course, and a careful examination of their papers might be useful. But he feared it was unlikely. By no means clear as to his next step, French returned to the Yard.

21

The Elusive Truth

Some further thought suggested to French that once again his most promising line of enquiry was the questioning of Stowe himself.

He therefore sent for him, and he was pleased to find it was a different Stowe who was shown in. Those hours of waiting had had their effect. Gone was the truculence, the aggressiveness and the scorn. Stowe was now frightened. He was anxious to do what he could to satisfy French and regain his liberty.

'A matter has arisen for which an explanation is required,' French told him. 'You may feel disposed to give it: you may not. But you will see that our future action depends on which you do. You told me that you spent the night of Sunday, the 11th of July, in your house?'

'Well, and what if I did?'

'Simply that the statement wasn't true. We know you were out that night. We are in a position to prove you left your house about eleven with Sir Richard Moffatt and returned about five the following morning. Do you care to give an explanation of this?'

French could see the man's alarm increase, but he was game and hid it creditably.

'How can you prove that?' he asked with assumed carelessness.

'That I can't go into. You'll have to take my word for it.'

Stowe sat silent, lost in thought. French could not help admiring him. He was doing what everyone ought to do in the crises of life and what so few accomplish: thinking the thing through before he made a move. No doubt he would come to a decision on the best that he could see, and then he would carry it through irrespective of the consequences. French did not interrupt him.

'Well, Chief Inspector,' he said at last, 'I must presume you know what you're talking about. Am I to understand that if you don't get the truth of this matter, you'll charge me with murder?'

'That's not in my hands. But you can form your own conclusions.'

Stowe nodded. 'I can see what that means. Then I must tell you where I was that night in order to satisfy you. It's true I left my house with Moffatt about eleven and didn't return till about five. I presume the source from which you learnt that told you also that it was not an uncommon thing for me to do? In fact it was a frequent thing. I don't go to business every day. I frequently spend the night out, and sleep late next day. You know that?'

'Please go ahead, Mr Stowe.'

'I go on these occasions to a gambling club in Brigadier Street. I suppose owing to your confoundedly muddled thinking all this about the club will have to come out. Very well, curse you, I'll tell you. It's my club. I've been running it for years. Roulette and so on. I give people what they want and what they're ready to pay for, but what our grandmothers in Parliament think is bad for them. Well, I've done no harm, even if it is against the laws of this mad country. If you must know, I was there on the night of Harrison's death. And so was Moffatt. Now are you satisfied? I suppose there'll be a charge for running illegal gaming rooms? Very well, get along and make it.'

'I suppose there will be a charge for that,' French said slowly, as he thought over what he had heard. This was a nasty blow. Not that he wished the man evil, but if Stowe and Moffatt were at this place, they were certainly innocent. And Stowe was not likely to put up a story which could so easily be tested, unless it were true.

'I should like a few more details,' French went on. 'The address, the manager's name, and so on.'

Stowe gave them willingly enough. However French could only tell him that his detention would, have to continue till they were checked.

At one o'clock on the following morning French and Carter presented themselves at the address in Brigadier Street. Knocking by the code Stowe had mentioned, the door was opened and he put his foot in it before it could be closed again. He showed his card to the porter.

'I know all about your gambling rooms,' he said, 'but I'm not interested in that at present. There's not going to be a raid and you needn't make a fuss. I want to see your manager on another matter. Kindly send for him and I'll wait here.'

Two minutes later an apprehensive looking manager entered hurriedly.

'It's not a raid,' French reassured him. 'I just want a word with you in private.'

Still extremely suspicious, the manager led him to a small office.

'I've come from Mr Stowe,' French went on. 'I've heard from him all about these rooms and the gambling that goes on and your name and the entering code of knocks and so on. I don't say there won't be a prosecution about it later, but I'm not interested in that now. What I want is a list of the people who were here on the night of Sunday, the 11th of July last. Mr Stowe tells me you have the information.'

The manager hesitated.

'I'm not bound to offer explanations,' French added, 'but it's a question of an alibi for a wanted man.'

The manager seemed relieved. 'I'll get you the names,' he said. 'The list will take a little time to make out, as our roll is not kept in the usual form. But you can have it in fifteen minutes.'

'That'll do.'

Twenty minutes later the manager returned with the list. 'It's a night I happen to remember,' he remarked as he handed it over. 'One of our members got a fainting fit and I was scared I should have to bring in a doctor. However he came round all right in a few minutes.'

'Is his name here?' French asked, pointing to the list.

'Yes, it's there. Henderson, if you don't believe me.'

'I don't question your statement,' French assured him while he mentally congratulated himself for this fortunate coincidence. Not only was there documentary evidence as to those present, but the attack would identify the night in question in their minds. He glanced at the list. Yes, Henderson's, Stowe's and Moffatt's names were all there.

'Can you tell me at what hour Mr Stowe arrived and left on that night?'

The manager glanced up quickly, surprise and consternation in his eyes. 'You mean—' he retorted, and as quickly checked himself.

French shook his head. 'Don't mind what I mean,' he advised. 'I'm just making general enquiries. Can you remember?'

'I can't answer the question,' the manager replied. 'I remember that Mr Stowe was here that night, as he and Sir Richard Moffatt and I discussed sending for the doctor when Mr Henderson fainted. But more than that I can't recall.'

'About what time did the fainting fit take place?'

The manager consulted the porter. They agreed it must have been about two in the morning.

If these statements were true it settled the larger matter for both Stowe and Moffatt. And French could see no reason why they should not be true. However he had enough information to settle the matter. An interrogation of those on the list would give him the truth. If a story were faked, with so many witnesses it was absolutely certain to break down on details.

To test the matter was French's next step. A careful examination of those who had been present convinced him that the story was true. He could not doubt that both Stowe and Moffatt had been in Brigadier Street for the greater part of that night.

French's disappointment almost amounted to consternation. He had four suspects and all of them had alibis. Entrican was at the Piccadilly Palace, Jepton in Edinburgh, and now here the remaining two were vouched for! It couldn't possibly be that he had made some fundamental error? He had succeeded well in the episode of the abduction. Surely he must be equally correct about the murder? He felt as if he were going mad.

Then his self-reliance rallied. He was not wrong! He had been done! One of those watertight alibis was faked. It must be. But which? He would soon see. He would go into them again, all four. One of them must break down before a more searching enquiry.

But as he considered them one by one the prospect grew less rosy. He took first the cases of Stowe and Moffatt. It really was impossible that all those who had been interviewed should have been mistaken or lying. First he had been to the man who had fainted, Henderson. He had confirmed the attack, as well as the fact that both Stowe and Moffatt were present and had helped him home. The seizure was so unusual that he had been alarmed about his heart, and next morning instead of going to business he had called in his doctor. French had seen the doctor, who had stated that Henderson was very much run down and might well have fainted as he said. He had a note of the call in his books, and this established the date. Further, all whom French questioned of those who had been present confirmed the manager's story. The proof that both his suspects were also present was therefore overwhelming. And nothing was more certain than that if they were in Brigadier Street on that night, they were innocent of the murder.

French turned to Jepton. With him the case was different. There all that had really been proved was that a man who had given his name as Jepton and who answered his description, had stayed in the Princes Street Station Hotel during the critical period. Was this man really Jepton, or had someone impersonated him?

The matter was so important that French felt he could not leave it in its present state. He must go himself to Edinburgh with Jepton's photograph. And if there still remained doubt he must bring someone who had seen the man in Edinburgh back with him to London, and arrange an identification parade.

He went north that night, and next day checked over what the Edinburgh police had done. And when he had finished, he was more worried than ever. He found himself absolutely convinced that Jepton and only Jepton had been there. Several people picked the man's photograph from a number of others of similar type, and all of them could not be wrong.

For some hours French's depression lasted. Then as he lay thinking the affair over in the up night express, a fresh idea occurred to him. Eagerly he seized on it and began turning it over in his mind. As he did so his spirits rose, they rose indeed until an eager excitement took the place of his former despair. Yes, he was on to it at last!

Entrican being the last suspect of the four, he had been considering his alibi more critically than ever. And suddenly he had seen how Entrican could have done all he said he had done, and yet could have been at Henley at two in the morning! That was it! He now had what he wanted!

Once again he went over the secretary's statement, making the necessary alterations and additions as he did so. Entrican had booked a room at the Piccadilly Palace in which he had changed. Probably he had changed to back up the tale about the woman, should he afterwards be called on to tell it. He had then gone out to Hampstead and dined with

Stowe and his companions. He had returned to the hotel about half-past ten and gone up to his room. There he had undressed, broken the glass, rung for another—thus impressing his personality on the chambermaid—and got into bed. So much was admitted but he could equally well have got up again and dressed: putting on other shoes, so that the pair he had been wearing could remain outside the door. He could then have slipped out, and avoiding the chambermaid, have gone downstairs and out of the building, retaining his key. He could then—

Here for a time French's theorising called a halt. How could Entrican have travelled to and from Henley? He would scarcely risk going by any of the public services—or would he? Unlikely, at all events. What then would he do? He must surely have bought or hired a car. Or could Stowe, Moffatt or Jepton have lent him one?

There was a difficulty here, but it could have been got over if Entrican had obtained a car. He could have garaged it before that evening, and left it in the garage again next morning. Again, quite easy.

Given the car, he could have driven down to Henley, parked somewhere out of sight, gone to the boathouse, taken out the boat and committed the murder, and driven back to Town. He could have slipped in to the hotel, and again watching his opportunity, he could have avoided the chambermaid and regained his room with nothing to show that he had left it.

French determined that that night he would himself go to the Piccadilly Palace and carry out the same scheme, so as to demonstrate its possibility beyond possibility of doubt.

But while he was now certain of what had been done, he saw that his case was by no means finished: it was one thing to know the truth, but quite another to prove it. For Entrican he had proved motive and opportunity, but he had not actually connected him with the murder. There was the fork for example. If only he could prove that Entrican had bought the fork, his case would be complete.

Suddenly it occurred to him that perhaps he had not been trying to find the maker of the fork in the best way. After all manufacturing firms make such small articles not by ones or twos but by the hundred thousand. The reason of course is that expensive tools and jigs are usually required, which only pay for themselves if used many times. Few of such firms would make a special small implement, as the work would upset their system. No, the place to get such a piece of apparatus would be the odd jobber: the private worker, the man who is so rapidly disappearing from the world. Most of those left are ingenious men who make their business their hobby, and in a small way make to order, probably with their own hands.

Yes, it did seem as if he had made a mistake there. The small man was the man to go for.

But how? The ordinary eliminative search would be a very tedious and costly business, particularly as Entrican would naturally have done what he could to cover his traces. Was there no other way?

Then it occurred to French that the kind of man he had postulated would probably read the *English Mechanic* or other similar technical journal. Suppose he were to make a list of these and insert advertisements? It mightn't work: but then again, it might . . .

It seemed worthwhile trying, and French spent the afternoon getting out his list and sending off his advertisement to each paper. He described the fork without giving dimensions, so that only the original maker would be interested, said it had been lost, and asked could the maker produce another at his own figure.

He had engaged a room at the Piccadilly Palace, and that night he carried through in detail the scheme that he had evolved by which Entrican could have faked his alibi. It worked without a hitch. He reached the hotel at half-past ten, went to bed, got up again and slipped out unseen by the chambermaid. He spent the night at his home, returning to the hotel a few minutes past eight. With a little care he had no difficulty in regaining his room while the chambermaid was occupied elsewhere. He had breakfast, paid his bill, and departed, leaving behind him as satisfactory proof that he spent the night in the building as had Entrican.

There now remained no doubt as to what had occurred. For Entrican he had early proved motive, and now there was demonstration of opportunity. He was satisfied that Entrican was his man, because elimination had told him so. There was no one else who could have done the job. Motive, opportunity and proof by elimination! It was good, but it was not quite good enough. He had still to find some one fact which would actually connect the man with the deed. A very trivial fact would be enough, but he felt it would be no good going to the public prosecutor till he had found one.

If only he could find it! But he could not. As day succeeded day the matter grew more and more serious. He must find it! He had practically completed his case, and he couldn't afford to fail for the want of one tiny further step.

In vain he reviewed the dossier, thinking over every fact in the hope of finding some contingent item which would represent a fresh line of investigation. He even did what he disliked a great deal more: he talked over every fact with Carter in the hope that putting the thing to another person would bring some light. But none came.

Then to his immense relief he received a letter which he thought would lead to the proof he needed. John Macdonald, the keeper of an amateur mechanics' requisites shop, wrote that he had made two forks similar to those described in the advertisement, that the price of a similar pair would be 15/6, and that on receipt of a firm order he would put them in hand.

The shop was situated in Kingston, and a couple of hours later French and Carter drew up at the door. Macdonald was an elderly man of the very type French had pictured when he put in his advertisement. He was tall and thin and stooped, with a straggling beard and slightly untidy clothes, and it soon became clear to French that he thought more of the things of the mind than of the body. His shop was one of those places in which mechanically minded amateurs delight: full of table legs, mouldings, plywood, hooks, hinges and little mechanical gadgets of all kinds. He was reading short-sightedly a copy of the *English Mechanic*, which he put down with obvious reluctance to attend to his customers.

French was accustomed to size up quickly those 'with whom he dealt, and now he decided to drop the fiction that he wanted more hooks made, and state his business directly. He found himself justified. The old man was perfectly willing to tell him all he knew.

'It was this way,' Macdonald began; 'a man called in here; it would be—' he paused in thought, 'I don't just remember when, but I believe I can turn it up for you if it's important: he called in and asked me if I could make him a couple of butterfly-net fittings to a friend's design. I asked to see the design, and he brought out scaled sketches. They were the usual thing: a tube about five-eighths inch diameter of heavy tin to fit on the end of a handle, and through it a bit of light brass quarter-inch tube, bent up to take the thin cane ring that carries the net. You follow?'

French followed.

'They were the usual thing,' the old man repeated, 'except for one point. The brass tubes in each fitting were of different lengths and were bent in an unusual and unnecessary way. I pointed this out and told him it would be much better and cheaper to have them straight. He said he couldn't tell about that: he really didn't know how his friend proposed to use them, but he thought he'd better have what the friend wanted, even if it should cost a little more. So I agreed to make them. I did, and he called a couple of days later and paid me and took them away, and that's all I know about the affair.'

'Very helpful to me, Mr Macdonald,' French said pleasantly. 'Do you think you could make me a sketch of the fittings, just to make quite sure we're talking about the same things?'

'Of course.' The man was an artist. The two hooks found by the diver sprang into life on the sheet of brown wrapping paper. French opened his bag and took them out.

'Oh, you've got them?' Macdonald exclaimed.

'I've got these,' French answered somewhat unnecessarily. 'Question is, are they what you made?'

Macdonald turned them over slowly. 'Yes,' he said presently, 'they're what I made all right. If there was any doubt about it I'd recognise that one by that drop of solder. I remember thinking I'd file it away for the sake of appearance, then finding it was awkward to get at and deciding to leave it. Oh, yes, if you want me to swear to them in court, I'll do it.'

'That's very satisfactory. Now there's just one other point. Here are some photographs. Is the man who ordered them among them?'

As the moment of obtaining his proof and ending his worry had arrived, French could not but feel a wave of excitement pass over him. But for the sake of his prestige he sternly controlled it. He sat back apparently quite at ease as he watched the old man turn the cards over slowly, examining each before he laid it down. Even when after a longer scrutiny he put one aside, French did not lean forward to see it, but waited while all the remainder were gone over in the same painstaking way. Then Macdonald picked up the one he had selected and again examined it.

'That's the man,' he said finally in an assured tone. 'I can swear to him also if you require it.'

'Full of thankfulness French took the card. Then suddenly he grew rigid. The thin rather worried features of Entrican which he had expected to see were not there. Instead there was the weak unhappy looking face of Locke!

22

The Final Elucidation

French gazed incredulously. Locke! Locke, whose case he had gone into, and whom he had acquitted in his mind! Locke, who had nothing to do with the abduction!

So Locke had been the dark horse of this puzzling and irritating case!

And yet French saw that, to be fair to himself, he had never really cleared him in his mind. Similarly, when he had conceived the idea that abductors and the murderers were the same, he had realised also that this was not necessarily true. It was likely: it was not certain. Where he had made the mistake was in following that idea too exclusively.

And yet he did not see how he could have done other-wise. As long as the guilt of Entrican and Company was probable, he must necessarily have followed the suggestion up until it was either proved or disproved. The fact that it was disproved did not alter his duty. The elimination of error was after all just as essential a part of detection as the establishment of truth. There had unhappily been an unnecessary delay in clearing the affair up, but he really could not blame himself for his action. He had done his best.

And, he told himself with a warm glow of satisfaction, that best had been a jolly good best. He had succeeded in what he set out to do. What remained of the case would be quickly completed. With what he now knew, the obtaining of the necessary corroboration would be child's play.

He went back to the Yard, and taking once again the dossier, set to work to think out his last moves.

Almost at once he received an unpleasant shock. There in the dossier, staring him in the face, was evidence which, had he only realised its significance earlier, would have saved him an immensity of time and trouble. He had in his hands proof that neither Stowe, Moffatt, Jepton nor Entrican could have been guilty! He stared blankly before him, wondering how he had come to miss it.

The evidence was connected with the decanter and lay in the juxtaposition of dates. Higgins had noticed the decanter was missing when he cleaned the glass on Saturday morning, the Saturday of the weekend before the crime. Therefore it was obvious that not only had the murder been decided on before that date, but preparations for it were then actually in progress. But Harrison's ultimatum to Stowe and Moffatt was not delivered until the Monday night following. Until then Stowe and his friends had no idea that Harrison knew who had abducted him. Until Monday night they had no motive for the murder. It was inconceivable therefore that they could have been preparing for it.

French could have kicked himself for having missed so obvious a point. Then he saw that while to blame, his offence was not so heinous after all. He had not known anything about the Monday ultimatum until Entrican had made his statement at the Yard, and since then he had been so obsessed with the idea of the quarter's guilt that he had not reconsidered the affair calmly. Very reprehensible of course, but still pardonable.

It was then that French saw that he had also missed the significance of a second piece of evidence—also connected with the decanter. This time nothing was proved by it, but he realised that it was very suggestive and clearly indicated the line he should have followed.

Higgins again was its source. Higgins had stated that after the others had gone to bed some nights before the tragedy, he had heard Locke and Harrison amicably discussing finance in the lounge. French now asked himself, was this likely to be what it appeared on the surface? Locke was desperately in love with Harrison's wife. Moreover he believed Harrison to be a swindler of the most callous type. Under these circumstances was this perfectly gratuitous and friendly conversation quite natural?

French doubted it. But if a further factor were taken into consideration, it became not only natural, but highly probable. At that time in the evening there stood on a table in the lounge, probably between the two men, a decanter of whisky and a second of brandy. Did not this alter the situation?

Sitting back in his chair with his eyes fixed on vacancy French mentally pictured what in all probability had happened. And at once he saw that the very fact which he had considered a proof of Locke's innocence, really indicated his guilt. In his mind's eye French saw him on this night getting Harrison to drink with him alone, on the pretext that he wanted his confidential advice about some shares. Locke holding the decanter by the neck after seeing that

Harrison had gripped its sides. Both men going to bed after their talk. Later in the night Locke creeping silently to the dining saloon, taking from the sideboard one of the empty decanters, returning to the lounge, transferring the whisky to it and leaving it on the table. Then carrying to his cabin the original decanter bearing Harrison's prints, wiping his own off its neck and locking it in a suitcase till it should be required for the hydrochloric acid. This, of course, was not proven, but French had little doubt that it had been done.

He felt anything but proud of himself. Circumstances, it was true, had misled him as to the value of these two pieces of evidence. But he shouldn't have allowed circumstances to mislead him. If he had been a little more wide awake he would have saved himself these mistakes.

However the thing was done and worrying over it wouldn't help matters. With a shrug he turned back to his plans for completing the affair.

First, there was the question of Locke's motive. As he had seen from early in the case, there was no doubt as to that. Locke was desperately and hopelessly in love with Letitia Harrison. For years he had hung on to his intimacy with her, not because he thought he would obtain his desires, but simply because he couldn't bring himself to make an irrevocable breach. And she appeared to be fond of him in a way. At all events she liked to have him to domineer over, and though she treated him with a scornful carelessness that at times reached actual cruelty, she always relented sufficiently to prevent him from breaking away.

That this had been going on for years he, French, had taken as an argument for the man's innocence. The circumstances, he had thought, had remained unaltered and nothing had occurred to spur Locke on to action. But again he saw he had been wrong. Something had occurred. Harrison had disappeared. What, French asked himself, would be Locke's reaction?

He saw that a dreadful hope would fill the man's mind. Knowing Harrison as Locke did, he would reject the idea of a voluntary disappearance. He would see death in the affair. Some accident—or *murder*.

An overwhelming excitement would sweep Locke away. Without stirring a finger the happiness he so desperately desired would be his. Because after all the encouragement Letitia Harrison had given him, he could not have doubted that she would accept him.

Could it be wondered then that when Harrison turned up as well as ever, this hope and excitement would be changed into the most terrible disappointment and despair? Locke would be desperate. Things would seem unbearable—a thousand times worse than before: as to be dragged back from a paradise which one was just about to enter would be worse than never to have seen it.

But the disappearance would mean more to him than that. By it a suggestion would have been presented to him and would no doubt have sunk deeply into his mind. Murder! He had thought that was to be his way out: murder by someone else. Could murder still be his salvation; but murder by himself?

French could imagine the idea preying on his rather weak mind, taking possession of it, germinating, growing, producing its hideous fruit. Inevitably the second idea would follow: How could murder be carried out? Locke was an ingenious man, a patentee, and as soon as he saw a way in which it could be done in absolute safety—as he thought—the die would be cast. No doubt he would fight the temptation. No doubt he would lose the battle.

And, as Locke had intended it, there would have been no scandal. A suicide while of unsound mind, brought on by overwork, would have been regrettable, would have carried no social or other stigma. Mrs Harrison's prestige would not have suffered. After a suitable interval she would have married again.

In his mind's eye French saw Locke making his preparations: getting the decanter, the bowl, the acid and marble, the cylinders of gas, the rubber tube, and all the other properties he required. He saw him slipping ashore, taking out the Colemans' boat—having already obtained a key of the boathouse, filling the cabin with gas, lifting in the bowl and decanter, replacing the boat and returning to his cabin. All the man had now to do was to sit tight and say nothing: and this he did. But—and once again French grew exultant— he hadn't reckoned with Joseph French. Though he, French, had made a mistake and had gone off on the wrong tack, he had got his man in the end!

But had he quite? He thought so. He had proved motive and opportunity, and the purchase of the forks was a direct connection between the man and the crime. One thing at least was certain. If he hadn't all he would like for court, he at least had enough for an arrest. He would carry this out at once, then a' short further investigation should surely give corroborative proof.

He went to Sir Mortimer Ellison's room and put his case. The Assistant Commissioner was complimentary. He considered the evidence French had obtained was convincing and at once agreed about the arrest.

That night Locke was lodged in the cells, and next day

French went with a search warrant to the man's bungalow near Sutton. There he carried out a detailed investigation. It was not long before he obtained further evidence.

Two points in particular removed any possible doubt of the man's guilt. The first discovery was the address of a famous theatrical supplies firm in Shaftesbury Avenue. French found it in Locke's engagement book under the date of a fortnight before the crime. He checked it up as a matter of routine, not expecting it to prove important. But it did.

It appeared that on the day in question a man called and purchased a Franciscan friar's robe with cowl attached. He explained that he was playing in some amateur theatricals. This man the attendant identified as Locke, first from a photograph and then from seeing the man himself in a parade.

French, highly excited by this news, asked if he could have a similar robe, and was supplied with a brown garment which still further thrilled him. He made the obvious enquiries suggested and found, first, that Locke's robe had been made from the same roll of cloth as had his own, and second, that it was of the same material as the pieces of wool he had found on the sides of the *Cygnet* and of the Colemans' boat.

This was more than satisfactory. The robe had clearly been obtained with the object of eluding the vigilance of the night watchman. Its use in the boat was probably a makeshift—the boat was found to be bumping and no other fender presented itself. What Locke had done with it afterwards French could not find out, though the man afterwards admitted he had rolled it round another gas cylinder and sunk it in the Thames below the boathouse.

French's second discovery was the result of following up

a very unpromising clue. In the pocket of one of Locke's overcoats he found a parking ticket. It was dated for ten days previous to the murder, and French was able to trace it to a certain car park in Birmingham. He went to Birmingham and walked the streets in the immediate vicinity. At once his attention was attracted to a chemical works. He called on the manager, and by dint of painstaking enquiries was able to prove that on the date in question Locke had purchased four cylinders of the gas on the pretext of experimenting with the production of a new soft drink. More suggestive still, he had had these fitted with reducing valves, ostensibly to assist his process, but obviously to prevent the hissing noise which would otherwise have been made by the escaping gas.

These two pieces of evidence completed the case against Locke, and though at his trial his counsel made a spirited attempt to break it down, he was found guilty and sentenced to pay the supreme penalty.

He had strenuously denied his guilt, but when his appeal was rejected and he saw that nothing could save him, he called for the Governor and made a formal confession. This showed that French had been correct in his reconstruction of the crime, though he had not learnt all the circumstances.

French was right in believing that the disappearance of Harrison had brought matters to a head with Locke. Before that no thought of obtaining his ends by violence had entered his head. But the disappearance had suggested to him that Harrison had been murdered, and his joy was overwhelming. Harrison's return had been an appalling disappointment, and the idea of himself killing the man had entered his mind and taken deep root. It happened that classes for anti-gas protection in war time had been held in his district shortly before, and these gave him his idea. He developed it and carried it out as French had supposed.

Two facts he divulged which French had not known. The first was that before joining the party on the *Cygnet* he had during the night brought down to the river the cylinders of gas, and hidden them in the water, attached just below the surface by a rope to a protruding tree root. After getting out the Colemans' boat on the night of the murder, he had simply pulled them up into it. Also, after throwing the fork and one cylinder overboard on his return journey, it had occurred to him that he might be seen getting rid of them from the *Cygnet*. He therefore dropped downstream some hundred yards before disposing of the remainder.

The second fact was that he had overheard Harrison's interview with Stowe and Moffatt when Harrison gave them his ultimatum. This had made him hasten his action. While he never for a moment believed that anything but suicide would be suspected, he thought that if by some miracle the idea of murder did arise, this blackmail would come out and Stowe and Moffatt would be suspected. To do him justice, he swore that he had had no idea of letting someone else suffer for him, but he didn't believe that either Stowe or Moffatt could be found guilty, when as a matter of fact they were innocent.

Though French received his A.C.'s congratulations on his successful handling of the case, he shivered when he thought how near he had been to making a terrible mistake. It was not of course a mistake from which a miscarriage of justice could have resulted, but it was a mistake all the same and it would have wiped out a good deal of his prestige. However so far as he was concerned, all was well that ended well.

He did not hear much about the Harrisons, but at least

one item was good. Strangely enough the affair proved the making of Rupert. He did not go to sea, but took over his father's business. With the help of Kemp he ran it, if with less success financially, at least with more humanity. But his mother and sister seemed simply to fade out. Mrs Harrison was broken by the affair and retired into obscurity, and Gloria broke off the Coleman engagement and went abroad.

'Poor people,' French thought as he looked back over the case, 'they played so much for their own hand that they missed their happiness.' He shook his head, shrugged and turned to the next item on his list.

By the same author

Inspector French's
Greatest Case

At the offices of the Hatton Garden diamond merchant *Duke & Peabody*, the body of old Mr Gething is discovered beside a now-empty safe. With multiple suspects, the robbery and murder is clearly the work of a master criminal, and requires a master detective to solve it. Meticulous as ever, Inspector Joseph French of Scotland Yard embarks on an investigation that takes him from the streets of London to Holland, France and Spain, and finally to a ship bound for South America . . .

'Because he is so austerely realistic, Freeman Wills Croft is deservedly a first favourite with all who want a real puzzle.'
TIMES LITERARY SUPPLEMENT

By the same author

Inspector French
and the Cheyne Mystery

When young Maxwell Cheyne discovers that a series of mishaps are the result of unwelcome attention from a dangerous gang of criminals, he teams up with a young woman who is determined to help him outwit them. But when she disappears, he finally decides to go to Scotland Yard for help. Concerned by the developing situation, Inspector Joseph French takes charge of the investigation and applies his trademark methods to track down the kidnappers and thwart their intentions . . .

'*Freeman Wills Crofts is among the few muscular writers of detective fiction. He has never let me down.*'
DAILY EXPRESS

By the same author

Inspector French and the Starvel Hollow Tragedy

A chance invitation from friends saves Ruth Averill's life on the night her uncle's old house in Starvel Hollow is consumed by fire, killing him and incinerating the fortune he kept in cash. Dismissed at the inquest as a tragic accident, the case is closed—until Scotland Yard is alerted to the circulation of bank-notes supposedly destroyed in the inferno. Inspector Joseph French suspects that dark deeds were done in the Hollow that night and begins to uncover a brutal crime involving arson, murder and body snatching . . .

'Freeman Wills Crofts is the only author who gives us intricate crime in fiction as it might really be, and not as the irreflective would like it to be.'   OBSERVER

By the same author

Inspector French
and the Sea Mystery

Off the coast of Burry Port in south Wales, two fishermen
discover a shipping crate and manage to haul it ashore. Inside
is the decomposing body of a brutally murdered man. With
nothing to indicate who he is or where it came from, the
local police decide to call in Scotland Yard. Fortunately
Inspector Joseph French does not believe in insoluble cases—
there are always clues to be found if you know what to look
for. Testing his theories with his accustomed thoroughness,
French's ingenuity sets him off on another investigation . . .

'*Inspector French is as near the real thing as any sleuth in
fiction.*'   *SUNDAY TIMES*

By the same author

Inspector French: Found Floating

The Carrington family, victims of a strange poisoning, take an Olympic cruise from Glasgow to help them recover. At Creuta one member goes ashore and does not return. Their body is next day found floating in the Straits of Gibraltar. Joining the ship at Marseilles, can Inspector French solve the mystery before they reach Athens?

Introduced by Tony Medawar, this classic Inspector French novel includes unique interludes by Superintendent Walter Hambrook of Scotland Yard, who provides a real-life detective commentary on the case as the mystery unfolds.

'I doubt whether Inspector French has had a more difficult problem to solve than that of the body 'Found Floating' in the Mediterranean.'   SUNDAY TIMES